# CRAZY LIKE A GOAT

Science Traveler Series

Book 14

# CRAZY LIKE A GOAT

Science Traveler Series
Book 14

J.L. Greger

Bug Press  Bernalillo, NM

Crazy Like a Goat

Bug Press
An imprint of IngramSpark
Bernalillo, New Mexico 87004
http://www.jlgreger.com



ISBN (paperback): 9798989418428
ISBN (EPUB): 9798989418435
Library of Congress Catalogue Number: 2025901861

# DEDICATION

To all those who as Dylan Thomas said,

"Do not go gentle into that good night

# CHAPTER 1: A Field Trip Gone Awry

*A Monday in August*

Sunlight streamed onto John's face as the blanket on the makeshift tent was lifted at one corner. A man in uniform flashed his badge. "Albuquerque Police. No one is allowed to camp in the bosque."

John sat up. He noticed Ab and Gus lay motionless on their stomachs, pretending to be asleep. "Officer, we weren't camping. Merely resting. Give us old guys a break. It's cooler in the shade of the bosque than on the sidewalks."

The blanket that had been the roof to their tent was pulled away. The uniformed officer studied John. "You, again." He turned to his partner who still sat astride a horse. "Find John Lindberg's address at one of the senior living facilities here in town."

His partner checked his phone. "Happy Days."

"Seems our wandering boy brought along two friends." The officer pushed an empty wine bottle away from Gus with the toe of his boot. "On your feet. You're taking breath tests before we give you a ride back to Happy Days."

Gus rolled over. "Happy now? I'm awake, but I'm still worn out from walking here." He rubbed his eyes. "Can't seem to see."

John figured he'd better take the breath test first because he was sure he wouldn't have a high blood alcohol level after drinking only two beers last night. If he passed, the officer might not test the other two who had drunk a lot more. John rose slowly. All his joints felt stiff from sleeping on the ground. *Maybe at seventy-six he was too old to camp.*

The officer snorted when he read John's negative results and extended his hand to pull Gus to his feet. Gus seemed to ignore him, tottered to his feet, and would have staggered toward the horse if the officer hadn't pushed a tube into Gus's mouth. "Blow into the device." After a few seconds, the officer said, "I'm writing you up for drinking alcohol in the bosque. Your blood alcohol isn't elevated much, but you were sleeping with a bottle." He turned to John. "This warning citation is the least of your problems. If you boys keep doing this, you'll be put in a memory unit." He chuckled. "If nothing else, Rosa Gonzalez is going to lecture you."

The officer was right. The manager of Happy Days—Mrs. Rosa Gonzalez—would be angry. They had broken her stupid rules. Like the way she required all staff and residents to call her *Mrs.* Gonzalez, not Rosa.

John shrugged. Of course, his friends' constant hijinks at the senior center were stupid too. It had earned them the nickname of The Three Old Musketeers. John didn't think he deserved to be included in the group, but Mrs. Gonzalez claimed he was the silent partner who egged on the other two.

John mused how he and his friends had gotten in this predicament. All three'd had successful careers at the University of New Mexico but were retired now. They were single because of death or divorce and had no close relatives in Albuquerque. Thus, they spent a lot of time remembering their past, avoiding widows looking for husbands, and plotting ways to confuse the bossy staff at Happy Days. They were bored.

One way they fought boredom was to take *field trips* to the botanical garden, the zoo, and sites featured in the news. The problem— he guessed—was they didn't bother to tell staff when they left on a trip. Mrs. Gonzalez had called the police twice before to locate them when they missed two consecutive meals.

The plan to camp overnight in the bosque—forest along the Rio Grande—developed as they reminisced yesterday about how they'd beaten the heat as kids by going camping in the woods. None of them felt like driving, so they had walked almost a mile to the Rio Grande and spent the night, even though they knew it was illegal to camp there.

John noticed Ab still lay on his blanket with a pillow over his head. John picked up the pillow carefully because he was wary his friend would shoot him with his squirt gun. He was not surprised to see Ab was grasping an almost empty bottle of Wild Turkey 101 Bourbon. While John and Gus drank mainly wine and beer, Ab liked his bourbon. When John removed the bottle from Ab's hands, he noticed Ab's fingers were stiff. John tried not to panic as he shook his friend's shoulders.

Ab didn't move.

The officer stepped toward Ab. "What's his problem?" He felt Ab's neck for a pulse and shook his head. "Better call for the medical examiner and backup.

# CHAPTER 2: A Friend in Need Is a Friend Indeed

Isaac Newson scanned the start of the police report while the morgue technician processed the body.

> *Seventy-eight-year-old man found dead in the bosque at 7 a.m.*
>
> *Two men of similar ages were found with him in a makeshift tent. One had elevated blood alcohol levels and claimed vision problems. Both acted as if they didn't know their friend was dead.*
>
> *Victim was found clutching an almost empty bottle of Wild Turkey 101 Bourbon. An empty wine bottle, two empty beer cans, and a bag of peanut shells were also found nearby.*

Isaac shook his head. Another senseless death. This year's heat wave had been brutal. He'd autopsied eleven elderly individuals who died of heat exhaustion this summer. Usually, they died alone in closed, hot homes. The bottle in the man's hand suggested he'd ingested ethanol, which meant he may have been dehydrated. That would make him more sensitive to the heat.

He looked at the report from the lab. The estimated the time of death was between two and three in the morning. Isaac was surprised the tech had sent the bourbon bottle and its contents for analyses. *Overkill.* He figured the victim or one of his friends was related to a politician, and the tech was covering her rear.

He glanced at the victim's name. *D***.* The victim—Ab Hess—had taught him anatomy in medical school. No wonder the tech was being careful. The report of his death was apt to receive attention statewide from physicians who had endured the med school hazing—known as gross anatomy—under his tutelage. Actually, Ab had been a kind instructor, but the rigor of dissecting a human being for the first time was traumatic for many students. Isaac sucked in his breath. He guessed it had bothered him too, but it had fascinated him more. He only regretted being a pathologist and then developed a drinking problem after his wife died of cancer. He'd autopsied too many cancer patients.

Isaac spotted the names of the two witnesses. One—John Lindberg—had been Isaac's colleague in the Department of Pathology here. He didn't know the other man—Gus Rinaldi—except by reputation. He had been a professor in the School of Pharmacy. The police reported both men seemed dazed, but only one had slightly elevated blood alcohol levels.

Isaac thought a minute. The last time he saw John was at the Pathology Department's holiday party last year. Isaac had forgotten the rules of Alcoholics Anonymous that night and had drunk the spiked eggnog. Then he'd enjoyed another drink and another. He didn't remember much about that party, but he was sure John Lindberg had been lucid. John was one of those men who had a disgustingly sunny disposition and who never smoked, never drank to excess, and seldom did anything improper. At the party, John had talked enthusiastically about continuing to be a docent at the National Nuclear Science and History Museum in Albuquerque even though he had sold his home and recently moved to Happy Days Senior Center.

*Wait!* He thought John had mentioned the move may have been a mistake. But Isaac wasn't sure.

***

The autopsy was troubling. There were no petechial—small—hemorrhages on the skin or viscera, although the cerebrum was edematous. Ab had not died of heat stroke.

The liver was somewhat cirrhotic—scarred—and had had been infiltrated slightly with a hepatocellular cancer. Alcoholism was the probable cause of these symptoms, but these chronic problems didn't explain Ab's death.

The edema in the brain included optic disc swelling and retinal damage. One of the victim's friends had complained of visual problems. Isaac suspected methanol poisoning.

That didn't make sense. These men were not skid row bums who bought cheap hooch potentially contaminated with methanol. He'd autopsied two homeless veterans in the last month who had died of methanol poisoning. VA social workers were frantically trying to educate homeless veterans on the dangers of methanol in various cleaning fluids, but their warnings were insufficient to slake the thirst of desperate alcoholics.

He emailed the lab and requested they screen the victim's blood and the fluid in the whiskey bottle for methanol. He advised them to get samples of the blood from the witness who complained of vision problems. He guessed his second request might be ignored. So, he called the Albuquerque Police Department (APD) and was surprised to learn the responding officers had taken John and Gus to the emergency room at University Hospital to have their blood checked for methanol immediately after they found them in the bosque.

Then he pondered the situation. Did someone intentionally add methanol to Ab's bottle of bourbon? That would be murder.

Isaac knew the local district attorney liked to transfer "poisoning or technical" cases to the federal court system because local juries were confused by scientific details and seldom found suspected poisoners guilty. He thought part of the problem was few of the local cops had the smarts or patience to gather clues in cases not dripping with blood. He sighed because he knew he was an intellectual snob, but he thought Ab deserved justice. Besides the FBI often stepped in to aid the APD on complicated murder cases. And the FBI office in Albuquerque had one scientist who specialized in such cases.

He sent emails to his boss, the officers who investigated the scene, their captain, the supervising agent in charge of the Albuquerque office of the FBI, the district attorneys for both the state and federal districts, and Dr. Sara Almquist. If nothing else, he'd enjoyed chatting with Sara even if he had to put up with her young, pretty-boy partner. Then to guarantee the case got attention, he sent an email to the New Mexico Attorney General.

# CHAPTER 3: Too Many Possibilities

*Tuesday*

Sara led Bug into the office of Paul Carbonne, the SAC (supervising officer) of the Albuquerque office of the FBI. Carbonne appeared to be concentrating on his computer screen while he listened to someone on the phone. She sat down at his table and played with her little black and white Japanese Chin. He was named Bug because she thought he was as *cute as a bug*. She looked up when she heard Carbonne clear his throat.

"We're busy enough. You didn't need to solicit a case." He winked.

Sara felt confused for a moment and then remembered Isaac Newson's email. "I didn't. I guess Isaac feels loyalty to his retired colleagues from the med school."

Carbonne pulled two diet colas from the refrigerator under the counter by his desk and sauntered to the table where Sara sat. "I know." He handed her a can. "Isaac's rationale was logical, and he covered his bases and cc'd everyone. The New Mexico Attorney General even called to give me advice." Carbonne shook his head. "Poor guy never stops campaigning for office. And senior citizens turn out at the polls in November. He thinks this case will make it look like he's concerned about them. He wants in on the action."

Sara laughed. "I figured you'd be forced to accept the case but not this fast."

"Don't waste a lot of time on it. The APD interviewed the manager, Rosa Gonzalez, of the senior center where the man lived. She was convinced all three men were senile and the death was due to a prank gone wrong." He took a long slug of cola. "You know the drill."

"It takes time to interview lonely, old people." She smiled. "It'll be a refreshing change from my last case where no one wanted to talk." Sara leaned down and patted Bug. "Before Bug and I leave, tell me what it's like to be a new father."

"Wonderful but tiring." Carbonne whipped a photo of an infant from his wallet. "That's the other reason I called you to my office. Barbara reminded me again this morning to ask you to be Willow's godmother. The christening is Saturday in Acoma. Will Sanders be around this weekend?"

"I was planning on visiting him in Washington this weekend. But we'll have to change our plans." She laughed. "Bug and I were dreading long delays in airports. Sanders won't mind jumping on a military plane due to land at Kirtland because he's wrapping up his work on the investigation of the US-Latin America drug trade for the Senate Intelligence Committee."

Carbonne shook his head. "Knowing Sanders, I'd think he'd be looking for his next assignment."

Sara sipped her cola. "Not this time. He's accepted an increased teaching load at Quantico and has gotten himself on the list of candidates for the director of the Bureau of Intelligence and Research in the State Department. 'Course that's a long way from getting the position."

Carbonne sighed. "So, he's finally achieved his dream. Having served as a young FBI agent under him in Cuba, I can tell you he's the best I've seen but..."

"He's stepped on lots of toes in the process. A weekend here will force him to relax." She led Bug to the door. "What time is the christening?"

***

Sara saw no reason to rile her partner, Jack Drum, and tell him about this new assignment until she had more info. Isaac had hazed Jack during his first month on the job by making Jack witness the autopsy of a putrid corpse which had been in the river for days. As a newbie, Jack had not known to enough to view the autopsy from behind the glass windows of the viewing room and had fainted. Sara thought even experienced agents would have gagged at the odors emanating from that *floater*. She was sure Isaac had put lots of salve scented with menthol in his nostrils before that autopsy.

She didn't think Isaac was sadistic. He was just a lonely, sixty-year-old man jealous of young, handsome men. Jack at twenty-eight looked like a star quarterback on a college football team. She knew Isaac would appreciate it if she stopped by the New Mexico Scientific Lab alone. Besides he was apt to be more candid in person than he would be if asked to reply to an email or a potentially recorded call. She emailed him to ask when he'd be available. She didn't want to arrive in the middle of an autopsy. Although Sara appreciated the value of autopsies and had seen dozens of them, she didn't have a desire to see more of them than necessary.

***

Sara studied the autopsy report for Ab Hess attached to Isaac's initial email. Isaac had suspected methanol toxicity because of the damage in the brain's optic areas. His diagnosis had probably saved the life of a second man, Gus Rinaldi, *but* she could tell Isaac was unsure. He'd used too many *weasel* words, which would be apparent to only someone with scientific training.

Lots of things could cause the liver damage Isaac had spotted besides alcoholism and methanol, including excess use of certain pain killers and vitamin A supplements, hepatitis B, metabolic diseases including diabetes, and exposure to molds. The effects of these diseases and toxins could be additive making an individual with an already damaged liver much more sensitive to methanol. *That meant anyone who knew the victim could have known how to target him.* Details would be more important than usual in this case.

Sara called the hospital for an update. The hospital lab had found high levels of methanol in the serum of Gus Rinaldi. He was now undergoing dialysis and treatment with fomepizole. When last checked, his vision had not improved.

APD officers had escorted the third man—John Lindberg—back to Happy Days and searched his apartment and car for sources of methanol. They had found no "windshield washing fluid or odd hand sanitizers." Sara assumed the police search had been cursory and requested search warrants. She wanted FBI technicians to catalog all cleaning supplies, medications, and supplements in the apartments and the cars of the victim and his two companions. She wanted their computers downloaded so staff could check for any animosities among the men. She also requested the judge approve a search of all the storage areas in Happy Days for cleaning and medical supplies because the three men involved were smart enough to not have kept a potential murder or suicide agent where it would be easily found in their possession.

She re-read the last paragraphs of the APD report:

> *Rosa. Gonzalez, the supervisor at Happy Days, reported Ab Hess, Gus Rinaldi, and John Lindberg were "constantly playing pranks and generally defying rules." This is the third time, she called the police to rescue the three men. Both arresting officers were involved in one of the earlier searches*

She forwarded the police report to the head of the FBI lab and requested Winslow Red Feather be assigned to be the prime lab technician on this case. Winslow was one of her favorite people in the building because he was energetic and enthusiastic.

She also requested Rosemary Garth, a young FBI computer analyst, to obtain a list of all staff and residents at Happy Days. Rosemary was new to the FBI and seemed to be having trouble integrating into the staff who were mostly twenty years older than she. Sara thought Rosemary—willowy, shy, smart—might appeal to Winslow or Jack. Both young men seemed to be having trouble finding female companionship.

Finally, she reviewed the case with Jack and suggested he interview Rosa Gonzalez when he served the warrants and accompanied Winslow to Happy Days.

She was now ready to have a serious talk with Isaac.

***

Isaac had shed his green autopsy gear and was waiting for Sara in a small conference room at the lab. She guessed he was trying to impress her with his gray slacks and lighter gray long-sleeved shirt. She'd only seen him that dressed up when he was testifying in court. The lines to his sagging jaw lessened when Sara pulled a bag of homemade cookies from her satchel. He inspected the bag. "Good. I like oatmeal with raisins better than chocolate chip cookies."

Sara waited until Isaac was chewing his second cookie. "We both know this case is not apt to be a prank by friends gone astray. These guys knew methanol was no joke. Could Ab have been targeted? Or could it be a suicide?"

Isaac stopped chewing. "I figured you'd understand why my autopsy report was so tentative. You missed one obvious possibility. Both Gus and Ab were targeted. Both were heavy drinkers and apt to be more sensitive to methanol."

"Was someone trying to frame John?"

Isaac shrugged. "Perhaps."

"Before we get into technical details, tell me about the three men. I assume you knew all three."

"Ab was the coordinator for the gross anatomy course for all medical students at UNM for over thirty years. I was in his first or second class." Isaac leaned back in his chair and closed his eyes. "He always seemed like a sad, quiet man. Probably because he was. He'd given up his research because he needed a more predictable schedule to care for his wife who had been badly injured in an accident that killed their ten-year-old son. She died ten years ago—about the time Ab retired and moved into Happy Days. When I saw him at the med school annual holiday party the last few years, he seemed like a different man—a heavy drinker and a prankster. Last year he was shooting everyone with a squirt gun if they asked him a question. I thought it might be a sign of senility."

"What about Gus?"

"Didn't really know him but rumors swirled around him for years. Went through two—no I think three—colorful divorces. We in the ME's Office used him as a resource if we suspected mold toxins were important in a case."

"Pretty rare in New Mexico. The arid climate doesn't foster mold growth."

Isaac shrugged. "That's why I never worked with him. I heard he got in a fight with the Pharmacy Dean ten years ago and retired early. Don't know when he moved to Happy Days."

"You knew John best?"

"John is a Midwestern farm boy. Never did anything in excess and always cheerful. He seemed to enjoy being a physicist in the medical school where his research focused on magnetic resonance imaging." He bit into his third cookie. "Why wouldn't he be happy? He only taught one course a semester. But at seventy, his wife died and his sons both had positions on the East Coast. He moved to Happy Days about two years ago."

Sara's phone pinged. She checked her text messages. "Jack needs me ASAP at Happy Days."

## CHAPTER 4: Jack Meets a Goat

Sara's attention to detail was annoying at times. Today it was infuriating. She'd written the most thorough search warrants Jack had ever seen. "You'd think we were searching the home of a major drug dealer," he told Winslow as they drove to Happy Days.

Winslow chuckled. "She doesn't do anything without a reason."

Jack sighed. "She read a feature article in the *Albuquerque Journal* last week about institutions—like nursing homes and assisted living units—claiming guardianship rights over wealthy New Mexicans who the institutions suggested were senile. The families of the alleged victims charged the institutions were milking the senior citizens of their whole estates. Now she's acting like a boomer, which she isn't." He shook his head. "Isaac, the boomer in ME's office, is egging her on."

"What do you mean?"

"She's got the crazy idea that this death wasn't the result of a prank gone wrong but part of some sort of scheme to get the fortunes of three elderly men or to silence them. But she can't even suggest a logical scenario. I think it's a stupid prank done by bored seniors."

Winslow pulled the FBI van into the parking lot at Happy Days. "Sara's a mother hen. She's trying to make our lives easier when she prepares detailed search warrants."

"Problem is all the other agents know she's protecting me and call me a momma's boy."

***

Happy Days looked like an upscale condominium complex. Brass-framed glass doors led to an airy atrium in the central building. An oak counter blocked direct access to a bank of elevators. A woman at the counter smiled and cheerily said, "Who are you here to see?"

"I'm FBI agent Jack Drum." Jack flashed his badge. "I have warrants to search the apartments and cars of Ab Hess, John Lindberg, and Gus Rinaldi."

The woman pushed a button, turned, and whispered into a receiver. She turned back to Jack and smiled. "You'll have to talk to Mrs. Gonzalez first. We're protective of our residents."

Less than thirty seconds later, a short, dark-haired woman in a gray suit strutted from an office by the elevators. She looked Jack and Winslow up and down slowly. "You can't search their apartments. We at Happy Days are responsible for our residents' privacy."

"A federal judge says we can. It's part of a potential murder investigation. You realize one of your residents died Sunday night, and another is still hospitalized."

Rosa Gonzalez traced her pointer finger down the page as she read the documents. "I could stop you."

Jack tried not to smile. "If you try, I will summon additional agents to watch the apartments and you until your attorney advises you it is unwise to defy well-documented search warrants." He smirked and waved his hand toward the five residents who had already congregated around Winslow and his assistant—both wearing navy FBI caps. "It will make your residents more nervous."

She gulped as she glanced at the residents. "Surely you don't expect me to also allow you to search our pharmacy, janitors' closets, kitchen, and storage areas for cleaning supplies and anything that contains methanol."

"Yes Ma'am, I do. The three residents of Happy Days found in the bosque were professors in the medical and pharmacy schools." Jack decided it was best not to say, *they may have gotten the solution with methanol from your cleaning supplies.* That implied Happy Days was liable. "They might have hidden their source of methanol among your facility's supplies. Stalling our search will only increase the vulnerability of your residents." He thought what Sara would say and waved toward the five gawkers "You wouldn't want one of them to call a TV reporter."

Rosa Gonzalez trembled slightly.

"One of my senior colleagues would be happy to speak to you." *This woman would be no match for Sara.*

"Stay here." Rosa Gonzalez turned and spoke rapidly into her phone, listened, and then sighed. "You may do your search, but I will have my social worker and head of maintenance accompany you." She snapped her fingers at Winslow and led the FBI team to Ab Hess's apartment on the third floor of the adjacent building.

A short, thin Hispanic man in khakis was waiting. He bowed his shaved head to listen as Rosa Gonzalez's whispered orders and said, "Yes, Ma'am," repeatedly.

                                                  

After she stomped away, he extended a hand to Jack. "I'm Diego Rivera." He lowered his voice. "That woman is *loco como una cabra.*"

Jack had to think. His Spanish was only so-so. *Had the guy really said Rosa Gonzalez was crazy as a goat?* He shook his head. "Did she annoy Ab Hess and his friends—John and Gus?"

The man waved the crew inside and shut the door. "Many here are *ratas.*" He eyed Jack and must have decided Jack didn't understand. "Rats. They tell her everything. They think she'll give them favors. Me—my brother is in the sheriff's office—I don't play her games. Ab, John, and Gus weren't afraid of her either. They annoyed her daily with their pranks. We should talk before the social worker gets here. She's the chief rat."

Jack sent the lab tech to walk among this apartment and John's apartment down the hall and Gus's on the second floor because he was concerned Mrs. Gonzalez might send someone to raid the apartments. *I'm becoming as paranoid as Sara.*

Jack turned to Diego. "Tell me about Ab, Gus, and John."

"Nice men. Smart. Funny. Ab and Gus drank too much. That annoyed Mrs. Gonzalez. But she hated John."

"Do you know why?"

"He gave good advice to other residents."

Before he could explain, someone pounded on the door. Jack admitted a prune of a woman—her overly tanned skin wrinkled over her thin face and bean pole legs and arms. Her long, black hair had gray roots.

"Evie, social worker at Happy Days." She extended her hand with its long, polished red nails. "Do you mind if I smoke?" She didn't wait for an answer. She took a long draw on her already lit cigarette. "I hope Diego hasn't given you the wrong impression. We all felt sorry for Ab, John, and Gus. They were so senile"

Diego winked and moved away to watch Winslow in the bedroom.

Jack was prepared to distract the social worker from watching Winslow. He didn't need to worry. She quickly began to recite what sounded like a memorized essay about the infirmities—mental and physical—of the residents. Every other sentence was: "We need to protect them—mainly from themselves."

On the third repeat, Jack said, "I don't understand. Are you saying you allow people to live in your independent living building when you know they are too ill to care for themselves? That would suggest criminal negligence on your part." He coughed. *I'm beginning to sound like Sara. Where is she? She should be here by now.*

Evie's hand trembled and her cigarette ashes dropped on the carpet. She frantically rubbed the soles of her red high heeled sandals on the ashes. "No, but... Must you record everything?"

"Yes." He thought flattery might calm her. "You are an important person here. We value your opinions and will need to talk to you more."

Jack's phone vibrated. He read the message from Sara:

> *In independent living building now. Need a key to get into John's apartment. He's not answering his door.*
>
> *The tech you had roaming the halls saw Mrs. Gonzalez lurking near John's apartment. She left when she spotted his navy FBI cap. He's coming to you to get the master key.*
>
> *I'll be interviewing one of John's neighbors—a single women. The men's relative wealth could have made them attractive to women. Maybe a romance went bad.*

*Another groundless hypothesis: an unhappy lover poisoned the men.* Obviously, Sara hadn't noticed how decrepit most of the men and women here were.

Jack decided he needed to distract Evie, so she didn't realize the search of John's apartment was about to begin. He seated her at the kitchen island. "Evie, I have a list of residents. Can you mark which ones you saw with Ab, John, or Gus frequently?"

He went to the bedroom to retrieve the master key from Diego, but Diego seemed to be taking Mrs. Gonzalez's orders seriously. He was reluctant to give Jack the key until Winslow announced he was almost through in Ab's apartment and would meet Diego at Gus's apartment after Diego opened the door to John's unit for Sara and the other tech.

Jack returned to the kitchen and found Evie still studying the list. Ashes were all over the page. *This is one nervous woman.* He pointed to the list. "I see you checked only three women's names. Was Ab looking for a girlfriend?"

"He was a wealthy man and drank too much. Women pursued him. It worried me. He was senile and needed to be protected. They all did." Evie only stopped her long list of the men's needs to snuff out one cigarette and light another.

                                                     J. L. Greger

He thought for a second. If this went to court, as a social worker she was apt to be a witness who would be asked to assess the mental status of Ab, John, and Gus. The tape of this interview could be used to suggest her judgment was biased. It was hard to believe Ab, Gus, and John were such bad alcoholics that they should be wards of the institution. Isaac was sure John drank only in moderation. Maybe Sara was right *partially*.

Jack's phone vibrated. He read a message from Winslow. *Strange he didn't yell from the next room.*

> *Hate to ask, but should we check the garbage for pitched bottles with methanol?*

*D***. No wonder he texted me.* Jack stood. "Evie, you've been helpful. We're going to Guy's apartment next. Diego will be there. We won't tell Mrs. Gonzalez if you want to take a break."

Evie sighed. "I need a break."

***

Jack stared while Winslow whistled when Diego opened the door to Gus's apartment. Although Ab's apartment was neat, Gus's was cluttered.

Diego chuckled. "Bet you find lots of trinkets from ladies in the bedroom. Gus likes women." He looked down as if embarrassed. "I heard he knew how to please them."

"Any special woman?"

Diego shook his head. "Too smart." He paused. "Evie was one of his..."

Jack waited for Diego to finish his sentence. He didn't. "How about Ab and John?"

"No rumors. They went to church on Sunday morning and to the museum on Tuesday and Thursday afternoons. That's when Gus entertained the ladies. Evie always on Sunday when Mrs. Gonzalez was at church."

"You'd better come look," yelled Winslow from the bathroom.

Winslow pointed to a shelf in the bathroom closet covered with mainly pink, red, and black bras and panties. Notes were pinned to each of them. "I opened the closet looking for cleaning supplies. I couldn't help but notice these. Does it constitute *plain view?*"

Jack shrugged. *Sara was good at warrants. Why take a chance?* "They might suggest a motive for the poisoning. I'll tell Sara to get a new warrant, so there'll be no problems if it comes to trial."

Evie rejoined them as they began the search of all the janitor's closets. She chain smoked six cigarettes as Diego led Jack and Winslow to the janitor's closets on each of the three floors of the independent living building and those on the three floors of the second building with the assisted living apartments and memory unit. They found no windshield wiper fluid or hand sanitizers containing methanol. However, in the women's staff bathroom in the main building—behind the elevators—Winslow found a plastic bottle with a methanol-containing hand cleaning solution underneath the counter.

Jack hated to give the next order. "Winslow, looks like the lab crew needs to search all the garbage for methanol products." He turned to Diego. "When is your garbage picked up?"

Diego looked at his watch. "In about an hour."

"Not today."

## CHAPTER 5: Sara Takes a Back Door Approach

Sara skipped the front desk—as Jack suggested—and went directly to the building with the independent living units. She knocked on John Lindberg's door. No one answered. The tech circulating through the building saw her and explained the situation. He quickly agreed to get the key from Diego and begin the search of John's apartment while Sara interviewed the neighbors.

***

A lumpy woman—obese with a puffy, pale face and sunken gray eyes—opened the door to the apartment next to John's and eyed Sara cautiously. She pulled at her loose pink top, which only partially covered the compression sleeve on one arm and the flabbiness of the other.

"Ms. Kline, I'm from the FBI. As you may know, one of the residents—Ab Hess—died Sunday in the bosque. I'd like to talk to you."

"Call me Deb." The woman giggled as if she was a preteen girl. "Everyone was talking about it at dinner last night. John, my neighbor, was in the bosque with Ab. Is John all right?" She looked expectantly at Sara. "Are you investigating John?"

"We're trying to learn more about Ab's and John's activities during the last couple of days. We were surprised they were in bosque at night."

Sara noticed Deb rubbed the arm encased in the compression sleeve constantly. *Did the arm hurt?* The rubbing might be a nervous tic. *Time to relax Deb.* "Do you like it here? This is just the type of complex I'm thinking about moving into in a few years." Bug added some *schmaltz* and sat down by Deb's feet without being pushy and jumping.

It worked. Deb stopped scratching and leaned down to pet Bug. "What a good dog."

"What do you like most about Happy Days?"

Deb went into a long explanation of the exercise facilities, which Sara guessed Deb never used. It appeared the main way Deb interacted with others was by playing Mah Jong and Mexican Train Dominoes. It was pathetic when Deb noted proudly a few men played those games.

"Did John, Gus, or Ab ever play those games?"

"John, Gus, and Ab are... were called the Three Old Musketeers because they did so much together. Exercised in the gym daily. Attended lots of lectures. Played poker two nights a week and spent their other nights in the Bistro. John dragged Ab along when he volunteered at the National Nuclear Science and History Museum."

*Deb must spend a lot of time watching John.* "It must have been nice living next to an interesting man like John. When was the last time you saw him leave his apartment?"

Deb bit her lip. "The walls are thin. I can hear when he opens the door to his apartment. I heard him enter around two yesterday afternoon and then leave about ten minutes later."

*She's nosy.* "Did you ever run into each other in the hall or eat together?"

Deb blushed. "Sometimes I join him at lunch on Tuesday and Thursdays when he eats at eleven because he's working at the museum in the afternoon." She bit her lip. "But he talks mainly about science stuff—not very interesting to me—or national news."

"How about social stuff? I know you have dances, game nights, and concerts here. Do the Three Old Musketeers go?"

"Yes." Deb looked at her lap. "They usually sit in a corner and ignore us ladies. Gus and Ab act like little boys and use their squirt guns while John pretends to nap."

Sara's phone pinged. She glanced at the message and pulled a small box of four chocolates with a card attached from her tote. "Thank you for taking time to talk to me. If you think of anything else, my card is attached."

***

The technician was waiting for Sara and rushed her into John's apartment. All the drawers in the kitchen, bedroom, and a study were open. "John left in a hurry, or this apartment was ransacked."

"The neighbor said he came home around two yesterday and left after a few minutes. She didn't mention hearing anyone else enter the apartment, but I didn't ask. Find any methanol?"

"Lots of cleaning supplies but none with methanol. Not many medications or supplements. No evidence of empty spaces in the medicine cabinet, so I doubt he took any with him."

"How about his computer?"

"No computer—just a printer here."

Sara nodded and texted Jack and Winslow:

***

The couple—Sandi and Bob Jones—living across the hall from John Lindberg were in their early seventies. Sandi was friendly and invited Sara in. Bob was less sociable He started to retreat to another room when Sara entered the apartment. Sara accordingly focused her first questions on Bob.

Bob replied, "I run into John occasionally. Mainly we talk about the local soccer team—New Mexico United—or baseball." He cleared his throat.

Sandi peeked a glance at her husband before she added, "He's the one we contact when we have problems."

"What do you mean?"

"Six months ago, Rosa Gonzalez started nagging us to update our durable power of attorney documents because our son and his wife had moved to Colorado. She suggested we use the service offered by the parent corporation of Happy Days—I forget its name. John suggested we authorize our granddaughter—who still lives here—to have durable power of attorney for us. She's a lawyer anyway."

"Seems strange that Mrs. Gonzalez would know John advised you."

Sandi touched her husband's shoulder before she said, "But she did. She warned us we could be evicted if we continued to 'procure' business for our granddaughter. She made it sound dirty. I was scared."

Bob pushed his wife's hand off his shoulder. "My wife is a silly ninny. Our granddaughter asked a senior partner in her law firm to look at our rental contract and our durable power of attorney documents. He wrote a letter to Mrs. Gonzalez. The old bag hasn't spoken to us in the last month."

Sara was glad she was recording this conversation. "Did Mrs. Gonzalez have other reasons to be annoyed with John?"

"She doesn't like where he parks his SUV in the garage. She also claims he makes work for the janitors when he takes his own garbage in used grocery bags down to the bins. Most of us just let the maid provide standard white garbage bags and haul them away twice a week."

Sara's phone pinged. The timing of Jack's message was fortuitous:

*Found a hand sanitizer with methanol in a staff bathroom by the front desk.*

*Authorized Winslow and crew to go through garbage to see if containers which once contained methanol have been discarded. The garbage was last picked up two days before the murder.*

Sara responded immediately:

*John Lindberg seems to have a running debate with Rosa Gonzalez about his garbage. She claims he makes work for the janitors by bagging it and delivering to the bins himself. Look for his used grocery bags. Most use standardized white garbage bags.*

*Did you find the men's vehicles?*

Sara pulled a box of chocolates out of her tote. "Please call or email me if you see John."

## CHAPTER 6: The Garbage Tells a Story

Sara followed a trail of elderly to the garbage dumpsters behind the assisted living building. Somehow many of the residents had heard the FBI was searching their garbage.

It was ninety degrees in the bright sunlight, and the asphalt pavement on the parking lot around the dumpsters radiated heat. Some of the garbage had been in the dumpster since Friday afternoon. It reeked.

She snapped photos of the scene. Winslow must have recruited additional help. Two technicians were scrambling to pull garbage bags out of a dumpster and tote them to the open lot where three technicians and Winslow were opening the bags and assessing their contents. A small pile of full gray grocery bags and a couple of white bags with bottles were behind them. Diego was re-bagging the debris not saved by Winslow and his crew and placing it in a nearby unused dumpster.

Mrs. Gonzalez stood near the gate to the garbage dumpsters shooing residents away. She repeatedly announced, "There's nothing here to see. Go back to your homes." Her shrill voice seemed to be a magnet that attracted a crowd. Sara guessed forty were milling around the parking lot and more were coming from the buildings.

Jack was nowhere in sight.

Sara wandered through the crowd listening. Rumors were flying. Several were convinced the FBI was looking for John's body. They all seemed to know no one had seen John today. Most were trying to spot their own garbage.

One man was telling others John's garbage bags were being saved. He said, "I heard Mrs. Gonzalez yell at John for not using the standardized garbage bags." Sara photographed the speaker. She might need to talk to him later. She noted several men and women nodded in agreement.

Two women claimed they'd started to do the same thing because it was a way to keep the grocery bags from accumulating in their units. "It's good for the environment." Sara photographed them. They might have to identify their garbage before the afternoon was over.

Sara's phone pinged. She read Jack's message:

*John's SUV and Gus's compact car are in the lot, but Ab's Honda is missing. I had an APB on it and John sent statewide.*

*I told Evie about the underwear with labels in Gus's apartment. I suggested she would be smart to admit if her underwear was in his closet before we identified it. I thought it might get her talking.*

Sara responded:

*Good. The expanded warrants requested will be issued in a couple of hours. Then everything in the apartments will be fair game.*

*Watching the crowd at the dumpsters. I can blend in better than you and will try to get statements from several residents.*

*Contact Lindberg's sons to see if they've heard from him. Ask if Lindberg has any friends anywhere in New Mexico who might let him stay for several days. Then check out the crowd at the Bistro. That's where John, Gus, and Ab spent a lot of their time.*

Sara guessed Jack would have trouble coaxing information from the old-timers in the Bistro. He did not look like them. She'd spotted no Blacks and only one Oriental couple in the crowd near the garbage bins. Most were White. She couldn't guess which had Hispanic heritage but doubted most did. She hoped she was blending in enough here so residents would talk to her.

She sidled up to the two women who claimed they used grocery bags for their garbage and encouraged Bug to sniff at their feet. One bent down to pet Bug. Sara said, "Do you know why Mrs. Gonzalez cares about how you dispose of your garbage?"

Both women stared at Sara. The taller one stepped closer. "You don't live here. Who are you?"

Sara showed her ID. "Can we talk?" She glanced toward Rosa. "Let's move to the shady area between the buildings."

The taller one whispered, "Ruth, I told you Ab didn't die of a heart attack like Mrs. Gonzalez claimed."

***

Karen Wright and Ruth Lopez had been business officers in the med school prior to their retirement. They'd known John, Gus, and Ab for years. Both women volunteered for OASIS—a volunteer program that focused on educating and entertaining senior adults in New Mexico. Through OASIS, Ruth served as a tutor for high school students. Karen was involved in developing the lecture programs that OASIS sponsored. Both indicated they didn't particularly enjoy the social scene at Happy Days but liked their apartments and thought the food was good.

Although both freely admitted they liked John and Ab, they never hinted of romantic interest. Both agreed John was a "private man" who would want to escape answering questions about Ab's death. They supplied the names of three of John's former colleagues in Pathology Department who might have allowed him to stay with them. Sara noted one was Isaac Newson. She suspected both women knew more than they admitted.

"Do you think Mrs. Gonzalez picked on John, Ab, and Gus?"

Ruth laughed. "Gus enjoyed frustrating Mrs. Gonzalez because she was so pompous and excitable." She pointed at Rosa. "Only a fool would stand out in the sun shouting like she's doing now. If she went inside, the crowd would disappear in five minutes."

"Do she and Evie Schoener try to encourage residents without nearby families to select a commercial guardian?"

They both looked puzzled.

"Have you ever been encouraged to change your durable power of attorney documents?"

Ruth looked upward and shook her head. "Gus and John have a silly notion." She shrugged. "What Rosa and Evie were doing was logical. Many residents here don't even have a will. It's a problem. When Evie bugged me a month ago, I told them my arrangements were on file with my lawyer and gave her his name. She never asked me again."

Karen nodded. "Same for me." She frowned. "Evie and our consulting psychologist may be more forceful with residents in the memory unit. John was particularly worried about two retired profs there."

"Names?"

"Don't know. John was careful about what he said in public places. There are so many tattletales here. He referred to them as the *Eds*."

Karen looked around the shady area between the building, pulled out a pen, and wrote on the back of an envelope:

*EDs might be faculty from pEDiatrics or mEDicine.*

Ruth watched Karen scribble the note and then looked at Sara. "John works all sorts of puzzles daily. He's cautious enough to use codes in his records." She pulled Karen's arm. "We should go before Rosa sees us."

"One more question. Can we trust the head janitor—Diego Rivera?"

Ruth smiled. "Gus does."

***

Sara led Bug to the edge of the parking lot. She saw the crowd of spectators was reduced to only about a dozen. She was surprised Rosa Gonzalez was still there. Now she was waving her hands as she spoke to Winslow. The team of five techs appeared to be efficiently sorting through the garbage but still had at least two more hours of work to do.

Sara didn't want to confront Rosa, sent several texts, and headed to the main building.

Jack was waiting for her by the door. "I left email and phone messages for both of John's sons. So far, no responses. I'm also didn't get much info in the Bistro. The residents don't seem to be in a talkative mood."

Sara thought they might be more talkative to a gray-haired, White man. There was no need to point out the potential problem to Jack—a young Black man. She smiled. "It happens sometimes."

"The revised warrants for the apartments arrived. I'm going to pull two techs from garbage duty and have them thoroughly search John's apartment for prints and DNA. Thanks for getting the judge to approve the rekeying of the apartments. I was afraid what would happen after we left otherwise."

Sara nodded. "I'm going to focus on finding John. He could have been kidnapped, or he could be hiding because he poisoned his friends."

"More likely, he just didn't feel like answering questions."

***

Sara reached John's oldest son at his medical office in Philadelphia. "Dad is so independent. It's typical of him to not call and tell me that he's in a jam."

Sara didn't want to alarm the son but needed info. "Has he complained about Happy Days?"

He hesitated. "Not exactly, but he told me a week ago the employees seemed terrified of Alejandro Smith, a bigwig in the parent company. Dad spotted him entering the main office several times."

"Did he say anything more specific? Like whom Mr. Smith visited? Or what staff said after his visits?"

"He said the supervisor—I think Rosa Gonzalez—ran from her office to greet Mr. Smith at the front door." The son chuckled. "It must have been funny. Dad's an engineer by training and personality. He's not colorful when he talks. But he said, she ran like a chicken with its head cut off."

"Do you think your dad kept any notes?"

"Yep, I suspect he'll have Mr. Smith's business address, email address, and phone number in his blue book."

"What blue book?" Sara had a sickening feeling.

"The small blue leather notebook he keeps in his desk drawer."

"Where is this desk?"

"In his study."

"We didn't find a blue notebook. His computer is gone too."

The son lowered voice. "You've got me worried. Mom gave Dad that blue notebook. He would never take it out of his apartment..." After a long pause, "...unless he was leaving for a long time. Far as that goes, he seldom takes his laptop out, except when he's doing a slide presentation at the Nuclear Museum."

"Would you mind if I transfer you to one of our data analysts? She may be able to use your past computer and phone contacts with your dad to track him." Sara decided she needed to be honest with the son. "I'm afraid your father could have been kidnapped or has gone into hiding."

***

Sara learned nothing more from her phone conversation with John's younger son.

Her calls to two of the faculty members in Pathology—whom Ruth and Karen had suggested as knowing John well— yielded little. One noted that John had brought Karen to the department's holiday party. The other noted John was still reading scientific journals. Last week John had told him about a scientific article describing the use of MRIs when families rejected an autopsy of a relative.

When she called the ME's offices, she was told Isaac Newson had left for the day. She couldn't reach him at home either. She was debating how to reach him when Winslow called.

"I have good news, and I have bad news. John was a shredder. His garbage bags are filled with shredded paper."

"Suggests paranoia?"

"Don't know, but it makes sorting easier. The two women who claimed to discard their garbage in grocery bags don't shred papers. The bad news is it will be difficult to read anything in John's six grocery bags of garbage."

"What type of shredder did he use?"

"A strip-cut shredder."

"Hope you didn't discard his garbage. An analyst might be able to scan the shreds in a bag and use artificial intelligence to sort them into readable documents."

"Jack figured you'd come up with a weird idea. He's ordered us to haul all the small grocery bags and any garbage bags with bottles that might have contained methanol back to our building. It looks like only two men refilled their cars' windshield washer fluid tanks. At least we found only two empty bottles of windshield wiper fluid with methanol in the garbage. We haven't identified the men yet. But we found ten full or partially-full bottles of hand sanitizer. All were in three large bags. Jack is talking to Diego now about the hand sanitizers."

"Sounds like your efforts were worthwhile. Thanks."

"Hope so. It was a bad job in the sun." He paused. "But that's not why I called. We only sorted through two of the John's grocery bags—to identify I guess you could say his type of garbage. In one, we found a non-shredded slip of paper with a phone number and a couple of receipts." He gave Sara the phone number.

She gasped. It was a number she'd just called.

# CHAPTER 7: Jack Underestimates a Woman

Jack felt good. He was no longer in the direct sunlight amidst the rotting garbage. The three apartments had been rekeyed. Now he only needed to complete the searches of Gus's and John's apartments.

He got off the elevator and saw a woman with a pink chiffon scarf around her head bent over Gus's doorknob. He tried to walk silently down the long hallway to Gus's door. He didn't call for back-up. He could outrun any woman here, even if she had a forty-foot lead.

The woman looked up and darted away.

He yelled, "Stop!"

The woman ran faster. He was only four feet behind her when she turned and sprayed something in his face. He lifted his hand reflexively to protect his face. She kicked him in his crotch and ran. *D***!*

The woman may not have been a star pupil, but she probably had taken self-defense classes. He limped down the stairs and saw her race to a car. He called Winslow for help. "Stop anyone leaving the front entrance in a white compact car. She could be dangerous."

Rosemary emerged from the independent living building and ran toward Jack. "Are you okay?"

Jack decided not to admit how bad he hurt to this attractive woman whom he barely knew. "Sure."

He called Sara to determine who at Happy Days drove a white compact car. As he explained the situation to Sara, he noticed Rosemary was looking at the ground and occasionally peeking at him but was not giggling.

***

Winslow took charge of the scene immediately. He rubbed a cotton swab around Jack's eyes and smelled the sample. "Not mace. Oily. Eyes look blood shot, but not bad." He stared at Jack. "Does it burn?"

"No."

He sprayed sterile saline into Jack's eyes and blotted them several times before he asked Rosemary, "Weren't you and another tech in Gus's apartment during the chase?"

"We didn't hear anything unusual until you called."

Winslow nodded and called Diego. "Bring examples of all the aerosol cleaning products and polishes in your storeroom to the back entrance to the independent living building immediately. We've had an accident. Hurry."

Jack couldn't believe his ears. "Why bother him?"

Winslow smiled. "I figure the residents lift cleaning supplies from the storerooms. It's something my *wa'wa*—really all the old women I know—would do. I might be able to identify the spray the woman used by odor and how it feels on the skin." He turned to Rosemary "You might as well go back and finish raiding Gus's computer and phones. Have the tech cataloging Gus's collection check Gus's front door for prints."

"Wait," Jack waved his hand. "She had on gloves—probably plastic."

Winslow sighed. "We aren't lucky today. Rosemary, have the tech check the door anyway."

Jack forgot his aches as he watched Rosemary walk away. In her miniskirt and sleeveless top, her long legs and arms looked toned and shapely. Thus, he didn't notice Deigo's approach until he set two bottles of cleaners in pump spray bottles and one can of furniture spray in front of Winslow.

Diego eyed Jack but spoke to Winslow. "We spray only these products."

Winslow sprayed a tile and counter cleaner on his arm, sniffed, wiped it off quickly. "Not oily." He sprayed a stainless-steel cleaner and polish on his arm. "Feels right." He sprayed the furniture polish on the back of his hand, rubbed his hand, and sniffed. "Smells wrong—too lemony." He read the label on the stainless-steel cleaner and polish. "Better have a doc check you out. Label says it's fatal if swallowed."

***

Two hours later, Jack stopped by Gus's apartment. Rosemary filled him on the lab's progress. "Winslow went back to the FBI building with all the techs who sorted garbage. I uploaded everything from Gus's computer including discarded emails."

"And?"

"I found several threats from women." She gulped several times. "It wouldn't surprise me if one or more of the women with pieces in Gus's collection might have sent him hate notes or tried to retrieve their underwear before we arrived. But there's no evidence." She led Jack to the bedroom where the other tech had laid out Gus's collection of bras and panties.

The male tech handed Jack a laptop with a detailed inventory. "The women's underwear appear to have been collected over several years. The earliest piece of underwear is dated more than seven years ago. The latest one was collected last month. Each was labelled with a scrap of paper."

Jack was surprised all the bras and panties were colored. He wondered whether old women didn't wear basic white or natural-colored underwear or whether Gus only kept brightly colored ones. It appeared Gus preferred thin women. Only one bra was bigger than a 36B cup.

As expected, Evie the social worker was on the list. So, was Ruth Lopez and Olivia Bend. Three of the bras were labeled with dates but no names. Jack figured one of the six women must have been the one who had kicked him.

Rosemary thought the collection of trophies suggested Gus was "exhibiting the regressive behavior of a teenager." The male tech thought the collection was "impressive."

Jack agreed with the male tech and ordered him to take the underwear back to the lab because they might be useful sources of DNA later.

His phone vibrated. Sara's email contained more bad news:

*Found five white compact cars. Owners are Evie Schoener, Sandra and Bob Jones, Ruth Lopez, and two kitchen workers. If you're up to it, check on the current location of these individuals.*

*The lab chief says only Winslow will be able to work on the garbage samples for a day or two. She's angry he recruited so many of her staff to sort garbage today.*

*Physicians claim Gus can answer questions now. Bug and I will talk to him before we quit for the day.*

***

Jack trudged to the apartments and offices of those with white compact cars. He found Rosa Gonzalez in Evie's office rifling through a file drawer. Jack was too tired to ask Rosa what she was doing and only said, "Where's Evie?"

Rosa didn't stop searching the files and sneered. "I thought she was with you."

He found the Joneses in the dining room. They had arrived late to dinner—if you considered five-thirty late—because Bob had an appointment with an optometrist. Jack noted the name of the optometrist and looked for Ruth. She wasn't at dinner, and she hadn't been in her apartment.

The kitchen supervisor, Cookie, eyed Jack angrily when he asked to speak to a line cook and a server. "Did Mrs. Gonzalez send you to spy on us? How could they have gone anywhere in the last two hours? It's not easy to serve dinner to two hundred old people at five. The residents start circling the area like chicken hawks around four and all but pound the tables if we don't have salad and beverages on the tables by ten to five. They eat their main dishes fast; some want dessert by five-fifteen."

"Sorry. This hasn't been a good day for me either."

She looked at the clock and then her nervous employees. "It's ten to six now." She sighed. "Go check out your cars with this agent. Then come back and clean up."

The dinner crowd had dwindled when he and the two employees returned to the dining area. Jack was surprised to see Karen Wright and Ruth Lopez were sitting with the Joneses. They must have just snuck in because their main dish hadn't been served yet.

As he walked to their table, he saw something pink and filmy poking from Ruth's purse. "What's that?"

Ruth looked offended. "It's my scarf. I had my hair done and didn't want it to get messed."

He frowned. "Isn't that unlikely on a windless, sunny day?"

Karen patted Ruth's hand. "Men don't understand."

## CHAPTER 8: Sara Meets a Dirty Old Man

"I'm Sara Almquist with the FBI." Sara lightly touched Gus's shoulder as he sat in his hospital bed.

Gus seemed to focus on her even though his eyes were covered with dark glasses. "I can only see shadows, but I judge you to be a tall, sexy dame."

Sara laughed. *Gus was a flirt.* "Your vision is really bad but thanks." She pulled up a chair. "Do you mind if my pet therapy dog Bug sits on your bed?"

"Great. I like anything warm and soft."

Bug on cue snuggled up to Gus's hands.

"I know you've answered lots of questions, but I'm going to bore you with more." She decided to start with easy ones that he'd answered before. "Who brought the cans of beer on your camping trip?"

"John. It was the lite stuff. Neither Ab nor I drink it. No flavor."

"Who brought the wine?"

Gus began to pet Bug. "Ab brought the rosé. I brought the Wild Turkey. Somebody gave it to me for my birthday last month, and it was Ab's favorite."

*At least Gus is consistent in his answers.* "Were all the bottles unopened?"

He shook his head. "I'd had a drink from the Wild Turkey a week ago with friends."

"Who?"

"Must I say?"

"Yes, I'll have to crosscheck everything"

"Figured you'd say that. Your voice suggests you're used to lecturing large groups of people. You didn't happen to be a minister or a professor?"

"Nice try. I'll answer your question after you answer mine."

"Ruth Lopez and Karen Wright gave me the bottle for my birthday and had drinks with me. Your turn."

"I was a professor of epidemiology at Michigan State." She remembered Gus had retired early amid rumors of a disagreement with his dean. "But I got tired of university BS especially from my dean."

Gus continued petting Bug. "You must have been more disgusted than I was. I only retired; you moved across the country and took a job with the FBI. Bet that's miserable most days."

Sara decided not to let him distract her. "Where did you keep the bottle after it was opened?"

"On a shelf in my kitchen. Everyone who knows me knows where I keep my booze. Our decision to go to the bosque was a last minute one at lunch on Sunday. It was so hot. I just grabbed the first bottle I saw and the blanket from my bed."

It was time to share info with Gus. It might make him more talkative. "The lab determined there was no methanol in the wine bottle or beer cans, only in the Wild Turkey bottle. So, let's determine how much bourbon you three drank."

"I assume you already know John is almost a teetotaler. He only drinks lite beer." He stopped petting Bug and rubbed his arms. "My skin itches. Guess it's a side effect of the methanol. Let's see. I took a slug of Wild Turkey before I handed the bottle to Ab. He handed me his bottle of rosé. It was cheap stuff but tasted good because he'd brought ice along. It was cold."

"Was that all?"

Gus scratched some more.

The area was red. "Do you want me call the nurse for an antihistamine?"

"They'll just lecture me to stop scratching." He began to tickle Bug behind his ears. "Let's see, we talked about the weather. Trying to remember when a heat spell had lasted so long in August. You know we should be getting monsoon rains in the afternoons now." He sighed. "I was drinking the rosé. Ab offered me the Wild Turkey again. Took another slug." He shrugged. "Didn't taste good. Went back to the rosé. Ab kept drinking the Wild Turkey and didn't say much."

"Okay. I checked. It was a 750 ml—about twenty-five ounces— bottle. How big do you think your slugs were?"

"I've been thinking about that, too. I think only a tablespoon or two each time—two ounces total." He stopped petting Bug. "I'd opened the bottle on my birthday when Ruth and Karen gave it to me. We drank a lot that night to celebrate—at least twelve ounces."

"There was less than an ounce left in the bottle."

"Means Ab drank ten ounces." He shook his head. "He probably spilled some. He was really wasted and sloppy that night."

*Gus's mind is still sharp. He did the mental calculations quickly.* "But a considerable amount of methanol—let's say twelve ounces—was added to the bottle."

Gus shook his head. "Come to think of it, the bottle did seem almost full Sunday night when I took my first slug. I didn't think about it at the time. But we'd drunk almost half the bottle on my birthday. Means Ab could have drunk more than twenty ounces of bourbon mixed with methanol."

"Now let's talk about why you and Ab use squirt guns."

"That's easy. It's a way to escape serious conversations when we don't want to talk." He chuckled. "And it annoys Rosa so much."

"You mean Mrs. Gonzalez?"

"Yes. She even had the on-call psychologist—Dr. Herb Snow—talk to me. He laughed as I explained that squirting Mrs. Gonzalez was a way to get her to clear out of the dining area. Everyone talks less when she is around."

"I'd heard several people tattled to her."

"That was Evie's only function, well almost...."

Sara waited for him to finish his sentence for thirty seconds. "Is she a good social worker?"

"She's fast at the paperwork when she transfers someone to the memory unit." His lips twitched. "Guess you've been in my apartment by now and know... She's good in the sack."

"Who else fed info to Rosa?"

"The sob story—Deb Kline. No one else would listen to her talk about her cellulitis after her breast cancer surgery. Sad, but enough is enough."

***

Sara checked her messages. No one from the Pathology Department or the National Nuclear History and Science Museum had spotted John Lindquist. Isaac Newson hadn't replied to her phone calls, emails, or texts. Sara sighed and drove to Isaac's home in the Northeast Heights of Albuquerque.

She thought she spied lights in the back of the two-story, beige stucco house. Sara wanted to leave Bug in the car in case she had to chase John and/or Isaac. But it was still too hot at seven in the evening. Instead, she led Bug to the front door and rang the doorbell twice. No one answered.

She opened a decorative iron gate and walked along a path at the side of the house to the back yard. A man stood with his back to her.

Isaac stopped turning kabobs on the grill when he saw her. "John, our company has *finally* arrived."

## CHAPTER 9: Sara Meets an Innocent Man?

The man who stood on Isaac's patio was about six-feet tall and one-hundred-fifty pounds with a thick head of silvery hair. John Lindquist looked like his photo. He motioned Sara to a teak table with three place settings and a big bowl of salad. "Isaac expected you an hour ago. He was getting worried we'd have to eat without you."

Isaac turned from the grill and bent down to offer a bit of beef to Bug. "The other agents claim you treat Bug like your partner—protectively. But of course, I wouldn't know. You've never brought Bug or your partner—except one time—along to the morgue."

*Not another joke about Jack.* Sara had planned to question John, lecture Isaac on professional courtesy—hiding a witness from a colleague was a no-no—and grab a hamburger on the way home. She could see it wasn't going to happen as Bug pulled on his lead toward Isaac. *Isaac had won.*

Sara let go of Bug's lead, called to remove the APB on John, and consulted with Jack. By the time she'd completed the process, Isaac had put a platter of grilled kebobs of beef, red peppers, onions, and cherry tomatoes on the table along with a large bowl of guacamole.

***

She had finished only a few mouthfuls when John said, "I need to explain. I know I look like the villain since Ab is dead and Gus is partially blind. *But* I'm innocent."

Isaac cleared his throat.

John ignored him and continued. "I hate to be paranoid, but I think I'm being framed. Isaac suggested I talk to you." He smiled at Isaac. "He's not guilty of anything but trying to calm a friend."

Sara decided to reprimand Isaac later. She smiled broadly. "Don't worry about Isaac. You need to answer all my questions completely and honestly even if the details are unpleasant. I'll record everything because my partner…" *Best not to admit Jack's latest problem. Isaac would use it to tease Jack.* "My partner is completing the search of Gus's apartment."

John's Adams apple bobbed in his throat. The stark white of his upper arms showed when he stretched across the table to pass the guacamole. He really looked like an aging Midwestern boy of the 1950s or 60s—earnest, muscular, with a tan that ended at the edge of his short-sleeved shirt.

"I've been thinking. No one knew we were going to the bosque unless they heard our discussion at Sunday dinner. We all arrived late to dinner—around twelve-thirty—because Ab and I had gone to church. We didn't start to make our plans until almost one-thirty. By then, the ladies who had sat our table had left." He blinked. "Doesn't sound nice, but we avoid making plans in front of the ladies. We don't want them to tag along."

Sara didn't often interview someone who seemed so forthcoming—almost answering questions before she asked them. *Could be an effective way to confuse an interviewer.* "Why don't you want the women's company?"

"None of us are looking for wives. Gus likes the company of women but prefers ones who don't talk much." He blushed. "You know what I mean if your partner has searched his bedroom."

Sara decided to try to relax John with a personal comment. "I understand. My boyfriend and I think living together all the time would destroy our relationship." *Enough of my personal life.* "Who was left in the dining room as you discussed your plans?"

"My neighbors—Sandra and Bob Jones and Deb Kline." His Adam's apple bobbed when he swallowed. "I doubt they could hear us. Don't remember any others."

Sara leaned down to give Bug a piece of meat. "Probably doesn't matter. I doubt anyone added the methanol to Gus's bottle of Wild Turkey that day. I imagine it had been added earlier. How long…"

John didn't wait for her to complete her sentence. "We went back to our units, took naps, and met at seven in Gus's unit. We'd decided it would be cooler then to walk to the bosque."

"Why his apartment?"

"His neighbors are less nosy."

"Why didn't you drive?"

"It was less than a mile." He gulped. "We needed the exercise."

"What happened at the bosque?"

"Strung a rope between two trees and spread two blankets underneath. I didn't think we should hang the blanket on the rope until nightfall. It looked too much like camping. Then Gus and Ab began to drink—really drink—and talk about their favorite conspiracy theory. I turned on my camp lantern, sipped my beer, and worked a Sudoku puzzle from the Sunday paper."

As he spoke, Sara reviewed the inventory of the items found by the Albuquerque police at the murder scene and Jack's notes. *Everything jives. Time to surprise him.* "Is there any chance either Gus or Ab laced the Wild Turkey with methanol? Either to commit suicide or to kill the other?"

Isaac gasped.

John dropped his fork. "No way. They've both lived at Happy Days almost ten years and were as close as brothers. Especially since they had developed their conspiracy theory."

"Tell me about their conspiracy theory."

"About five years ago, they'd noticed several—I think six—of the residents in the independent living unit developed the DTs—delirium tremors. Anyway, all were moved to the memory unit and died there within a few months. Ab thought it strange because he didn't think three of then drank much. He was sure two hardly drank at all. He obtained their death certificates and autopsy reports." John glanced quickly at Isaac.

Isaac suddenly found it necessary to tend to the empty grill.

"Remember I'm a physicist who was employed in the medical school, not a biologist or a pharmacologist like Ab and Gus. So, I may not get the details right. As I understood it. Liver cancer was listed as the cause of death for all six of them, but only two had been autopsied." John looked down at his plate. "Anyway, that sparked Gus's interest. He became obsessed with looking for what he called liver toxins in the food at Happy Days. He collected certain foods and sent them for analyses."

Isaac turned from the grill. "Better add one detail. Gus's research specialty was aflatoxins—liver toxins. He knew aflatoxins could cause cirrhosis and liver cancer."

John straightened in his chair like a student proud he knows the answer. "Yes, and a major source of aflatoxins is mold on peanuts. Gus sent several samples of the peanuts served in the Bistro to a commercial lab."

Sara was intrigued. "Wasn't that expensive?"

John shrugged. "Money wasn't a problem for Gus. He'd done lots of consulting as a professor and collected large fees. I think one of his past students ran the contract lab he used. Anyway, the peanuts served from five to three years ago had high levels of aflatoxin."

"Odd in this dry climate."

John shrugged. "Gus and Ab talked to Ruth. She was in the financial office at the med school and used to tracking invoices. I'm not sure how they did it, but they discovered a vendor who sold peanuts to Happy Days had been hit hard when FDA recalled most of their products about five years ago because of high levels of aflatoxin."

"Okay? What did Gus do?"

"He sent anonymous letters to the New Mexico offices that monitor nursing homes and food safety. He thought no one knew what he'd done because Ab convinced someone else to let Gus use their computer and printer."

Sara was afraid to ask whose computer and printer. She looked at Isaac.

He sighed and took the dirty plates into the house.

*It will take days to confirm this story.* "Any changes in behavior by Rosa Gonzalez or staff after the letters were sent?"

"Not really. Evie Schoener may have stopped by our table more. Ab thought Rosa Gonzalez had ordered Evie to pump Gus." John blushed. "Gus claimed it was because of his charm and bedroom skills. I think Ab was right."

"What do you think? About their theory?"

"There are holes in their theory, but the management of Happy Days is hiding bad secrets. That means the management might try to silence Ab, Gus, and—I suppose—me. I got them the squirt guns at Christmas because it made them look senile and harmless."

Sara remembered a point from Jack's notes. Diego Rivera the janitor at Happy Days, claimed Mrs. Gonzalez *was crazy like a goat*. Sara thought the phrase could be used to describe the Three Old Musketeers, too.

# CHAPTER 10: Wishful Thinking

*Wednesday*

Sara's phone rang at five-thirty in the morning. "Sorry, I'm early but I have a lot to do today." Sanders didn't stop for breath. "Your emails got me thinking. I found three sterling silver teething rings in my mother's old horde of expensive junk. I doubt my daughter will ever want them. She and her boyfriend show no interest in starting a family. They might be good christening gifts for Carbonne's child."

*He's really wound tight today.* "Hello, dear. I like your idea. I was going to buy *onesies* in a couple of sizes for Willow."

"What are onesies? And why multiple sizes?"

"Body suits for babies. Most people only give clothes for newborns, and babies grow rapidly. A silver teething ring would be a classy addition to my practical gift."

"Why not all three rings? They are no good to me."

"Your daughter is twenty-five has just started a law clerkship with a federal judge in Manhattan. It's natural that she has no interest in a family now. She may change her mind by the time she's thirty-five. However, I doubt she'll want more than two children. Are the silver teething rings already engraved?"

"No. They are in a pristine—albeit tarnished—state. My mother probably bought them as gifts and then forgot them. Would they be an appropriate gift?"

*Useless, but showy.* "Yes, one would be a nice memento. But I can't get it engraved here if you don't arrive until Friday afternoon."

Sanders moved to his favorite topic. "The senator from New Mexico agreed to support my candidacy for director of the Bureau of Intelligence and Research in the State Department. That's important because the position carries the rank of Assistant Secretary of State."

Sara wanted to shorten the dialogue. "I know that means the appointment would require Senate approval. What else did the senator from New Mexico want?"

"He and the chair of the Senate Intelligence Committee would like me to work on one more project before I leave in October to assume a larger teaching assignment at Quantico."

*That was news.* Sara hadn't known until now *when* Sanders planned to leave his interim position with the intelligence committee. She understood his unhappiness with his current assignment, but it had been a way for him to "not look defeated" after losing his appointment as the Interim Ambassador to Brazil. "Okay, can you talk about this new project?"

"No."

"Don't let your..." Sara considered her word choice carefully. "...eagerness for a potential position cloud your judgment." She didn't pause to give him time to object. "If you can't fly to New Mexico this weekend, it's okay. I'm sorry I've made your life harder by not coming to Washington this weekend as planned. But as the godmother, I must go to the christening."

There was silence. "I'll get back to you later. I'll send the teething ring by overnight mail to you." He hung up without saying, "Love you."

*This was a first.* He always before ended calls and emails with the word *love.* Their relationship often had rocky spots, but Sara thought they were approaching a major divide. Her inability—if she was honest, her unwillingness—to fly to Washington this weekend was a breach of their tacit agreement to support each other. It was a symptom of their deteriorating bonds.

Sanders wanted a full-time helpmate, who could disappear when he was busy and reappear as needed. It was an impossible task for Sara. Thus, she had continued to be a science consultant for the FBI and other agencies. It gave her a focus and ironically made her more interesting and useful to Sanders. *Perhaps not a healthy, but until now a functional, relationship.*

She emailed a peppy note of encouragement to Sanders and checked her freezer and pantry. She'd better have the supplies for quick meals just in case he changed his mind and visited Albuquerque this weekend.

***

"Sorry to bother you, but I didn't want to put my comments in writing." Sara plunked in a chair at Carbonne's conference table and seated Bug at her feet.

Carbonne had not bothered to look up from his computer until she said, *didn't want to put it in writing.* He stared at her for a second, pulled two diet colas from his undercounter refrigerator, and sauntered to the table.



J. L. Greger

Sara shook her head after taking a long slug of cola. "Isaac Newson in the ME's Office may have been too involved in my case to have done the autopsy. If this goes to trial, he may appear to have abetted criminal activity."

Carbonne sighed. "Do I need to alert the ME?"

"Probably. Isaac is friends with the victim and his two friends—who must now be considered potential suspects in the murder. They were convinced the management of Happy Days was involved in some sort of scheme to gain access to accounts held by residents by claiming they were senile."

"That charge has been made against several nursing homes and assisted living facilities in New Mexico. It could be true."

Sara nodded. "They also seem to have shown the management of Happy Days knowingly served peanuts that were contaminated with dangerous levels of aflatoxin."

"What does that mean?"

"FDA may fine the vendor and maybe Happy Days. Families of residents of Happy Days who died of liver cancers after eating the peanuts might sue."

"Where does Isaac come in?"

"He gave them copies of the death certificates and autopsy reports of all residents who died at Happy Days during the last six years."

"Yep, he violated the rules of the ME's Office."

"But Isaac, Gus, and Ab could be considered whistleblowers. The problem with the guys' theory is excess alcohol intake, as well as aflatoxin, causes cirrhosis and liver cancer. John is a second-hand source of info, but he said six residents in the memory unit died of liver cancer around five to six years ago." Sara paused. "That suggests alcoholism is a problem at Happy Days. However, Ab and Gus claimed most of these individuals didn't drink excessively." She frowned. "But Gus and Ab might not have been good judges of what constitutes excess intake of alcohol."

"What do you want to do?"

"Give the data to FDA. I think the FDA can use the data to levy a large fine against the company—American Peanut Supply—and maybe a smaller fine against Happy Days. That should trigger the New Mexico Health Department to investigate procedures at Happy Days."

"What will that achieve?"

"It's the right thing to do." She petted Bug. "The FDA and New Mexico Health Department investigations will make people at Happy Days nervous and talkative." Sara smiled. "Someone will slip, and we'll learn who added methanol to the bottle of Wild Turkey Bourbon that Gus brought to the bosque." She smiled again. "Then Isaac can be considered a whistleblower, and the ME probably won't fire him.'"

Carbonne frowned. "Since when, did you believe in fairy tales? Your scenario has more *ifs* than I can count."

"Got any better ideas? The Attorney General of New Mexico likes showy cases where he can demonstrate he's protecting voters. Perhaps we'll be able to shift much of the work for this case to FDA and state agencies. The federal district attorney should be pleased if we lighten his load."

"I don't know. My basic problem is which agency to call first." Carbonne drained his can of soda. "I guess the US Attorney for New Mexico." He shook his head. "Why did Isaac have to get you involved in this case? This will waste a lot of time. I'll expect you to sit in on my call later today."

Sara stood and led Bug to the door. "It looks like Sanders won't be coming to the christening. He's wrapped up in a new investigation for the Senate Intelligence Committee."

"I thought he was leaving the committee's staff soon."

"He is, *but* he's convinced the senators on the committee will support his nomination for assistant secretary in the State Department if he does them one last favor."

"Bet they're probably all laughing at him and his ambition." Carbonne shook his head. "He obviously has the right record for the job. But do those in power *like* him? One more favor won't change their attitudes toward him. Makes me glad I got married and forgot any wild ambitions." He frowned. "But I don't have his family background, professional experience, or you." He walked to the door and put his hand on Sara's shoulder. "He'd never admit it, but he needs you. You ground him and make him more likable."

"Do you mind if I put in a call a friend in the FDA? It might stimulate their review of American Peanut Supply and Happy Days."

## CHAPTER 11: Jack Develops Empathy?

Jack felt sorry for Winslow. The lab director had clipped Winslow's wings. Only Winslow would be analyzing data on the case today.

Jack slapped Winslow on the back and said, "I guess Sara and I should take it easy today and not create work for you."

Sara, who had blown into the meeting at the end, winced. "What Jack means is: we'll be grateful for anything you do. If possible, check out the materials I got from John and Isaac last night." Sara pulled several pages from her tote and began to hand them to Winslow. Suddenly, she pulled them back. "Never mind. Forget what I just said."

Jack darted a look at Sara and rushed her out the door. "What are you talking about?"

***

At first, Jack was annoyed that Sara had gone to Carbonne before discussing her findings from last night with him. As he listened to her convoluted explanations, he was almost relieved. He doubted this mess of charges would benefit the residents of Happy Days, let alone elderly in what she'd called "poorly run senior facilities" throughout the state. *What a dreamer. And what about Ab's murder?*

They agreed as soon as they departed for Happy Days that Jack should talk to Diego. Sara said, "I'll try to distract Rosa Gonzalez and Evie Schoener, so they don't notice what you're doing. But I don't want to confront them." Sara was quiet for the rest of the trip but smacked her gum loudly.

*Bet her plan is a doozy.*

Jack lagged as Sara raced from the back parking lot to the main building. First, she stopped at the Bistro to read the sign and stare through the glass door. Then she progressed to the beauty shop. It looked as if she was making an appointment.

Jack doubted it was for herself. Sara had never mentioned going to beauty shops or spas in the six months he'd worked with her. He knew she cut her own blonde hair—which was not her crowning glory—in what she called a bob. His mother, who was a hair stylist, had met Sara a couple of months earlier and suggested Sara should get hair extensions. Sara had wisely ignored the advice. Jack thought hair extension looked great on his mother, but thought they looked weird on White women—especially ones of his mother's age.

Sara joined him on a bench under the shade of several pear trees in the grassy area between the buildings. "The Bistro is closed today until five. So, I figured the best place to hear gossip was in the beauty shop. I'm getting a manicure in ten minutes."

Jack snorted but knew enough not to say, *Why bother?* He changed the subject. "Strange they're not opening the Bistro until five today."

"Not really. They appear to be replacing the carpeting. I saw Diego supervising the work."

Jack nodded. "It will be hard to pull him aside for questions if Rosa is monitoring the work, too."

"Maybe not. The woman I talked to at the FDA was eager to talk to Rosa."

Jack stared at Sara. "I thought your scheme was a fantasy. I didn't know you've started the ball rolling. Does Carbonne know?"

"Of course."

***

Rosa Gonzalez was lecturing Diego at the back of the Bistro. Even at a distance, Jack could see that Diego was unhappy as he directed two men to roll up the old purple and blue carpet. Jack decided to avoid Mrs. Gonzalez and check the locks on John's apartment.

When he returned, Rosa was gone. Rolls of old carpet lay near the doorway of the Bistro. Jack bent down to study them. They seemed to be dirty with a lot of embedded grit. *Maybe peanut shells.*

Diego was talking on his phone. One assistant was vacuuming and the other stacking the old baseboards and trim in a garbage can. Diego held up op one finger when he saw Jack. He ended his phone conversation and turned to his crew. "The carpet guys will be here in forty minutes. Have it ready."

Diego muttered as he walked past Jack. "Meet you at Gus's apartment in five."

***

Diego was breathless when he arrived at Gus's apartment. "After you left yesterday, I got thinking. Bob Jones sometimes stands up at lunch and announces when he buys a new bottle of windshield wiper fluid. Then he and John top off the fluid in other residents' cars."

"How did John get involved?"



J. L. Greger

"He's John's neighbor. I asked Bob yesterday afternoon if I could get some windshield wiper fluid from him. He said he used up his supply and threw out his last empty jug on Sunday. It might be one of the empty jugs you found in the garbage."

*Darn. Means John had access to methanol.*

"So, am I a good detective?" Diego self-consciously rubbed his hands together and stared at Jack. "Maybe, you can help me get a job with the police. Anything is better than here. Mrs. Gonzalez is *loco como una cabra.*"

Jack felt guilty exploiting the poor guy. He'd tell Sara. She had a soft spot for sob stories. "What's up with Rosa today?"

Diego shook his head. "This morning, she decided—no warning—to get new carpet for the Bistro. I told her months ago I couldn't get the carpets clean—so much junk embedded in the fibers." He shrugged. "She had said, 'The old drunks can't see in the dark Bistro.'"

Jack nodded and motioned for Diego to sit on Gus's sofa. "Who ordered all the full bottles of hand sanitizers be discarded?"

"Mrs. Gonzalez, of course. On Monday afternoon, she called me into her office and said it was dangerous to have methanol around all the 'old drunks.' I didn't know what she was talking about. She pulled a bottle from under her desk and ordered me to pitch all the bottles of hand cleaner with the same label." He shook his head. "I'd just finished that job when you arrived on Tuesday."

Jack thought for a moment. "Did she discard the bottle in her office?"

"How would I know?"

"Why didn't you pitch the bottle in the staff bathroom?"

"We did. The bottle you found appeared after I had checked that bathroom." He looked at his watch. "I've got to get back to the Bistro."

***

Sara was waiting in the shade of the pear trees.

"Let's see your hands."

Sara wiggled her fingers in front of his face. She'd been smart and hadn't selected fake nails or a bright polish. Her nails glistened a bit and were more uniform than usual.

"The manicurist couldn't do much for what she called 'my workaday' hands. Doesn't matter. I learned a bit about the Three Old Musketeers. Basically, John and Ab are considered catches—wealthy and polite. Less so Gus. He has a reputation as a swinger. Everyone seemed to know about his collection of women's underwear."

"Nothing new."

"Two of the women noted Gus avoided married women." Sara chuckled. "The old girls must watch Gus constantly. Their estimates of when he 'courted' Olivia Bend, Ruth Lopez, and Evie Schoener correspond well to the dates on the bras' labels."

*No wonder the guys felt like prey.* "Don't you think the women's comments are weird?"

"According to the CDC, STI infections in those over fifty-five doubled between 2012 and 2022."

Jack's lower jaw dropped.

"CDC is the Centers for Disease Control and Prevention. STIs are sexually transmitted infections."

"I'm not a baby. I know the abbreviations. What I don't understand is: where do you get stats like that?"

Sara smiled. "I gather info from a variety of sources at the start of the case. It helps me understand motives better. So, I found Gus's behavior less surprising than you did. I think we'd better check with Gus to be sure none of his trophies are missing." She checked her phone. "One more thing, the women didn't seem to know about aflatoxin in the peanuts served in the Bistro." She bit her lower lip. "But then they—at least the four in the shop—didn't know anything about our three men except their food and drink preferences and their relative wealth. Nothing about what they thought."

"I guess I'll talk to Gus this afternoon while you talk to the US attorney or one of his assistants."

"Two more points. They all complained that Evie Schoener kept asking them about their estate plans. No one thought Gus, Ab, or John were senile, just rude."

***

Gus was in a pensive mood when Jack arrived at his room in the hospital. "They think I'll never regain my sight completely. All I can look forward to is blurred images and no driving." He looked at Jack. "You look like a handsome dude. Would you want to buy 1962 Thunderbird Sports Roadster in Diamond Blue?"

Jack gasped. "That's one heck of a car. It could be worth more than thirty thousand."

"Try forty thousand. Worth it to a young guy like you. It's a chick magnet."

"Not the type of woman I'm looking for."

"Oh, you're serious like Ab and John. That's too bad. I'd give you a discount."

Gus seemed to enjoy talking about his collection of women's underwear. Nothing seemed to be missing in the inventory, but he refused to name the owners of the underwear without names labels. All he would say was sets were from residents and an employee at Happy Days. He also refused to discuss his relationship with Evie Schoener or Ruth Lopez, except to say they were "nice women."

In contrast, he was eager to talk about Olivia Bend. "Olivia was the best—smart, funny, kind." Gus cleared her throat. "And not an alcoholic like Rosa Gonzalez claimed when she died. That's why I recruited Ab, Isaac, and Ruth to help me stop Rosa Gonzalez."

Jack knew Sara would give the man a hug. *He couldn't. It wouldn't look right.* He wondered whether he could end up like Gus some day—a lonely old man who put too much emphasis on his career. "Could Mrs. Gonzalez have been following orders from her boss?"

"That's what John thinks."

# CHAPTER 12: Is Sara in Trouble?

The video conference with an assistant US attorney—Ted Cottingham—started well. He liked the idea of letting the Office of Criminal Investigations (OCI) in FDA assess the possibility the liver cancer deaths among present and past residents of Happy Days was due partially to ingestion of aflatoxin in illegally obtained peanuts. He agreed with Sara that the FDA might be able to prove the management of Happy Days knowingly bought the contaminated product and was criminally liable as was American Peanut Supply.

As Cottingham spoke, Sara was reminded of a guy she had a crush on in high school. Both had ruddy complexions, blond hair, the same last name, and similar frowns. *Guess that's not a good omen. The guy in high school was a snob.*

The middle-aged lawyer peered over his reading glasses. "I decided to take this case instead of letting the younger attorney who usually works with you handle it because it's..." He coughed. "...complex."

Sara tried not to act nervous. She feared his next questions. Carbonne had warned her that Ted Cottingham was a stickler for details. "I've watched Cottingham reduce several agents to tears."

"Did you share the illegally obtained death certificates and autopsies John and Isaac gave you last night with anyone?"

Sara thought a second. "I gave a copy to Carbonne." She glanced at Carbonne and was struck by his frozen stare. "He shared them with you I assume."

"Yes, unfortunately."

"I almost gave them to Winslow Red Feather in the FBI Lab but didn't." She pulled her phone out of her tote. "I recorded our conversation."

"Odd. Convenient."

"No. I record almost all my conversations with anyone but my partner Jack Drum and Carbonne." She gulped. "It's safer that way. I knew the death certificates and autopsy reports Isaac shared with John, Gus, and Ab could be considered *fruit of a poisonous tree*. But I thought last night it was logical when John offered them to me. This morning, I suddenly realized I didn't want to involve the FBI lab in what may have been my mistake."

Sara watched the screen behind Carbonne's desk and saw an aide hand Cottingham several documents. He flipped through them. "Whistleblowers create messes every time."

Sara gave a quick smile. "It may not be so bad. The OCI investigator I talked to this morning didn't want copies of the autopsy reports I had. She thought FDA could legally request them based on tips from the whistleblowers—that is copies of the anonymous letters John, Ab, and Gus sent to state agencies."

Cottingham loosened his tie. "You dodged a bullet. I'll confiscate your phone."

"Oh, one more thing from my conversation with the FDA official. She was impressed with the lab analyses. Gus's past student evidently runs a lab that frequently provides data for the FDA."

The aide placed a phone in front of Ted Cottingham. He squinted at a message. "Your FDA contact emailed us. She claims she seldom works a case where law enforcement officers are so organized and helpful." He frowned. "Don't let it go to your head."

Carbonne emitted a soft sigh.

Sara wanted to take control of the conversation while she was on a roll. "I assume I can use the death certificates and autopsy reports if I get copies from the FDA. Can I use the letters John provided to put pressure on the employees at Happy Days during the murder investigation of Ab Hess?"

The aide shoved a page in front of Cottingham, who studied it for a moment. "You've determined Gus Rinaldi brought the contaminated bourbon on the camping trip. Why isn't he the prime suspect?"

Sara didn't let him gain control of the conversation. "Gus is partially blind because of drinking the bourbon laced with methanol now."

"He's could have been desperate."

"He had no motive. But there are those who had motives."

"Like those managing Happy Days? Don't confront them until FDA has officially gotten the death certificates and autopsy reports in a legal manner and launched their investigation. Is that it?"

The aide coughed, fumbled with a phone, and shoved it at his boss. Cottingham chuckled as he read.

Sara guessed he was reading Winslow's report on Gus's apartment. "I think you can see. Several women may have had a reason to kill Gus Rinaldi. He's quite a Romeo."

Ted stared at the camera. "The guys here warned me about you. Does Carbonne dislike you and give you weird cases? They tell me your last one in the ghost town of Golden Gully may have had the strangest murder weapon ever."

Carbonne coughed. "Quite the contrary. Sara was my favorite partner before I became the SAC in the Albuquerque office. She's thorough. I trust her with complex cases even though she's not an agent." He reddened slightly. "But I gave her this case because Isaac Newson requested her. He wanted a scientist to read Ab Hess's autopsy report. His boss—the ME—agreed." Carbonne shrugged. "I thought I was giving her an easy one—a prank gone astray."

Cottingham continued to study his phone. Sara thought it odd that he was so interested in women's underwear. Finally, he muttered, "These are racy for someone my mother's age."

*Better not chide him for his ageist comment.* "One set is particularly interesting. Evie Schoener is the social worker at Happy Days. My partner texted me a few minutes ago. Gus claims she became flirtatious with him after he started investigating the deaths of his friends."

"So, we're back to the poisoned peanuts again?"

"Yes. I'm hoping FDA's investigators will make people nervous and talkative." She gave a quick glance at Carbonne. "He doesn't want me to say this, but the New Mexico Attorney General is always running for office. He might be willing to encourage the New Mexico Health Department to join FDA in investigating the management of Happy Days."

Cottingham's voice boomed. "And what will that accomplish?"

"It will probably result in news stories and increase the pressure on the management of Happy Days. Residents and employees are apt to become talkative." Sara saw his face had become redder. "You might even be able to return this murder investigation to APD and state courts. That would simplify your life and mine."

"Stop dreaming. You and I will have to clean up this mess together. Are we through for today?"

Carbonne raised his hand. "I should notify the ME of Isaac's inappropriate actions. She'll blow a gasket. Sara would like to protect him because he's a whistleblower."

Ted frowned. "Dr Almquist is not a legal expert."

"But I was on faculty committees at Michigan State which considered scientific misconduct cases based on the findings of whistleblowers."

Cottingham reddened more. "Mr. Carbonne does Dr. Almquist always offer her opinion so freely? Does she respect your decisions as the SAC?"

Carbonne coughed. "I always win *if* I insist."

"Good. Tell the ME that Dr. Newson has created a legal situation but warn her not to punish him until we have more evidence. She should not allow him to perform any more autopsies that might be associated with this case or transfer any more info on this case to anyone not with the FDA or New Mexico Health Department."

Ted pointed at Sara. "Immediately inform me if Dr. Newson tries to communicate with you. Somehow, I'm sure that will occur." He sighed. "Sara, you can leave."

***

An hour later, Carbonne wandered down to Sara's office. She and Jack were huddled over an organizational chart for Happy Days.

Jack looked up first. "Rosa Gonzalez has irritated a lot of the staff and residents at Happy Days. Several stopped me today and wanted to speak to me outside the building. Sara thinks we should first focus on Rosa Gonzalez's bosses, the medical director of the memory unit, and the psychologist on call—Dr. Herb Snow."

Sara leaned down and picked up Bug and began to pet him. "At this point, I feel like our interviews aren't productive because we're not asking the right questions. So, I got an organizational chart for the facility off the WEB. It didn't mention a parent company per se. But John Lindquist's son mentioned Alejandro Smith was a bigwig in the parent company—Golden Years Management—usually called GYM. Evidently, John had spotted Smith twice at Happy Days. We're brainstorming how to covertly..."

"Get the big picture." Jack smiled. "Without tipping our hand."

Sara peered at Carbonne. "But you didn't come to my office to chit chat."

Carbonne plunked into a chair. "I was worried today. Ted Cottingham usually handles cases where law enforcement officers have screwed up."

"Am I in trouble?"

"No, but I may be. Seems someone contacted Ted's boss and wanted to know if you could be moved to another state. Ted wouldn't name who made the request. Ted took this case because he wanted to observe you in action." Carbonne stared at Sara. "Are you planning to move to be nearer Sanders?" He paused, "I'd understand."

"Relax. I'm not planning on going anywhere."

Carbonne sighed. "Could Sanders have tried to find opportunities for you?"

"I doubt he'd do it *without* telling me first. He's not the most sensitive man, but he's not a fool."

# CHAPTER 13: Is Sanders a Wily Coyote?

Sanders knew Sara was right. He was being used by the senators on the intelligence committee. They were worse than a conniving wife with a long *honey-do* list. However, the special assignment they'd outlined sounded more interesting than the routine scut work done by committee staff. It would also get him out of Washington. It was beastly hot this summer. Of course, so was his planned destination.

The senators wanted to learn about the stability of several Central American governments. The attempted coup by the drug lord in the Amazonas State of Brazil had scared them. They feared drug cartels had infiltrated the police and military of several other nations besides Brazil. They—evidently the senators on the intelligence committee and unnamed State Department officials—thought he, as a disgraced former ambassador, could get info that other couldn't. *Jerks.* They could have cleared him quickly of wrongdoing but found it useful to keep a slur on his record.

Two members of the Senate Intelligence Committee had told him this morning. "Your *vacation* in the Yucatan of Mexico, Guatemala, and Belize would be more plausible if Sara accompanied you."

Sanders agreed, but there were two problems. Sara couldn't—or at least wouldn't—drop a case to accompany him. He suspected this trip could be dangerous. Sara had been a great backup for him in Brazil, but it wasn't fair to endanger her again. He had told the senators, "Sara won't be accompanying me. Do you still want me to spend a couple of weeks visiting local officials in Central America? I'll tell them I'm thinking of running for the U.S Senate and am trying to learn ways to improve the relationship of the US with its neighbors."

Both senators had snorted. Sanders hadn't asked which part of his statement annoyed them.

***

He rushed to Andrews Air Force Base and caught a military transport headed to Kirtland Air Force Base in Albuquerque. Instead of working as he usually did on the flight, he studied a couple of books on photography that he'd loaded on his e-book reader. He'd promised Sara and himself that he would try to develop interests besides his work. During his last visit to New Mexico two weeks before, he'd bought a camera and the books but hadn't bothered to use the camera or read the books during the intervening weeks.

When he arrived at two, he reviewed his email messages. Sara and Carbonne had survived an *unpleasant* video conference with an assistant US attorney. He almost pitied the man because he'd knew Sara and Carbonne were a wily pair of coyotes. He watched how they confused foes several times. They acted harmless at first but alternately pushed their agenda and circled their victim without ever signaling to each other— much like coyotes in the wild. *Funny how Sara had changed him.* He'd never considered the hunting techniques of coyotes until Sara had talked about how they killed unsuspecting dogs left to run freely in the bosque.

He decided to not interrupt the plotting at the FBI Building. He'd rent a car, take the silver teething ring to a jeweler to be engraved, and start dinner at Sara's house. His only regret was that he couldn't pick up Bug. *Poor dog loved Sara but was bored in her tiny office.*

***

He laughed when he entered Sara's house. Her crock pot on the kitchen counter was full of corned beef. She must have put the meat on low when she left for work and figured it would be ready if he arrived early and was hungry. He was surprised she had bothered. He had ended their conversation abruptly this morning.

On the other hand, he wasn't surprised to see Sara was preparing corned beef. He had mentioned earlier this week that the FDA recalls of deli meat nationwide were changing his food habits. Normally, he was a fan of deli meats and salad for quick suppers during the week. The bowl of coleslaw in the refrigerator and a fresh loaf of homemade rye bread on the counter meant Sara, as usual, had tried to please him.

He sliced the bread. Sara couldn't seem to get her rye breads to turn out like good deli ryes. Hers had a softer texture and a sweeter flavor probably because she used molasses. The bread slathered with a cheese spread made a great snack.

He tasted a bit of meat. *Tender.* Then he spied the brown sugar and unopened jar of Dijon mustard on the counter. He put the slab of cooked meat in a casserole dish, covered it with a mixture of brown sugar and mustard, and set it in the refrigerator. It would slice better when cold. He hated to admit how he and Sara were like a pair of coyotes, too. They'd adjusted to each other's style of cooking and lifestyle in general.

     

He texted her and settled down at the kitchen table to plot his trip in Central America. It would begin in Mérida where he'd rent a car.

Maybe Sara would fly to Mérida with him and stay two days while they visited Uxmal and Chichén Itzá. Then she could fly home, and he'd continue with the real business of the trip. He'd been to Chichén Itzá with his ex-wife and daughter twenty years before. It had been their last vacation together before the divorce. Then he realized he wasn't much different than he was then. He was too work oriented and expected those close to him to have similar interests as his. No, that wasn't true completely. He was sure Sara liked archaeological ruins. His ex hadn't.

# CHAPTER 14: Knowledge Doesn't Always Change Attitudes

*Thursday*

"Happy Days has had seven medical directors since it was founded ten years ago. The first was a semi-retired physician who died of a heart attack about six years ago. The rest have been nurse practitioners. Each left the job after about a year." Sara sighed. "Three told me they signed non-disclosure agreements with Happy Days and refused to answer any questions. I couldn't locate two of them. I think I won't even approach the current one until I have more info from residents."

Jack yawned. "Sounds fishy."

"Hmm. Why don't you pump Diego more? This background info might help. He and his brother both served as MPs in the army. Afterward, his brother was hired by the Bernalillo County Sheriff's Department, but Diego had drifted from one dead-end job to another with several arrests for petty theft but no convictions. I think he was lucky to get the job of lead custodian at Happy Days. Money is a problem. He has a six-year-old son and no wife."

***

"People don't really change. They just get better at hiding their true selves as they age." Karen Wright pulled her iron gray hair behind her ears and looked at her lap. "I bet you disagree. Were you one of those egotistical profs who thought they could change their students?"

Sara was surprised. It was not often she met someone whose philosophy on education was so cynical. She decided it was okay to be distracted into this aside because this woman was apt to have insights on the three faculty members at the heart of this case.

"I partially agree with you. As a faculty member, I thought I could increase the knowledge levels of students, but only receptive students change their attitudes." She paused. "I guess I didn't want to change their attitudes per se—just help them to become well-informed professionals."

When Karen raised her head, Sara noticed the woman seemed to have permanent winkles descending from her lips to her chin. Otherwise, this thin woman was attractive and looked younger than sixty-eight.



J. L. Greger

Karen's wrinkles deepened. "I've met a number of profs in the med school who had God-complexes and thought they could change students."

*Wonder who she's got in mind?* Sara leaned forward and touched Karen's hand. "You worked too long at a university."

"Thirty-six years after I served a few years as a supply clerk in the army."

*Not an exciting life.* "I expect you saw faculty members' worst behavior in the financial office of a med school. As a professor, I saw profs—who went to church weekly and spouted platitudes on ethics to their students—proposition every post doc in sight and lie on their travel records." Sara shook her head. "One prof in my department always found excuses to attend conferences in New York City where he had a girlfriend. I doubt he ever attended more than one session at those conferences."

Karen looked up. "Bet he had a wife back home."

"Yes. Did Ab Hess have a God-complex?"

Karen stared at her lap. "Ab was a man with no options. His wife liked the prestige of being married to a successful professor but had no interest in his work. I got to know him when he brought his grants into the grants management office of the med school. He had a good sense of humor, loved his work, but had no pretensions about being a great scientist or teacher. A nice guy who did his best. We celebrated when he submitted each new grant proposal by having lunch together." She looked into the distance.

Sara guessed Karen was remembering more than lunches. "Funny how you can become a close friend with a married man. Know his thoughts better than his wife."

Karen grabbed Sara's hand. "You understand. We were together when his wife had her accident. The police had trouble finding Ab, and he didn't get to the hospital before his son died. He never forgave himself. Neither did his wife. For the next thirty years, he lived under her thumb."

"Did he change after she died?"

"He retired shortly after she died ten years ago and immediately moved to Happy Days. I came here a couple of years later. I had high hopes, but it was too late. He had become an alcoholic and was rude to everyone." She shrugged. "I suspect Gus encouraged Ab to express the resentment that grew during the thirty years that he taught gross anatomy and nursed his crippled wife."

*Karen has a motive for killing Gus.* She'd had access to the open bottle when she, Ruth, and Gus had drinks on his birthday. *Time to startle her.*

"Do you think the person who added methanol to the bottle of Wild Turkey you and Ruth gave to him wanted to kill Gus alone or his friends, too?"

Karen gasped. "I don't know. Everyone knew John drank only lite beer." She paused. "Are you sure the methanol was in the bottle of bourbon?"

*Strange answer.* "I'm sure. Why did you and Ruth give the Wild Turkey to Gus for his birthday? You don't seem to like him much."

"Ruth likes him. Thinks he's funny."

"Did you process his grants, too?"

"No, he wasn't in the med school, but Ruth knew him. She transferred from accounting in the pharmacy school to accounting in the med school fifteen years ago. I met him when I moved here."

Sara wondered whether Karen knew or guessed that Ruth had been intimate with Gus. She saw no way to finesse it. *Might as well be direct.* "Was Ruth a close friend of Gus before she moved to Happy Days?"

Karen snorted. "She was his steady for three years between wife two and wife three. If you want to learn about Gus, ask Ruth. I only know what she's told me."

"Okay. What about John?"

"He's what he seems to be. A nice man with no secrets—as far as I know."

***

Ruth was the opposite of Karen—short, pleasantly rounded, and with a great smile. She greeted Sara at the door to her apartment warmly. "I've been expecting you." As Sara was seated, Ruth said, "I know you've searched Gus's unit and must have seen his collection. Some men never grow up. I know it should annoy me, but I always liked Gus's impish side."

"Okay. I'll be blunt. Your bra was labeled with a tag for seven years ago. Are you still close to Gus?"

Ruth didn't seem surprised. "No, he met Olivia Bend shortly after we rekindled our relationship seven years ago." She bit her lip.

"Is that the only reason?"

"Gus was obsessed ever since Olivia Bend died. He was ready to make her wife four. She's why he developed his preposterous theory that the management of Happy Days targeted seniors with no close relatives and poisoned them with aflatoxin-contaminated food. Then the parent company could become their guardians and control their estates. He wouldn't accept Happy Days was like many greedy businesses—always looking for the best deal, even if they had to cut some corners. Their action may have caused seniors here to die, but it wasn't their intent."

"Like buying FDA-recalled peanuts."

Ruth smiled. "You must have seen the invoices from American Peanut Supply. John and Gus sent a lot of letters, but none seemed to have gotten into the right hands."

"They have now. John and Gus indicated they used you as a consultant. Did you notice anything else?"

Ruth walked to a desk and pulled out a file. "Gus obtained invoices for the purchase of other foods and drugs. He gave me ones in which the prices seemed unusually low." She handed ten pages to Sara. "I couldn't find any FDA recalls for these products on the WEB. I don't know why Happy Days got them at such good prices." Ruth pulled another file. "I think I know why Happy Days got such good buys on these products."

Sara thumbed through four invoices and saw notes on each. She gulped. "Do you know how Gus got these invoices?"

"No, and I didn't ask." She winked when Sara hesitated to take the pages. "Frightens you, too. That's why I'm not as close to Gus as I was. He makes me nervous."

As Sara rose to leave, Ruth said, "Gus isn't senile. Using a squirt gun is an act. He has a source of information that he hides from everyone, even John and me. It must be a staff member. I suspect several of them hate Rosa Gonzalez and only pretend to be her spies."

***

Sara sent copies of her recorded interviews to Ted Cottingham. She wondered how long it would take him to learn that her summaries were as useful as the full interviews and a lot quicker to digest. Maybe he was a slow learner. Jack hadn't been. She sent Jack only a copy of her summary of the interviews.

Then she thought about another slow learner—Sanders. Last night he'd been intent on getting her to take a four-day trip to see archaeological sites in the Yucatan. She was sure he wanted to see Mayan ruins and had correctly guessed she'd enjoy seeing them too. *But what were his motives for staying longer after she returned home?*

They had reached a compromise. They would both go to the christening in Acoma this weekend. He'd go to Mérida before her flight next Thursday. They would take day tours from Mérida to archaeological sites on next Friday and Saturday. He would travel in Central America for at least a week after she left.

She hoped she'd convinced him not to do something foolish for the Senate Intelligence Committee during his time—without her—in the

Central America. *Sanders isn't a slow learner. I just haven't given him enough information to change his attitudes.* She knew he wouldn't do anything that was illegal or amoral to get the assistant secretary position, but he would take huge risks.

## CHAPTER 15: Jack Talks to Nervous People

Jack found Diego in the custodian's closet by the kitchen reading a long, hand-written note from Rosa Gonzalez. "The boss lady says a shipment of nuts is due in this afternoon. Cookie says she has no space in the kitchen. I'm stuck in the middle and must convert a janitorial closet on the second floor of this building into a food storage closet." He shook his head. "Why would she buy five hundred pounds of pinion nuts? Cookie says that's enough to serve pesto fifty times to the residents. We agree Mrs. Gonzalez is *loco como una cabra*."

"Sounds strange. Who will sign for the nuts when they're delivered?"

Diego frowned. "Anyone in the kitchen or at the loading dock at the time." He must have guessed Jack's next question. "We leave the signed packing slips in a box near Cookie's office."

"What's Cookie's real name?"

Diego pointed to a heavy-set woman in white pants and a white T-shirt with her red hair pulled into a bun. "Think her real name is Pat…" He paused. "…O'Hara." Diego scanned the area. "Can't talk now. Mrs. Gonzalez is apt to show up soon to check on my progress."

"I understand." Jack watched Diego rush to the stairs and then ambled over to Cookie.

"Mrs. O'Hara, may I speak to you."

"That was my mother's name. I'm Cookie." She looked around the kitchen. "You with the FBI?" She didn't wait for him to answer. "Been expecting you. I usually take a break around one-thirty when lunch rush is over. Meet you at my red Honda parked by the loading dock then." She pointed to the back door of the kitchen and bustled away.

Jack thought the woman spoke and moved more quickly than he expected of a heavy-set, middle-aged woman. He figured she too expected Mrs. Gonzalez's imminent arrival. *Like to see it without being seen.*

He exited through the kitchen's back door and was studying the loading dock when he heard Rosa Gonzalez. "Cookie, we need to talk." Jack noticed a window and thought it might be in Cookie's office. He peeked in and withdrew. Rosa was entering the office with Cookie trailing. He stepped back.

"I got the pinion nuts at an amazing price."

"No one needs five hundred pounds of nuts."

"The residents like a vegetarian option every day. Your pesto made with pinion nuts is good."

"Still too much."

"You'll find a way. Can you develop and print out a new set of menus for next week?"

He heard curse words, a file drawer slam, and a chair squeak. He peeked in again. Cookie was typing and Rosa was standing by the printer. *Rosa may not be crazy, but she is pushy.* He stepped back and almost tripped on a kitchen staff member who was smoking. *When did she appear?*

The thin Hispanic woman flicked her cigarette ashes. "Saw you the other night. You got everyone nervous. Are you looking for *undocumenteds?*"

*Where did she get that idea?* "Is that a problem here?"

The young woman with her hair in a braid down her back flicked her cigarette again. "Kinda dumb for a Fed to ask. It's a kitchen." She inhaled as she studied him. "Maybe you aren't with immigration. You haven't insulted me yet."

Her comment suggested undocumented aliens were working in the kitchen. *Not my problem.* "Relax. I'm with the FBI and won't report anyone to the immigration service."

The woman snuffed out her cigarette on the concrete steps to the loading dock. "Are you looking for who killed the old man in the bosque?"

*The grapevine is healthy here.* He nodded.

"Nice old man. He often left his change on the table at dinner time, especially if we gave him an extra dessert. Never at lunch time. Mrs. G would see it then."

"Why would Mrs. G care?"

"She says it gives a bad image to place." She shrugged. "Like Diego says she *loco como una cabra.*" She started to walk away.

"Why do you say Mrs. G is crazy like a goat?"

"She's like a goat. Smarter than she looks. Nosy. Only goats are funny. She's not."

He heard Cookie in the background grumbling about the work created when she had to change menus at the last minute. He decided it was more important to talk to the Hispanic woman. "What about Gus and John?"

"Gus is—how do you say it—a dirty old man. He pats all the women staff. We learn to move quickly around him. He gives bigger tips than Ab but asks strange questions."

Like what?"

She lit another cigarette. "Like names on food delivery trucks. Or the names of the drivers."

*She's right. That's strange.* He noted the name tag on her white apron said, *LOLA.* She might be a reliable source of info. "What about John Lindquist?"

"He's quiet. The ladies like him because he helps them into their chairs and hold doors for them." She blew a smoke ring. "Never uses a squirt gun."

"Is he nice to the staff?"

"Doesn't notice us."

"What do you mean?"

Before she could answer, he heard. "I smell smoke. Cookie, I told you to not let workers take smoking breaks on the loading dock."

The young woman crushed her cigarette with her foot, jumped off the dock, and ran into the parking lot ducking between cars. *Better get out of here.* He ran down the stairs of the loading dock and raced around the corner of the building. The closest door was a back entrance to the assisted living building. He rushed forward fearing the door would be locked. He lucked out. A woman with a walker pushed open the door. He caught the edge of the door and helped the woman roll out.

Behind him, he could hear Rosa Gonzalez complaining about ashes on the loading dock. He hoped she was too busy to notice him as he walked beside the woman with the walker to the dining hall.

The glass doors to the dining room were closed but seniors with wheelchairs, walkers, and canes clogged the hallway. Inside the dining room, Lola was now placing pitchers of water on each table. He studied her. She was more than thin; she was scrawny.

Then a walker rammed him, and he tripped on the front foot pad of a wheelchair. He fell face forward onto the lap of an old woman His left knee grazed the spokes on the wheelchair. It hurt, but his biggest concern was the woman.

She screamed, "Young man, look where you're going."

The good part about the misadventure was everyone stepped away. He uttered apologies and limped to an empty lounge across the hall from the dining room. As he moved, elderly women pointed at him and tittered.

One old man waved his cane at Jack. "Get a cane. I use mine to knock the old hens out of my way."

Jack sat in the lounge and watched the crowd. Teenagers waiting in line to buy tickets to a rock concert were more polite than this group. *Is this a special meal?* He stood to read the menu posted nearby. The entrees were macaroni and cheese and spicy meatloaf. *Didn't sound special.*

The noise from the crowd increased as Lola opened the doors to the dining hall. The seniors moved rapidly to what appeared to be preassigned tables. Lola latched the door open and waved to him after the last of the crowd dispersed.

He bet she had entered the US illegally and would talk if he could make the right offer. He had nothing to offer her. He texted Sara and waited.

***

Jack closed the door to Gus's apartment and scanned the hallway through the peephole in the door. No one had followed him. He heard Sara before he saw her in the kitchen. "I can't believe inspectors from the Department of Health would okay the use of a janitor's closet to store food."

Diego was slumped at the kitchen table. "It's what Mrs. Gonzalez wants." Suddenly, he smiled. "I place a secret call tonight."

Jack wondered how Diego got that idea but didn't know how to begin that discussion. Sara was more direct. "How do you know who to call?"

Diego looked down. "I have my ways."

"Tell me about them." She must have noted Diego's hesitancy. "I think Gus knew lots of secrets about this place. Ones he didn't share with John and Ab. Are you one of his informers?"

"No." Diego stared at her. "I know who to call because Evie was stupid. She talks too much when she drinks. One time, I caught her leaving Gus's apartment at dinner time. She pointed to a number on a sheet of paper and said, 'This is Mrs. Gonzalez's worst enemy.' Then she cackled like a hen, made the page into a ball, and dropped it on the floor. So drunk."

"And you retrieved the crumpled paper?"

"Sure. I called the number. It was a food inspector in the health department."

"Have you ever talked to the inspector?"

"No."

Sara tapped her fingers on the table. Diego lowered his head. "I left a message at that number a few months ago when Cookie complained we got cold cuts that didn't smell right, but Mrs. Gonzalez insisted they be served."

Sara gave a reassuring smile. "That was brave of you. Did anything happen?'

Diego nodded. "Many of the residents got sick. Lots of vomit to clean up. The next day Mrs. Gonzalez screamed a lot in the kitchen." He smirked. "But she was quiet when Cookie pitched all the remaining cold cuts."

Sara grooved on this type of story. Jack flinched as he remembered her tale about a local restaurant which catered a banquet where the speaker had run to the bathroom halfway through his after-dinner speech. *Sure enough.* Sara not only recorded Diego's comment but wrote a note to herself. It was his chance to ask Diego questions. "Do you think others might have called the health department? I talked to Lola. She doesn't like Mrs. Gonzalez much."

Diego looked down. "Mrs. Gonzalez pays some people in the kitchen less. Lola claims it's because they can't complain."

"What does Cookie say?"

Diego shook his head. "She doesn't argue, but she looks the other way when kitchen staff take leftovers home." He looked pleadingly at first Sara and then Jack. "It's hard for any of us without papers or with police records to get jobs. This place is our last hope."

Sara patted Diego's shoulders. "You'd better get back to work before anyone notices you are missing" She handed him two of the candy boxes she prepared for residents. "Your son might like these."

After the door closed, Sara said, "I think one of the staff shared info on the dirty secrets of Happy Days with Gus. Might be…"

Jack completed her sentence. "Cookie." He paused. "I'm supposed to meet her at her car at one-thirty. Until then I'll interview janitorial staff. All the kitchen staff are too busy to talk during mealtimes."

# CHAPTER 16: A Fast Exit

Sara bit her tongue and didn't mention the tear in his slacks at the knee as Jack left Gus's apartment. She wondered whether someone had purposefully tripped him. He was a good-looking, young guy. That was a rarity at Happy Days.

Sara quickly scanned Rosemary's report on the backgrounds of staff at Happy Days.

Evie had worked fifteen years as a social worker in the New Mexico department known as CYFD—Child, Youth, and Family Department. Less than a week after Evie had certified the parents of two school age children to be capable parents six years ago, the father had beaten one child to death and maimed the other. Rosemary had provided a copy of an article that appeared in the *Albuquerque Journal*. The photo of the room where the surviving child had been found was disgusting—bloody debris and rats. Evie had resigned immediately but had not been charged with any crime. Shortly afterward, she took the job of social worker at Happy Days.

Dr. Herb Snow, the consulting clinical psychologist for Happy Days, had resigned from CYFD after ten years of service but his name had never been associated with any scandals. For the last five years, he'd consulted for several senior living facilities.

Although the two men working in the kitchen had police records—disorderly conduct and brawling, Pat O'Hara had a clean record. She'd been a cook in the US Marine Corps for twenty years and retired with a rank of staff sergeant. Rosemary reported three of the five women working in the kitchen were immigrants. Two had green cards. One— Lola Lopez—had a temporary student visa. Sara texted Jack:

> *Attached is info on kitchen staff. One may be an immigrant working illegally. Might be true of cleaning staff, too.*

Rosa Gonzalez's history also had a nasty twist. Rosa had worked a nurse at the VA hospital in Albuquerque for twenty years before she was hired to manage a memory unit at an assisted living facility. Less than six months after her arrival, one patient had strangled another in the unit with ribbon from a birthday gift. Rosa had been fired because her cost-cutting measures had facilitated the murder.

Rosemary also noted Rosa Gonzalez was raising two high school aged kids. Her husband had been killed in a gang-related shooting fifteen years before. *Bet Rosa's strapped for money.*

Sara thought it odd that Happy Days employed so many with shadows in their background—Rosa, Diego, Evie, and much of the kitchen staff. She checked the hiring policies for Happy Days and its parent company Golden Years Management, Inc. Then she looked for job vacancies and compared pay scales of employees to those in other senior management companies.

As expected, GYM had no policy of trying to hire minorities or *disadvantaged* people. The salaries offered were low but typical of those offered the industry. *Bet a lot have interesting side hustles.* She performed one more computer search.

***

Jack reached for his gun when he heard a knock on the back window of Cookie's Honda. "Sara, what are you doing here?"

"Thought you might like some help." She opened a back door of the car and slid in.

Cookie turned to see her. "I assume you're the boss or at least the experienced sergeant. Jack here is a boot."

"Excuse me." Jack frowned.

Cookie chuckled. "Guess you aren't military types."

Sara smiled. "You've judged us right. He's a new agent. I'm a consulting scientist." She shrugged. "But I think you knew that. I found your name on an interesting website."

Cookie didn't move a muscle in her face.

*Bet she's a good poker player.* "You're on the advisory board for *Undocumented UNM."*

Jack stared at Cookie. "So, you were Gus's informer?"

Cookie chortled. "We sometimes had mutual interests. After I retired from the Marines two years ago, I certainly didn't want to go back to the family farm in Kansas."

"So, why Albuquerque?"

"Little snow. Vibrant culture, not like vanilla Kansas. I also wanted to continue to make a difference. Pretty obvious, plenty of people in Albuquerque need help—homeless, immigrants, victims of crime. And I remembered my experiences as a line cook right after high school. Only one other person in that hospital kitchen in Chicago twenty-five years ago spoke passable English. I figured a good place to find immigrants who needed help was in an institutional kitchen in Albuquerque. Happy Days had a reputation for hiring individuals with police records."

Sara nodded. "So, you figured they didn't check immigration documents carefully either. How did your and Gus's interests coincide?"

"Gus was convinced that the management if Happy Days was trying to gain control of the estates of residents here."

"Was he wrong?"

Cookie frowned. "I think so. Like many over-educated people, he always looked for complex answers when simple ones were staring him in the face." She pushed her seat back so she could see Sara more easily. "All GYM cares about is the bottom line and no headaches. They want help who can't complain about their low wages and vendors who offer cheap supplies."

"Why did they hire you?"

"They knew I was retired military and didn't care about GYM's benefit package—which isn't good—and wanted flexible vacation times. I can take off for a week anytime with only two days' notice."

"Who is they? I doubt it's Rosa Gonzalez."

"This isn't your first rodeo." Cookie chuckled. "She's the front who delivers messages. Alejandro Smith makes all the important decisions. That was the first detail I shared with Gus. Then he and his two friends kept tabs on Alejandro."

"Why didn't you track Alejandro?"

Cookie turned to Jack. "Boots, close your mouth. I was stuck in the kitchen and couldn't watch the front desk. They could, but I knew when certain key decisions were made."

"What constitutes a key decision?"

"Someone was fired, quit, or was hired. Or food arrived that I didn't order, and I was asked to adjust menus and my next orders."

Jack reached out and touched Cookie's arm. "Like the arrival of five hundred pound of pinion nuts?"

Cookie removed his hand. "I don't allow any familiarity with officers. Policy, I learned in the Marines." She seemed to think for a moment. "I was surprised Lola was sloppy enough to smoke on the loading dock." She studied at Jack. "I can see why you distracted her. She can't afford mistakes."

Sara wanted to bring Cookie's thoughts back to the original topic. "Did Gus agree with your list of key decisions?"

                                                    J. L. Greger

"No, he considered movement of a resident to the memory unit a major decision. John plotted all the data on a calendar."

"And?"

"There appeared to be no relationship between Alejandro's visits and movement of residents to the memory unit, but we had no way to monitor Alejandro's or Rosa's phone conversations or emails" She straightened and smiled. "However, Alejandro always visits in the week prior to a hiring or a firing."

"What about the odd food orders?"

"They don't appear to be related to his visits. Might be Rosa's side hustle."

Sara pushed three invoices for food in front of Cookie. "Did you give these to Gus?" She decided it best not to mention Ruth had given her these copies.

Cookie studied them. "No. I shared the dates on invoices but never gave him copies of the invoices. I couldn't help the homeless or veterans if I got fired."

"Okay." Sara put the invoices back into her tote. "Who did you help? How?"

"I helped Lola Lopez gain a student visa and enroll in the Culinary Art Certificate program at UNM. Of course, she could lose her ability to stay in the US with political changes, but the training should help her no matter what. I worked with the VA and hired two veterans in the kitchen while they were on probation."

Cookie's comments meshed with facts Rosemary had uncovered. Sara nodded. "Do you think they'll stay with Happy Days?"

"No. They know I'll write them a good rec when they want to move on."

"Training new staff is a lot of work."

"But it's the right thing to do."

Sara liked Cookie but thought she probably had done more for Gus than she admitted. *But we won't pull it out of her now.*

Jack suddenly slumped in his seat. "I think Evie Schoener is walking toward us."

Cookie grimaced and drove out of the parking lot, waving to Evie when she passed her. "Evie's snooping again. Rosa really has her by the tail. If she asks, I'll tell her I was talking to prospective employees. She probably didn't recognize you because of my tinted windshield."

"Doubt we'll be lucky. New Mexico doesn't allow that much tint on windshield."

Jack looked in the rear-view mirror. "I think someone is following us in a compact white car."

"Let's be sure." Cookie did a U-turn and drove out the front instead of the back entrance of Happy Days.

The white car did the same.

Cookie frowned and took the first right after leaving the entrance to Happy Days. Then she turned right again one block later and then left a block later. Each time the white car followed.

"Better go to I-25." Jack shook his head. "That's the easiest way to lose them."

Sara texted for help. "It's all right to speed up. Maybe we'll get lucky, and an officer will stop us."

Cookie nodded, sped up, zigzagged to Montgomery, and took the ramp onto I-25 going north.

Jack watched the traffic and called instructions to Cookie.

Sara kept studying the white car. There was no booster license on the front. No apparent dents or scrapes. The car stayed far enough behind that Sara couldn't describe the driver, except he or she had short hair. *Useless.*

I-25 did its magic. Cars changed lanes as if they were racing in a computer game. Within a mile, Cookie had lost the white car.

"Now exit the freeway onto Paseo del Norte and head east."

Cookie nodded. "I'll drop you off near a bus stop on Louisiana. You shouldn't try to return to Happy Days to retrieve your car for a couple of hours. Or better yet get someone else to claim it."

Sara handed her a business card as she and Jack left the car. "Call us if you feel threatened."

"No problem. I'm a Marine."

## CHAPTER 17: The Rescue

Winslow stopped the FBI evidence van near the bus stop at Louisiana and Montgomery. Most of those waiting for the bus in the midafternoon of this ninety-degree day looked like derelicts. A young Black man with a tear in his tan slacks and a flushed, middle-aged, White woman dragging a large tote waved him down. He opened the side door of the van. "Not every day I pick up such a rough looking crowd."

Sara threw the tote in, and Jack pushed her up the step into the van. She immediately started to fan herself with a file. "Let Jack drive this van. He'll drop you off a block from Happy Days. You can walk to our car and drive it back to the building."

"Don't you want an update before you decide? You could be missing a golden opportunity."

"Okay, pull off and we'll talk."

***

Winslow pulled to the curb on a shady side street and turned off the van. "The lab chief wasn't pleased by all the garbage in the freezer. I decided the first thing I needed to do today was complete the sorting of the garbage bags."

Jack thumped Winslow on the back. "You mean she ordered you to clean it up."

"Yeah." Winslow pulled out his phone and appeared to study his notes. "You'll remember we kept only the large standard garbage bags with bottles of windshield wiper fluid or hand sanitizer and the small garbage bags like John used to dispose of his garbage."

Jack rolled his eyes. "There's nothing wrong with my memory. What's new?"

Winslow lowered his voice. "It seems that I—we all really—missed a major source of methanol. As I sorted through one of the small bags without shredded paper. I found a small bottle with an interesting smell. Er… like isopropyl alcohol or methanol."

Sara had tried to be patient, but enough was enough. "Spit it out. What was it?"

"Nail polish remover." He bit his lip. "It seems many brands of non-acetone-containing nail polish remover contain methanol. How would I know?"

"It's all right Winslow." Sara sighed. "We all forgot about that source of methanol. Can I assume the FBI crew wouldn't have noticed bottles of nail polish remover in the garbage bags sorted on Tuesday?"

Winslow looked at his lap and nodded

It was rapidly becoming warm in the van with the engine off. Sara started to fan herself again. "At least a quarter of the women at Happy Days wear nail polish. The beauty shop must use at least a bottle of polish remover every day."

Winslow looked up. "I talked to those at the lab who sorted the garbage. Only one remembered seeing small plastic bottles that might be nail polish remover."

"But a defense lawyer could say we prejudiced our search and only looked for select sources of methanol." She studied Winslow who was still slumped at the steering wheel studying his phone. "What are other potential sources of methanol?"

"Canned fuels used to keep chafing dishes warm." He looked up quickly. "None of us remembered seeing any of those cans in the garbage."

Jack whistled. "Maybe we lucked out. I don't think the residents cook much for themselves but…"

"They drink a lot. Even at a distance I saw dozens of glass wine and liquor bottles in the garbage." Sara kept fanning herself, but her face remained red. "And they might serve hot hors d'oeuvres."

Winslow lifted his head. "Maybe not. Bags with booze bottles usually were filled with napkins and empty bags of chips and empty salsa jars."

"We can't prove that now." Sara sighed. "Did you find any other sources of methanol?"

"Booze especially bourbons have traces of methanol." He added quickly, "But probably a million-fold less methanol than we found in Gus's bottle of Wild Turkey."

"Maybe that's why Gus and Ab didn't notice an off flavor. I wonder if our murderer knew all these details." Sara stopped fanning herself. "Stop saving fuel and turn the engine back on. I'm cooking back here."

Jack laughed. "The killer knew Gus and Ab were sots and didn't even taste the booze anymore." He wiped sweat off his forehead. "Looks like sorting the garbage was a waste."

                                                    J. L. Greger

"Nice pun." Sara moved around in her seat trying to catch the blast from the van's air conditioner.

Winslow shook his head. "The guys in the lab will never forgive me. They spent hours in the sun."

"They'll forget with time."

Jack snorted.

Sara wanted to end the pity party. "At least the freezer is cleaned out. Did you learn anything positive this morning?"

"Oh yeah." Winslow looked at the notes on his phone. "Found fingerprints on several of the bottles of windshield washer fluid and on a bottle of nail polish remover in a small bag with no shredded paper—probably from Karen Wright or Ruth Lopez. But I don't have their prints for comparison."

"Karen was in the military. So, hers should be in the system." Sara shook her head. "I don't think most of the residents—at least ones we want to focus on—will give fingerprints or DNA without a warrant. And I don't want them calling lawyers for advice before we have better evidence." She smiled. "Let's focus on what we can do. Winslow, after you get our car, check with Rosemary to see if she found anything useful in the shredded garbage using artificial intelligence programs."

Jack and Winslow changed seats. "After Jack changes his slacks, he and I can needle Alejandro Smith and Dr. Herb Snow."

Jack pulled from the curb. "Annoying Snow and Smith sounds like fun. At least better than dealing with computer program that decodes shredded garbage."

Sara felt sorry for Winslow. "Let's be honest. Working with the AI program takes more patience than you and I have at this point, Jack."

Winslow snickered.

***

"Dr. Snow is a busy man. I can't get you in until next week."

"This is a police murder investigation." Sara tried to sound respectful. She lowered her voice. "We're with the FBI and appreciate the doctor's expertise. Please. We know he treats patients at Happy Days."

The receptionist traced her index finger along a line on her computer screen. "If you can wait five minutes, he should be available for ten minutes before his next patient."

***

After a few basic questions about the memory unit at Happy Days, Sara asked Herb Snow, "How do you handle patients if they have no kin nearby or Happy Days or its parent company Golden Years Management is the patient's guardian?"

Herb cleared his throat and began a recitation of legal details.

"What is happening now with Joseph Nowak and Georg Cernak?"

"That's confidential."

"A whistleblower has mentioned they are being held unlawfully, and the two men have info related to the death of Ab Hess."

"That's not possible."

Sara suspected he was right on the latter point, but it was a logical bluff. "You can save us and yourself a lot of time if you answer our questions. We suspect you've seen a lot of mistakes made in protective care of juveniles and older patents over the years. You left CYFD after ten years." Sara gave a small smile. "Was that out of disgust or fear?"

Dr. Snow swallowed hard and became cooperative. "Professors Nowak and Cernak have no close kin in New Mexico. They have impaired memories and need help with medications."

"But are they dangerous to themselves or others? Doesn't the assisted living facility routinely help its residents with medications."

Snow bit his lip. "Their relatives—I believe a nephew in each case—didn't object when GYM sought to become their guardian. A judge granted Mr. Alejandro Smith's request. It was all legal."

Sara smiled. "Do you remember a patient at Happy Days from five years ago—Olivia Bend?"

Snow closed his eyes as soon as Sara said *Olivia*. He muttered under his breath, "How could I forget?" He opened his eyes. "I think I want to talk to a lawyer before I answer more questions."

***

Sara had barely closed the car door, when Jack asked, "Who are Joseph Nowak and Georg Cernak?"

"Remember Karen gave me a note on Tuesday about the *two Eds* in the memory unit?"

"The word puzzle one?"

"Right. Karen thought the two men were once faculty in medicine and pediatrics at UNM. Rosemary and Winslow identified them this morning." She shrugged. "Not sure why Rosemary needed Winslow's help. He must have wanted a break from sorting garbage."

"And you bluffed with Snow?"

"I just followed up on John's and Gus's hunches, which all began when Gus saw how Olivia Bend…"

"His girlfriend."



J. L. Greger

"Yes. Gus thought she was treated badly before she died."

"Looks like Winslow rescued us again. I bet Snow has a lot to say if US attorney can make him the right offer."

## CHAPTER 18: A Grouchy Risk Taker

Sara's phone pinged. "Uh, oh. Carbonne wants to see me in his office ASAP."

"Who do you think tattled on us: Dr. Snow, the driver of the white car, Cookie, or someone else at Happy Days?"

"Don't know. We seemed to annoy everyone today."

***

Sara knocked timidly on Carbonne's door. The door swung open, and Bug tried to jump into her arms. She picked him up so he could lick her face. "I missed you, too." Then she saw Sanders. "I guess I didn't keep you updated today."

"I figured you were busy."

Carbonne looked away from his computer screen. "You barely managed to notify me before I got complaints three times today. The lab chief wanted the garbage removed from her freezers. A woman called Cookie was worried about you. And Dr. Snow's lawyer asked to meet with you and me tomorrow. Evidently you scared Snow."

"That's my girl." Sanders leaned over and kissed Sara on the cheek. "I decided to learn the details on the baptism on Sunday and invite Carbonne and his family to dinner. We've already talked to Barbara."

"And what did she say? Taking a month-old baby out isn't easy."

"Carbonne and I made an executive decision." Both men laughed. "We ordered food from a Thai restaurant, which will be delivered to his home at six."

Carbonne winked. "I would have said we could eat earlier but I was afraid you and Jack wouldn't be through riling everyone by five. By the way, where is Jack?"

"He was glad you only summoned me. He thought we had gotten a complaint from Snow and thought I deserved all the credit." Sara laughed. "Coward." She shook her head. "I swear the old women of Happy Days are out to get Jack. Today they tripped him on the footrest of a wheelchair. He tore his slacks." She sat down next to Sanders. "Did he admit to you, one kicked him in the crotch yesterday when he tried to chase her? She got away."

"Ouch." Carbonne frowned. "What's causing the hostility?"

"Everyone's nervous at Happy Days. But I suspect, the ladies are flirting with Jack in a pre-adolescent way."

Carbonne muttered, "I doubt he wants to join more old farts for supper."

***

"I know it's only four, but I can't face another problem. Let's get a drink."

Sanders glanced at Sara. "This must have been a bad day. It's not like you to want a drink."

Sara opened the door to her office, threw her tote on a chair, and checked for notes from Winslow or Jack. There were none. "I'm dehydrated from the heat. Bug and I need water. What you drink is your choice." She turned and kissed him. "This will give you time to update me on your plans for visiting the Yucatan."

"We could party here." Sanders squeezed her tight.

"I think not." She waved her hand around the room. "There's three chairs, a small table, and a dirty floor."

Sanders backed out of the door. "Let's take your SUV. There's an odd odor in my rental car. Not worth returning it, but not that pleasant." As Sara closed the door, he said, "I read in the *Albuquerque Journal* this morning about a new brewery—Turkey Strut Brew House. They claim to have a large patio, and it's only a couple of miles from Carbonne's home in the east foothills of Albuquerque."

***

The Turkey Strut was a disappointment. It was filled with a young, noisy crowd already at four-thirty. Heat radiated from the stone patio around the front of the A-frame structure. The side patio was shaded but filled with a large group playing Karaoke. Sanders, Sara, and Bug settled in a quiet, shady corner in back—unfortunately not far from the garbage bins. Sara didn't mind because her mint iced tea was refreshing, the patio pavement was clean for Bug, and Sanders seemed happy after a couple sips of a pale ale.

"There are lots of quaint, old hotels in Mérida. One of them might be fun." Sanders studied her face.

Sara suspected he was hoping she would change her mind and extend her stay in the Yucatan. "This trip is last minute, and summer is the busy season for police in New Mexico." She tried to be funny. "The natives get antsy in the heat. I'm certainly willing to do whatever you want during my stay in the Yucatan." She regretted her last comment immediately. She didn't want to go roaming in the jungle without a guide because she didn't want to participate in another spy mission.

Sanders eyed her silently. She felt uncomfortable and slipped an ice cube from her tea to Bug. With his flat face, chewing even a small ice cube was real challenge, but Bug adroitly chipped at the ice with his little teeth, dropped the ice on the napkin, and then retrieved the ice and tried again. When she looked up from Bug, Sanders was still staring at her. *He doubted my last comment.*

"Two all-day tours back-to-back is a bit much. I think we should spend a day wandering around Mérida and its markets."

"Fine with me. When I was there twenty years ago, I thought you could buy anything in the main market *if* you asked the right questions."

Sanders seemed to relax in his chair. He sipped his ale. "Anything you're particularly interested in?"

"You know me. I love to look at pretty and odd things."

"But you seldom buy."

"I learned years ago that accumulating exotic trinkets meant more to dust. I prefer a single postcard or photo as a memento."

Sanders groaned.

Sara wondered if he'd considered her last comment as judgmental. His condo was packed with valuable antiques and exotic items from around the world. *Time to refocus the conversation.* "I did a quick WEB scan of drug cartels in Mérida today."

"No worry. Mérida is considered the safest city in Mexico."

"I wasn't worried, but I like to understand the situation before I visit a new locale."

"And you thought I would underplay problems?"

"I didn't say that." Sara decided the best way to avoid an argument was to change the subject slightly again. "I also learned about the Mérida Initiative in 2008." She saw Sanders was still frowning. *Better keep going.* "I hadn't realized this initiative was the basis for Congressional appropriations of billions to Mexico." She paused and hoped her next comment would get Sanders talking about the real reason for this trip. "It was awfully broad and outlined plans on a range of issues from targeting drug trafficking organizations to improving border control."

Sanders leaned back. "Too broad. Neither side met their goals. In 2021, the US and Mexico issued a so-called Bicentennial Framework for Security, Public Heath, and Safe Communities." He frowned. "Its title explains the problem. The two parties didn't agree on many issues, except that drug—especially fentanyl—problems had increased." He took several sips of his ale. "And you guessed right. Several of these issues are why the Senate Intelligence Committee wants me to unofficially meet with officials in the Yucatan and Central America." He finished his glass. "Enough said."

***

Sara and Sanders arrived at Carbonne's house fifteen minutes before the takeout delivery. Sara used the time to listen to Barbara talk about the joys of motherhood. Barbara was dreading the end of her maternity leave and having to leave Willow with a nanny daily. But she missed her job—recruiting minorities in the Southwest to work for the FBI.

When the food arrived, Sara helped Barbara set the table. Before she called the men in from the backyard, Barbara whispered, "Paul said Sanders seemed particularly irritable this afternoon."

Sara tried not to smile. Carbonne had imitated Sanders and refused to use his given name for years. Barbara had refused to honor this quirk and always called her husband by his given name: Paul. Sara had avoided arguments and never used Sanders's given name: Eric. *That was the only thing to smile about.* Sanders was irritable. It was partially but not entirely her fault. "He's concerned about our upcoming trip."

"Is that all?"

"I don't know. I can't wait to get him away from the Senate Intelligence Committee. The senators are manipulating him to make risky choices."

Barbara nodded. "Paul made a similar comment. He said he couldn't decide if Sanders had a death wish or if someone on the committee wanted to eliminate him permanently." She slid the door to the patio open and called the men to dinner.

## CHAPTER 19: The Scam

*Friday*

Sara settled Bug in his car seat as Jack revved the engine of the FBI car. "We didn't get a dud today."

Sara laughed. "Surely, we won't need to make a fast get-away again today."

Jack nodded. "Why are we interviewing John before Gus? University Hospital is closer to the FBI building than Isaac's house? That's where John is staying—right?"

"John will be more cooperative than Gus."

"Why do you doubt Gus?"

"The ophthalmologist treating Gus made an off-the record comment yesterday. He couldn't understand why Gus's vision hadn't improved more because they had successfully lowered Gus's blood methanol levels within four hours in the hospital." She scanned her phone. "Of course, Gus arrived at the hospital probably seven to eight hours after ingesting the methanol. But…"

"What are you trying to say?"

"Gus had been on a mission for at least three years—since the death of Olivia Bend. He's proven he's an actor—pretending to be senile by using the squirt gun and to be a lady's man with his collection. What else is he pretending to be?"

"And John?"

"He's what he seems to be."

"Are you sure, you don't trust John more because you two share a midwestern farm background?" Jack drove in a silence for several minutes. "I think John would be easier to interview if Isaac wasn't present."

"I agree. That's why we waited until eight to leave the building. Isaac likes to start his first autopsy by seven. Even if he was running late, he'd be out of his home by now."

Jack seemed engrossed in the view in his rear-view mirror.

After a couple of minutes, Sara turned to look. "Am I seeing right? Is a white compact car following us again? When did you first notice it?"

"About the time we turned east on Montgomery."

Sara called for backup and got standard advice. "Don't go to your planned destination. Try to lose him as you return to the building."

Jack took the last protected left turn off Montgomery before the light turned red. Sara saw the white car was blocked from turning by heavy oncoming traffic. Jack went only one block on the side street before he turned right. After a block, he turned right and continued zigzagging until he was on San Mateo. All the time, Sara fielded questions on the phone and looked for the white car.

Finally, the dispatcher announced. "Agents are at Happy Days found the cars owned by the kitchen staff but can't find the white compact cars owned by Evie Schoener, Ruth Lopez, Bob Jones, or Diego Rivera. The ABQ Real Time Police System should find them soon if they pass any of the system's thousand cameras."

Jack muttered under his breath. "We'll be back at the FBI building before that occurs."

Jack was right. He drove into the FBI parking lot as the dispatcher announced. "Car owned by Ruth Lopez just returned to parking lot at Happy Days. She told agents she'd gone grocery shopping. Bottled orange juice and canned soda were found in a bag in the car."

A moment later, the dispatcher announced, "Agents determined Evie Schoener and Diego Rivera arrived at Happy Days and clocked in to begin their workday in the last five minutes."

Jack whistled. "Means if we start now, we shouldn't be bothered unless Bob or Sandi Jones is stalking us. If we stay on Montgomery all the way to Tramway, the cameras are apt to catch them. Let's go."

Sara wanted to say, *No*. She didn't feel like taking risks and didn't want to lead a murderer to John. "I guess."

"If they re-appear, we'll have the evidence to get a search warrant on them. The Joneses don't appear to be into guns, and I can out-drive them."

Instead of arguing, Sara searched the records of the NM Department of Public Safety. Only one of the employees and residents at Happy Days had a permit to carry a concealed weapon The results didn't make her feel better. The one was Rosa Gonzalez.

By the time she had finished the search, Jack had parked a block away from Isaac's home.

Sara had alerted John of their arrival and the possibility of problems. He answered the door before she rang the doorbell. "I don't know where to stay if this house isn't a secret location. What do you suggest?"

Sara shook her head. "Jack will work on that issue while I interview you." She looked around. "Let's sit at the island in the kitchen."

Sara settled Bug at the foot of her stool and started with an easy question. Both she and John needed to relax. "When did you first meet Gus? What was he like?"

John closed his eyes. "Gus and his various wives and live-in girlfriends lived down the street from me for over twenty years. After his third wife left, he quickly found home maintenance inconvenient, retired, and moved to Happy Days."

"Were you surprised?"

"No, Gus never spent much time at home. He consulted a lot and expected his wife or live-in girlfriend—whoever was in the position at the time—to hire help as needed." Jack looked at the ceiling. "I won't say he is rich, but it's rumored he doubled his salary most years through consulting."

"Who paid him so much?"

"Companies who were faced with huge claims for selling products contaminated with aflatoxin or other mold toxins. I guess the big money came when he testified in court." John squinched his face. "Although Gus bragged about his conquests in bed, he never talked much about his professional successes. Too bad. The latter were more interesting—at least to me."

"So, Gus became a joker after he came to Happy Days?"

"I guess. I didn't see him much for the first few years after he moved to Happy Days. I was still working and taking care of a sick wife." He stared into space. "When I moved to Happy Days two years ago, I noticed he'd developed a split personality. He was a joker in public, but he was obsessed with his conspiracy theory and aflatoxin poisoning when he was alone with Ab and me. That's one reason I encouraged us to spend so much time at the Bistro. It was a public place, and he didn't talk about his conspiracy theory."

"So, you didn't take his conspiracy theory seriously?"

"Not at first. I thought the way Rosa and Evie encouraged residents to name Golden Years Management as their guardian was annoying. It became scary after they moved Georg Cernak and Joe Nowak to the memory unit. It was so fast. One quick meeting with Dr. Snow and they were transferred to the unit."

"Tell me about the transfers."

"Georg screamed during the move until Dr. Snow injected him with something."

Sara tried not to seem alarmed. "Anything else?"

"Joe left a note at my door saying he didn't want to go to the memory unit."

"Do you still have that note?"

"Yes. It's with my blue notebook." He stood and rummaged through a pile of papers on a table in the living room.

"Why did Joe leave a note with you?"

John kept shuffling through the pile. "He lived one door down from me—on the other side of Deb Kline." He shook his head. "Now there's one who needs Snow's help. She's crazy."

"Had you known Joe before you moved to Happy Days?"

"I collaborated with him years ago. He provided me with pediatric patients when I was trying to improve the use of MRIs in children."

"So, you were close?"

John held up a blue leather-bound notebook. "Not really, but I liked him. He was a model pediatrician—caring and kind."

"Had he deteriorated a lot since you worked with him?"

John sat down on the stool next to Sara. "No. That's why I came to believe Gus's theory. Joe had severe osteoarthritis. His hands looked like claws, but he was mentally sharp. He showed me a manuscript on the use of MRI on patients with osteoarthritis about four months ago and asked my opinion. He had correctly identified flaws in the design of the studies." He pulled the note from the notebook.

Sara read:

*Help me. I signed a paper Dr. Snow gave me yesterday. I didn't have my glasses with me. He assured me it was just routine. Now I'm worried.*

*Dr. Snow talked to Georg two days ago and took him to the memory unit this morning. Dr. Snow is coming to see me tomorrow. I know I need help in taking my medicine. I take five different medications, BUT I'm not crazy. Neither was Georg. He's deaf.*

*Call my nephew.*
*Thanks*
*Joes*

"What did you do?"

"Told Gus and Ab. Called the nephew. The nephew told me to mind my own business. Dr. Snow had already convinced him that Joe had Alzheimer's disease."

"Did you do anything else?"

"I called a lawyer. She did some checking and advised that Joe was lucky to have Golden Years Management as his guardian." He handed Sara the letter. "That lack of advice cost me five hundred dollars."

Sara noted the letter was cc'd to Dr Herb Snow, probably because the lawyer quoted Dr. Snow as saying, "Jospeh Cernak should remain alive at least ten more years in the protective environment provided by the memory unit at Happy Days."

John shook his head. "I didn't know how to argue that quality was more important than length in life."

"Did Gus and Ab agree?"

"Ab drank more. Gus wanted to get a gun. That's why we went to the bosque last Sunday. To talk about how to help our friends… and ourselves."

Jack entered the kitchen and interrupted Sara's and John's conversation. "I've come up with a plan to trap the person stalking Sara and me. I expect he or she wants to get to you, John. Are you game?"

Sara watched John's face. He became pale and his hands shook.

"Is it necessary?"

Jack nodded. "Yes. I think things may develop quickly after Sara and Carbonne interview Snow and his lawyer…" Jack looked at his watch. "…in two hours."

Sara bit her lip. "I need to talk to Gus before I interview Snow. So, I can't stick around here to help."

"Hence, my plan. Zeke Grant from the Evidence Room is driving here in the duplicate of the car we're using today. An agent in an unmarked car is following him at a distance."

"Why Zeke?"

Jack shook his head. "Sara, don't act dumb. He's Black. I'm the only Black agent in Albuquerque. Most of the residents of Happy Days wouldn't notice differences between Zeke and me"

Sara compared the gaunt, fifty-year old Zeke to Jack in her imagination. "Doubt that."

Jack ignored her. "The agent in the tail car already reported in. He thinks he's spotted the white car on Montgomery following Zeke. When Zeke gets here, you and Bug will go out to the car and greet Zeke as if he were me and get in. The agent in the unmarked car won't enter this street. He'll park a block or so away and walk through back yards to this house. That's when John will go out to work in the yard and try to attract the attention of the person in the white car—we assume he or she will have followed Zeke at a distance."

John looked at Jack. "Do you know who is in the white car?"

"Looks like a woman, but it's Bob Jones's car. Probably Sandi Jones." Jack smiled when his phone vibrated. He turned to Sara. "Time for you to act."

Sara led Bug to the car and opened the door and yelled, "Jack you're late." She scooped Bug up, got into the car, and waved to John as he sauntered out of the house.

# CHAPTER 20: Bluffs Work

Sara stroked the long black and white hair around Bug's ears and then offered to let Bug sit on Gus's lap, but the man refused. Maybe his reduced sight had made him nervous. He had also resisted talking about his vision problem or reminiscing about Ab Hess this morning. He reminded Sara a bit of Sanders—a silent, grouchy man. She decided direct questions were necessary. "Tell me about Joseph Nowak and Georg Cernak."

Gus tapped his fingers on the arm rest of his wheelchair. "Why do you ask?"

"John said they didn't belong in the memory unit."

Gus stopped fidgeting. "You talked to John?"

Sara nodded.

"Then you know that Joe is crippled by arthritis and Georg doesn't hear well. Snow confused them." Gus moved his wheelchair to a table and grabbed a glass of water.

*He doesn't move like a recently blinded man.* Sara decided to test Gus's vision. She yanked a snarl from the hair behind Bug's ears and watched Gus. He flinched.

"I think your vision is pretty good now. You flinched when I pulled a snarl in Bug's hair. I also saw your lab results. I'd bet your vision is only slightly or occasionally blurred now."

"Since when did you become doctor?"

"Only a Ph.D. in medical epidemiology, but I've interviewed enough suspects for the FBI and research subjects to know when someone is being secretive."

"You had no right to see my medical records."

"A judge approved a search warrant of your medical records. Now answer the question."

"You could get her killed."

"Who could I get killed? Karen? Ruth?"

"No."

"Rosa Gonzalez? Or the medical director at Happy Days?"

Gus smirked. "The medical director walks quickly through the memory unit at seven every morning and then spends two hours in the assisted living unit. She leaves by ten most days. I doubt she ever actually talks to Snow who doesn't appear before noon"

He's trying to distract me. *I'm getting war*m. "Or the most logical person—Evie Schoener?"

"Why is she the logical person?"

"As the social worker, she works with Dr. Snow whenever a person is transferred to the memory unit."

He stopped fidgeting. "Are you pleased? You've now put Evie and me in danger. I'll probably either be dead or in that d*** memory unit within twenty-four hours. You should know—Evie and I didn't sleep together. We thought the best way to hide the intent of our meetings was to let everyone think we were an item."

Sara had accomplished her goals. She had the info she needed for the interview with Herb Snow. But she hated to leave. Gus wasn't acting now. He was scared. *Why?* She doubted he needed to remain in the hospital. She called Carbonne and had a frenzied conversation.

***

"Gus, do you trust me? Will you let me roll you out of the hospital and take you to the FBI building?"

Gus began to roll his wheelchair out the door of his room before Sara called Zeke to bring the FBI car to a back entrance of University Hospital. She caught up to Gus as he announced to a young nursing aide, "I'm going to the gift shop. I want this agent to deliver a gift to a friend."

The aide smiled. "You really shouldn't do outings on your own."

"I did yesterday." He rolled past her.

Sara ran to the elevator. Gus rolled in, looked around, and pushed the button for the fifth floor not the lobby. He stood as soon as the elevator moved. "Push it out when the door opens if no one is there."

Sara noticed Gus was pulling the white gown off. He had on sweatpants and a T-shirt underneath. He was amazingly steady on his feet.

The door opened. No one was waiting for the elevator. She pushed the wheelchair out. Gus punched the button for the lobby and smirked. "I've been planning my escape for days. Yesterday I checked out which floor was the best place to dump the chair."

"So, you didn't lie to the nursing aide?"

"I never lie."

"What about telling the ophthalmologist you couldn't see?"

"That was a fib."

They walked out the back door of the hospital to the waiting car.

***

Sara walked into Carbonne's office at one minute after one. "I'm sorry I'm late."

Carbonne bluffed cleverly. "I told Dr. Snow and his lawyer that you had picked up a biological sample from the hospital and had to deliver it to the evidence room." He smiled. "This is your case. Why don't you begin?"

Sara smiled. "People have filed complaints on how patients were transferred to the memory unit at Happy Days." She placed copies of two documents on the table: the handwritten note from Joe to John and the lawyer's letter to John.

Dr. Snow examined each one and whispered to his lawyer. Carbonne seemed distracted and she noticed he was wearing an earpiece. That meant he was receiving instructions from someone. She wondered if he'd told Snow and his lawyer that someone from the US attorney's office and/or the state attorney general's office was listening to the conversation before she arrived. *Now's not the time to ask.*

Snow's lawyer said, "The lawyer's letter to John Lindquist says it all. You have comments from senile men. Their comments won't hold up in court."

"Doubt that. John Lindquist claims as recently as four months ago, Joseph Nowak reviewed a technical article on osteoarthritis." She shuffled through papers in her tote. "About that time his physician noted in his medical records that Nowak had a 'high level of understanding' of his osteoarthritis."

Snow whispered into his lawyer's ear. The well-dressed, middle-aged lawyer steepled his fingers. "Jospeh Nowak signed the papers which allowed Dr. Snow to move him to the memory unit."

"True, but he didn't have his glasses with him. He couldn't read the document. Besides, how can a man, who you claim is mentally impaired, legally sign commitment papers?"

More whispering. "Mr. Nowak's mental incapacity is a double-edged sword. How can a jury believe his statements?"

Sara didn't want to identify Evie. Gus might be right. "The walls are thin at Happy Days and lots of people have little to do but listen."

Carbonne left the table and whispered on his phone. When he returned to the table, he winked and smiled at her. She guessed that meant someone in the FBI had talked to officials at the hospital and arranged for Gus's departure to be recorded as the *patient signed himself out.* At least she didn't need to worry about kidnapping charges. However, she saw that Snow and his lawyer assumed Carbonne's conversation was pertinent to them. Snow's lips trembled.

She decided to be aggressive. "Then we have the autopsy report on Olivia Bend." Sara handed the report to Snow. "You'll note the pathologist found limited signs of cirrhosis in her liver considering she had hepatic cancer. He also noted her emaciation seemed extreme considering the early stage of her cancer His report is consistent with statements from her friends. They claimed she was a moderate drinker and starved herself to death because she was so unhappy in the memory unit. There is no evidence in her medical records that you treated her for depression."

Snow gasped.

"Do you really want this info aired in open court. You'll look bad no matter what you say."

Carbonne leaned forward. "As I told you when you arrived, federal and state attorneys were monitoring this conversation. The New Mexico Attorney General has decided he wants to prosecute a potential case or cases of elder abuse against you and the management of Happy Days. Who gave you the orders to force so many residents of Happy Days into the memory unit unnecessarily?"

The lawyer whispered into Snow's ear. Snow shook his head.

Sara wanted to push him a bit more. "So far, I've identified these three records but am told Golden Years Management—better known as GYM—became the legal guardians for at least forty residents of Happy Days and committed most of them to the memory unit in the last five years."

Snow right hand was shaking. He placed his left hand on top of it to stop the shaking.

"I suspect you were threatened—maybe blackmailed is the better word—because of events when you worked for CYFD."

The lawyer glanced at Snow—who finally nodded—and turned to Carbonne. "What can you offer us?"

## Chapter 21: Jack Hits a Dead End

John waved to Sara as the FBI car pulled away from Isaac's home. He pulled Creeping Jenny weeds from the gravel for ten minutes—as Jack had instructed—before he sauntered into the house.

Jack immediately locked the door and ushered John to the kitchen island. He motioned to a muscular man with a shaved head and a Hawaiian-style shirt. "This is Agent Leroy Elroy."

Leroy stopped peering through binoculars out the sliding door between the kitchen and the patio for only few seconds to wave a hand at John. "The cameras in my car indicate a white compact car drove past but didn't stop. I've seen no one on the path I took through back yards when I walked here from the car."

Jack pulled a bottle of water from the refrigerator and placed it in front of John. "You must be thirsty after working in the blazing sun."

John took a gulp of water and watched Leroy.

"Leroy's black Chevy SUV is parked two blocks block away. If we think you are in danger, he will lead you to it." Jack gulped. "Here's an extra set of keys to the SUV. Use them, if neither of us can escort you to the SUV. In that case, drive directly to the emergency entrance of University Hospital. Help will be there."

John blanched. "My God."

Jack put a hand on John's shoulder. "We think we have everything under control, but I believe you should know what to do in an emergency. Leroy saw the white car follow Zeke onto this street before he parked his black SUV. Zeke and Sara don't think the white car followed them to University Hospital."

John lifted his hand. "I understand. I'm bait. I saw a white car drive past while I worked in the yard."

"So, did I." Jack continued to pace between the kitchen and the front door. He never stepped in front of the picture window in the living room but peered around the corners of other windows. "We hope the driver of the white car now assumes you are here alone. She saw a Black man—who we hope she presumed was me—and Sara drive away. If she noticed the black SUV, we hope she thinks it belongs to someone in the neighborhood."

John looked worried as he watched Jack pace. "How soon do you expect action?"

"We have no idea. While we wait, why don't you tell me about your neighbors Sandi and Bob Jones. You must have been in their apartment many times."

"Not many. They're private people. So am I."

"Don't you and Bob top off the windshield wiper fluid in residents' cars together? What did he talk about as you worked? For example, did he ever complain about Rosa Gonzalez, mention a gun or hunting, or talk about Gus and Ab?"

"Let me think," John took a swallow of water. "He and Sandi were annoyed when Evie tried to convince them to name GYM as their guardian."

*Ruth already told Sara about that incident.*

John leaned forward. "I don't think Bob liked Gus much. He avoided me at the Bistro if Gus was with me."

"How do you know he wasn't trying to avoid Ab not Gus?"

"Ab didn't talk enough to annoy anyone. Besides, he played bocce ball with Ab and me several times."

"What did he talk about?"

"Gossip. Wait. He mentioned hunting deer in Colorado when he was young."

Jack stopped pacing. "Do you think he still hunted or kept a gun?"

"I doubt it. Sandi and the women—Ruth, Karen, and Deb—one day at lunch got into a discussion of their least favorite food. They all disliked venison. Gus argued that they hadn't eaten properly prepared venison." John took a sip of water. "I agreed with women. Never like gamey meats."

"What about Bob?"

John smiled. "He's a happily married man because he knows not to express his opinions when they differ from his wife's. Something Gus never learned."

*John sees only the best in others. Bob could have an unregistered hunting gun*
"Okay." Jack couldn't believe he was using Sara's favorite word: okay. "Can we assume it's unlikely Bob and Sandi squealed on other residents to Rosa or Evie?"

"You can't make that assumption at Happy Days. Everyone says negative things about Rosa and Evie, but some still tell secrets to them."

"Like whom?"

"Deb Kline and probably Ruth."

"Ruth?"

"Ruth is everyone's friend. There's a price, but Gus claimed that's how she could weasel so much info for him." John swallowed more water. "But no one ever said Gus was good judge of women."

*Maybe John's comments are less sunny than I thought.* Jack phone vibrated. He was shocked by what he heard. An agent had located Bob in the Bistro at Happy Days. He said Sandi had announced this morning the best way to beat the heat was to go shopping at Coronado Mall. Bob thought she planned to take friends because she told him to eat lunch and supper without her.

Jack wanted to scream. He'd wasted time questioning John about Bob. He should have been asking about Sandi and her friends. Jack switched positions with Leroy because he believed the back entrance might be easier to monitor while he questioned John.

"John, we have new info. Agents have talked to Bob. He's not the stalker. He claims his wife left this morning with friends without giving him details. Is that unusual?"

John studied Jack. "Pretty obvious you're not married. Like I said they're a good couple which means they don't sweat petty details." He shook his head. "And before you ask, I'll answer your next question. Sandi plays mahjong two afternoons a week. Usually, only women play that game. I usually see her with Ruth, Karen, and Deb at social events. I doubt Bob could give a much better answer."

Jack thought he saw someone walking along the far side of the black SUV on the camera feed. The camera showed a person's lower legs. He hadn't realized until now how poorly Leroy had placed the cameras. The legs were thin. He assumed it was a woman with blue flip-flops.

He studied the continuing camera feed. *False alarm.* A young woman with long blonde hair was walking past the black SUV.

"John, tell me about Deb Kline."

"Nosy. Sometimes she seems to stalk me, but I can get rid of her if I talk about the nuclear museum."

"I've heard she squeals to Rosa Gonzalez and Evie Schooner."

"Squeal suggests she'd intentionally trying to be hurtful. Deb is like a leaky faucet. She talks continually without thinking."

"You don't like her much. Why do others, like her?"

"They pity her." John leaned forward. "What happens now?"

***

Thirty minutes later, the white car pulled up in front of Isaac's house. Leroy quickly identified Deb Kline as the driver. He muttered as he watched her apply lipstick and comb her hair, "Lady, you need more than that." Then she appeared to be playing with something in her lap for over a minute.

Finally, she struggled out of the car, pulled her too tight purple dress down to cover her seat, picked up what appeared to be a decorated bag, and tramped to the front door. She stood for at least a minute before she pushed the doorbell.

Leroy shook his head. "Don't see any obvious weapons."

Jack held his fingers to his lips and pulled John to the door. "Don't open the door until I signal that I'm in a position to grab her."

Leroy added, "Don't take the bag. Could be a bomb."

John opened the door but left the screen door in place. "Deb, what are you doing here?"

"I was worried about you. You left without saying goodbye." She reached to open the screen door. "I brought you a gift."

Jack pushed the screen door open and stepped out. "Put your hands in the air. My partner has a gun aimed at you."

Deb screamed, "My gift?"

Jack frisked her, grabbed the gift, looked inside the bag, and groaned. Two cans of a lite beer were in the bag. He set the bag on the gravel and pulled Deb inside. He looked around and saw John had retreated to the kitchen. Jack led her to the living room and pointed to an easy chair.

She resisted. "If I sit down on the recliner, I won't be able to get up. I prefer to sit on a straight chair in the kitchen." She started to walk toward John.

"Stop." Jack touched her arm. "Ma'am, you stalked FBI agents this morning and circled this neighborhood for hours. What are you trying to do?"

"See my friend." She batted her eyelashes and smiled at John, who seemed to shrink on his stool by the kitchen island.

Jack almost laughed. Deb was either one cool character or dumb. "Ma'am, if you stand still, I will bring you a chair." He pointed to Leroy. "Remember he'll keep the gun aimed at you until you convince us that you aren't a danger to John and us."

Deb tittered, "Oh my. This isn't a nice welcome for a lady. John, tell them I'm your friend." She began to wring her hands. "I can't stay long. I'm supposed to meet the girls at the back entrance to Macy's at the

Coronado Mall at four. Sandi let me borrow her car so I could deliver my gift. Oh my, it's still out in the yard. I'd better get it." She stood.

Leroy stomped his foot and pushed Deb back on the chair. "Lady, are you crazy? We're ready to arrest you for stalking. Why did Sandi let you use her car?"

The droop of Deb's eyelids lessened. She looked like she might understand her situation. "It's simple really. The others wanted to shop. I told them I needed to quickly pick up a gift and deliver it. Sandi let me borrow her car. That's why I need to leave. They expect me at four." She stood.

"Sit." It sounded like a command to a dog. "What about yesterday." Jack enjoyed watching Leroy. He treated Deb like she deserved.

"It's obvious." She smiled. "If I used my car, the agents would have known I was following them. And I knew Sandi kept at extra set of keys by her door. I just borrowed the keys when I stopped by the Joneses yesterday morning—after I saw the lady detective leave Karen's apartment."

"In other words, you could be charged with stealing the Joneses' car?"

"Oh, no. I returned it." She stood again. "I really need to get the beer from the front yard before it gets warm." She waved to John. "He likes his beer cold."

"Sit." Leroy pointed at her. "I still don't get why you followed Sara and Jack."

She shook her head. "I watch police shows on TV. I know police routines. After the lady detective entered Karen's apartment, I stood by the door and listened. The lady detective never asked where John was. So, I knew the FBI had him. I thought he might need to be rescued." She turned to John. "They didn't force you to stay here, did they? You know police sometimes do terrible things."

John stood and whispered in Jack's ear, "Now you know why I avoid her. She means well but she creates havoc wherever she goes."

Leroy tried one more time. "Lady, do you understand that we could charge you with stalking federal agents and stealing a car?"

"Oh, no. You couldn't."

Although Jack found the conversation between Deb and Leroy amusing, her shrill voice was beginning to grate on his nerves. "Ma'am, we're going to get a restraining order against you. If you come closer than fifty feet of John, you will be fined and may be jailed. Agent Elroy and I will escort you to Coronado Mall and talk to your friends."

"Must you? I don't want them to know John didn't like my gift. I tried so hard."

Jack wondered why Evie and Snow hadn't put Deb in the memory unit. He knew what Sara would say: *Her estate must not be worth much.*

## CHAPTER 22: A Miserable Day

Sara didn't think she was needed during the rest of the video conference with Snow, his slick lawyer, and federal and state prosecuting attorneys. Administrative scuffles were Carbonne's domain. "I'd like to get back to investigating the murder of Ab Hess."

Cottingham cleared his throat. "Not so fast. You need to hear this discussion because you will be the liaison between federal and state offices working on these related cases. Carbonne doesn't have the time."

Carbonne grinned.

"Please update us on the status of the murder case."

Sara gulped. "My partner just informed me that one lead we were following appears to be moot. The woman—Deb Kline—who has been tailing us for two days doesn't have sinister designs against us or John Lindquist. Well, except to trap John into marriage. Jack thinks she senile and wonders why Dr. Snow didn't move her to the memory unit."

Snow snorted. "You aren't the first to suggest Debra Kline was deluded. Rosa Gonzalez has ordered me and the medical director to follow up on Debra's disruptive behavior several times. Our medical director reported Debra's breast cancer hadn't metastasized and the cellulitis in her arm is under control. I found her memory was better than most young adults. She's not senile, but she has a narcissistic personality disorder which is basically untreatable."

Sara couldn't resist. "Gee, I misjudged the situation. I thought her estate must be too small for GYM to be interested in acquiring her guardianship."

She heard laughs from the federal and state attorneys. Snow's lips quivered. His lawyer turned red.

Carbonne coughed. "I think Sara is showing signs of frustration with these cases. She'll update all of you when she has something *positive* to report on the murder investigation."

Sara left his office quickly.

***

She decided it was a mistake to respond to Sanders's or Jack's emails when she was in a foul mood. Instead, she and Bug took a walk.

Only a short part of the walk was outside. It was ninety-five degrees, which is hot even in the shade. While the heat only increased her annoyance with the world, it was dangerous for Bug. As a Japanese Chin, with a flat face, he couldn't dissipate heat as well as most dogs. Thus, Sara and Bug wandered the halls in the basement for ten minutes before they went to the evidence room where Sara had left Gus with Zeke Grant before her meeting with Carbonne and the lawyers.

Zeke almost ran to the Dutch door at the entrance of the evidence room when Sara appeared. He leaned out of the open top of the door. "Get Gus out of here. He's driving me crazy. I finally told him he had to sit at the desk and not move."

Sara saw Gus was thumbing through the procedure manual for the evidence room and taking notes. "I hate to ask. Why is he taking notes?"

Zeke glanced at Gus as he whispered, "He says he wants to be sure he gives you clues you can use." Zeke chuckled. "Sometimes I envy agents. Not today. He's all yours."

"I'm not an agent."

"That's why you're stuck with this case. No agent, except poor Jack, would walk twice into Happy Days. At least, if Gus is typical of the residents. He's like a hyperactive child." He pulled Sara with him as he approached Gus. "Dr. Almquist is going to take you to a conference room where you'll be more comfortable."

Gus looked up from his notes and smiled. "This manual is interesting. Can I take it with me?"

Zeke turned from Gus to stare at Sara. "Please."

"No, I think Zeke is required to always keep a printed copy in the evidence room. Let's see if I can find something for you to read."

She texted Jack and learned he and Leroy were bringing John and Deb Kline—in separate cars—to the FBI building after they talked to Sandi, Karen, and Ruth at Coronado Mall. Jack wanted Sara to find two separate rooms for John and Deb because John feared Deb would tackle him if they were left alone in a room.

***

Sara thought Bug might amuse Gus but was afraid Gus might give the dog dangerous snacks. She finally settled Gus in a small conference room with a pitcher of lemonade, sandwiches, and three brochures on the history of the FBI. She texted Jack to bring John to that room and escort Deb to her office.

Sara and Bug awaited their arrival by calling Sanders. He was evasive and unwilling to talk about his plans for their trip to the Yucatan. Finally, she said, "Did you book our flights yet?"

"I booked your flight to Mérida for Thursday of next week."

"And yours?"

"I'm leaving Sunday evening. By my calculations, we need to leave Acoma by two on Sunday. Won't the christening be over by noon?"

"Yes." Sara guessed they'd have to skip the lunch after the christening. "I'm surprised you can get a flight from Albuquerque to Mérida that leaves late on Sunday afternoon."

"I found a way."

*He's being secretive.* Sara was worried but knew she'd only annoy him with questions. "Why don't we make tonight special. Should I pick up lamb chops or steaks on the way home?"

She guessed he was pleased when he answered. "I haven't had lamb chops in ages. Try to get home by six."

***

Sara walked to the conference room and found Jack had left John with Gus. John handed her a note. "Jack was afraid you might not read your emails and texts."

> *I deposited Deb in a locked interrogation room with the camera and recorder on. I thought it was dangerous to leave her in your office. I gave her the sandwiches and soda you left for John and a magazine. John didn't care as long as he wasn't in the same room with Deb.*
>
> *Leroy and I are going to talk to Sandi, Karen, and Ruth. We planned to do it before we dropped Deb and John off, but Leroy couldn't stand to in a car alone with Deb any longer.*

As she read, she listened to John's and Gus's conversation at a subliminal level. *What did John just say? He visited Gus in the hospital.*

Sara decided Deb could wait, and John was more apt to give a direct answer than Gus. "John, how did you find Gus in the hospital? We had him in a private room under a false name."

John gulped. "Gus called and gave me his room number."

"When?"

"Tuesday night?"

Sara frowned at Gus. "I'm sure there was no phone in the room when I visited you around five on Tuesday. How did you get a phone?"

Gus shrugged. "Where's there a will, there's a way." He gave an irritating smile. "I saw a nurse's aide using a phone to make a call. I pushed my help button. While he fussed over me, I pulled his phone from his pocket. The rest was easy."

"Do you still have the phone?'

Gus looked insulted. "I'm not a thief. I placed the phone on the floor. The aide found it thirty minutes later. Probably when he was going to make another call." He flashed his irritatingly toothy grin again. "I knew he wouldn't mention the incident because he shouldn't have been making personal calls."

"Okay." She turned to John. "Did Gus call you before or after I visited with you and Isaac on Tuesday night?"

"About fifteen minutes after you left." John licked his lips. "That was good because I don't lie well."

"What did Gus tell you to do? I want every detail."

"He said his vision had returned to normal but to tell no one, not even Isaac, until we could figure out who poisoned the Wild Turkey. He said you had him 'under wraps.' I couldn't get to him, but he thought he could get to me on Thursday. I should wait by the gift shop at the main entrance of hospital between ten and two." He paused. "And to bring him a set of sweats."

Gus interrupted. "I asked John to sit in one of booths for the food court that's near the gift shop. No one would notice him if he nursed a drink and pretended to read. By then I knew I could bribe one nurse's aide."

"The aide I saw this morning." Sara had forgotten how clever faculty members could be in getting around rules. *One of the things that made faculty meetings so unpleasant.*

Gus winked at Sara. "That's the one. Sweet young thing and not too bright. She rolled me to the food court on Tuesday after my dialysis. Then the doctor decided I didn't need any more dialysis." Gus rolled his eyes. "I could have told him that already on Monday. On Wednesday and Thursday, I conned the aide into letting me roll myself to the food court." He shrugged. "It was easy I promised to bring her a chocolate shake."

John nodded. "I was worried and got to the spot by the gift shop by nine-thirty. I shouldn't have worried. Gus rolled up at exactly ten. I brought a notebook. We made a list of everyone—including cleaning staff—who had been in Gus's apartment since he'd opened the bottle of Wild Turkey and poured drinks for Karen and Ruth almost two weeks ago."

Gus interrupted and grabbed Sara's hand. "You helped us a lot. Your questions on Tuesday night helped me organize my thoughts."

Sara pulled her hand away. *Gus is a schemer to his core.* "Do you have the list?"

John slid a wad of paper from his slack's pocket. Before he had unfolded the two pages, Gus began to speak. "The same maid comes every Tuesday. Evie stopped by once to complain that John had counseled several residents to not list GYM as their guardian. She wanted me to tell John to shut up."

"Then why is her name crossed out?"

"I made him."

John nodded. "I crossed her name off because Gus swore that he watched her constantly and had her out in less than a minute."

Gus pointed to the next name. "Bob and Sandi stopped by on the day Bob announced he'd top off everyone's windshield wiper fluid. That would have been Friday a week ago."

"Why did they stop by? I didn't think you helped John and Bob top off the windshield wiper fluid in residents' cars."

John shook his head. "Gus is all thumbs around cars. Don't know how he managed a lab."

Gus poked him. "That's the key word—managed. I liked chemistry but didn't like working in a lab." He didn't pause as he switched the subject. "They stopped by because they and John were out of rags." He anticipated Sara's question. "Sometimes they overfill the tank with fluid and need rags to clean up."

"Why did you list only Bob?"

"I left Bob at the dining room table while Sandi and I looked for old towels in a bathroom closet. I can't vouch he didn't touch my bottle of Wild Turkey."

Gus appeared to be honest and meticulous in his assessment. She saw the next three women on the list. "Why did you let Deb in?"

"Karen and Ruth stopped by to ask me—more like order me—to stop using my squirt gun. Deb pushed in behind them."

"Odd." John frowned. "Although Deb is always following me, she usually avoids you."

Gus glared at John. "She darted around my apartment while I tried to talk to Ruth and Karen." He scratched his chin. "I don't think any of them touched the booze shelf in kitchen, but I can't be sure." He pinched Sara's arm. "As you've learned, Deb adds confusion wherever she goes."

Sara looked at the last line on the list—*Management.* "What about this?"

Gus shook his head. "I'm sure I didn't let anyone else in during the last two weeks, but it doesn't matter. The management—Rosa, Evie, and Diego—have keys to all our apartments."

The men's list of possible poisoners was like hers. Were they trying to be helpful or were they—or at least one of them—building a diversion with the list? After all, Gus's charade in the hospital made it seem possible that he consumed a small amount of Wild Turkey—and accordingly methanol—to give himself an alibi. She decided to continue to play along.

She pointed to checkmarks on the page. The only names checked were Diego's and Bob's. "What do the checkmarks mean?"

"We figured one of these two had to be the poisoner because they were the only ones with access to windshield wiper fluid with methanol."

"Yes, but everyone had access to hand sanitizers."

Gus smacked his lips. "Most of them were gels. The Wild Turkey wasn't thickened."

"We've learned many nail polish removers contain methanol."

Both men looked startled. Gus said, "All the women on our list occasionally wear nail polish."

Sara decided she'd toyed with them enough. "The lab is starting to catch up. They assessed the prints on the bottle of Wild Turkey."

Gus sighed, "At last."

"Don't get too hopeful. Yours, Ab's, and Karen's prints were on the bottle. There were also two other set of unknown prints. Winslow Red Feather of the FBI lab convinced Mrs. Gonzalez she could stop nasty gossip about Happy Days if she let him collect prints and DNA from all the staff. The two unknown prints aren't the prints of any of the staff." She didn't add two points. Winslow hadn't located Ruth, Sandi, or Deb because they were out when he stopped by Happy Days. Bob had refused to provide his prints and DNA.

Gus's jaw dropped. "That means Ruth, Karen, Deb, Sandi, or Bob could be the poisoner." He shook his head. "We haven't shortened the list much."

"Actually, there are two other possible poisoners." She stared at Gus and then John. "Your names belong on the list."

## CHAPTER 23: A Bad Day Improves

Jack's email suggested he was frantic:

> *HELP. Deb is now dancing around the conference table, bobbing her head up and down, and mumbling the lines of a song—we think—"I can't get no satisfaction."*
>
> *Leroy is convinced she's a danger to herself. I removed the soda can, pens, and pencils from the room. I called a psychologist to evaluate her. He promised to be here ASAP.*

Sara replied:

> *Save the can and send it to the lab. It should have Deb's fingerprints. Did you get Ruth's and Sandi's prints when you spoke to them at the Coronado Mall?*

She stepped back into the conference room.

John spoke first. "We want to convince you that we didn't add methanol to the Wild Turkey. We'll take a lie detector test." Gus nodded in agreement.

"Lie detector tests can't be used in court. Your best defense is to help me solve the two other cases related to the murder. The New Mexico Attorney General—well at least the director of the Division on Medicare Fraud and Elder Abuse—agreed this afternoon to pursue indictments against anyone responsible for coercing residents into the memory unit. They are initially focusing on the cases of Georg Cernak, Joseph Nowak, and Olivia Bend."

Tears welled up in Gus's eyes.

"FBI analysts haven't had a chance to study your files, particularly your paper files thoroughly." She thought for a second. "Do you have anything on your computers or in your paper files that would give us reason to get the records of Dr. Snow, Evie Schoener or Rosa Gonzalez? Or for that matter the medical records of everyone in the memory unit?"

Gus smiled. "Copies of all the questionable invoices are in a file named *IPS* on my and John's computers."

Sara hated to disappoint him. "Ruth already gave me the printed copies."

"Yes, but I also have copies of most of the packing slips in the file." Gus must have noticed Sara's smile. "You talked to Cookie. You've been busy."

John pulled a page from his blue notebook and handed it to Sara. "Here's what you need. It's from the MU file on my computer."

"No," Gus shook his head. "That will send Evie to prison. She's helped us so much. Surely, she can be protected from prosecution."

Sara didn't feel like explaining. The NM Attorney General's office would probably only grant immunity from prosecution or lessen the prosecution of one person in the management team of Happy Days. Snow would probably be the protected person. And the decision wasn't hers. She patted Gus's arm. "I only investigate the cases. Attorneys decide who to prosecute."

Sara scanned the page and forwarded it to Carbonne, Jack, and Rosemary. "I'm locking you in here. I'll be back ASAP."

***

"Sara, you did it again. Your cases always break on Friday afternoon or during the weekend. I must leave by five." Carbonne waved toward a screen where a man and a woman appeared to be arguing. They were the director of the Office for Medicaid Fraud and Elderly Abuse in the New Mexico Attorney General's office and Jerry Maggio. Both had participated in the previous video conference. Carbonne pushed a button to turn on the audio feed when Jack entered his office a moment later.

Sara spoke immediately. "We have new evidence. I hope you haven't signed a plea agreement with Dr. Snow. I believe the person who can give you the most info and who is the least culpable is Evie Schoener"

Maggio screamed, "No."

His boss's jaw dropped. "Why?"

"We just found a statement from Evie Schoener—the social worker at Happy Days—explaining how residents were admitted to the memory unit. She referred prospective patients to Dr. Snow if she and nursing staff thought the residents were feeble physically and/or mentally. She also provided Dr. Snow with other info—an assessment of their wealth and info on whether they had a guardian residing in the Albuquerque area. She noted Dr. Snow usually admitted all those who were financially well-off and were under the guardianship of GYM—the parent company of Happy Days—to the memory unit. The others went to assisted living if they weren't already there. She also admitted Alejandro Smith gave Dr. Snow and herself bonuses every time Snow admitted a patient with GYM as his/her guardian to the memory unit."

Maggio yelled, "How could you have missed this statement?"

Sara knew enough to keep her cool even when Carbonne's face turned red. "Mr. Maggio this case is complicated. Retrieval of info from files was delayed because my partner and I used a lot of the FBI staff on Tuesday to sort garbage at Happy Days."

She saw Jack turn gray when she said *my partner*, but he said nothing. Instead, he kept on sending one text after another.

"The net result is no analyst was available to analyze all the records of two—we thought minor—suspects in the murder. They are both retired faculty members—Gus Rinaldi and John Lindquist. I basically trusted them. This morning, I learned one—Gus—had been lying to his physicians at University Hospital. His vision was not impaired by methanol after the first day."

"What are you rambling about?" Maggio was literally bouncing in his chair.

Sara decided to treat him like an unpleasant student. "I'm telling you Gus was clever enough to fool medical authorities for several days about his condition."

Carbonne coughed.

Sara continued, "I read Gus and John the riot act. They finally started sharing details—mainly this statement from Evie."

Maggio jumped from his chair and strutted to the door of apparently his boss's office. "Bet it's a fake. How did they get it?"

His boss ignored Maggio as she studied her computer screen—presumably looking at a copy of the document. "How sure are you that the memo is real? How did they get it from her?"

"John Lindquist gave me this paper copy…" Sara held it up. "…and told me where to find it in his computer files. An FBI analyst located it in John's computer files, forwarded it to you and Carbonne, and is now determining if it's been altered." Sara frowned. "I don't know how John got it." Sara bit her lip. "John's a med physicist and seems to be normal and honest, but I won't guarantee anything at this point."

Jack whispered in Sara's ear.

"My partner thinks we have another problem. Evie Schoener is convinced Alejandro Smith will kill her when he learns of the note. Jack has asked Agent Leroy Elroy to pick her up. She prefers to be here rather than in her home."

"D***." Carbonne picked up a phone and started whispering.

Sara looked over at Carbonne's back. "I suspect Carbonne is arranging to put Evie in protective custody over the weekend. That will give our analyst time to examine all the computer files of the three med school faculty." Sara saw the confused look on the lawyers' faces. "The files of the victim and the two clowns I spent the day with."

The woman attorney looked annoyed. "John Lindquist and his wife were my godparents."

Sara gasped while Jack laughed. "I'm sorry, but he and Gus have created so much work by keeping secrets."

The woman lawyer shook her head. "I've also met the old lecher, Gus Rinaldi. I've seen the Three Old Musketeers in action when I visited my mother at Happy Days." She pursed her lips. "My husband won't be happy, but I think I'll have Mother stay with us until these cases are solved. I don't want her to be targeted."

***

As soon as the attorneys signed off. Jack looked at Sara and then Carbonne. "What do we do with Deb, Gus, John, Evie, and Snow?"

Carbonne didn't look up from the note he was scribbling while he mumbled into his phone.

Sara walked to Carbonne's under-the-counter refrigerator and pulled out three diet colas. She gave one to Jack. "Let's start with the easiest first. I think John will want to go back to Isaac's house. Gus could go back to the hospital."

"I already checked. They said he checked himself out, and they won't readmit him."

She handed a can to Carbonne who sounded like he was begging the person on the phone. *Best to ignore him.* "We can dump John and Gus at Isaac's house and get ABQ Police to circle the neighborhood regularly this weekend." She sighed. "We should separate them so they can't agree on their stories, but I don't have the energy to arrange separate housing for them. They'd outsmart me anyway."

"What about Evie, Snow, and Alejandro Smith? Evie's the key person now in the State's case. The other two have funds to leave the state."

Sara looked over at Carbonne. "Both Carbonne and I must leave by five today. We don't have time to try to prepare papers to arrest anyone. I suspect he's…" She nodded toward Carbonne. "… trying to arrange protective custody for Evie this weekend."

Carbonne held up a finger.

Sara assumed she'd guessed right. "Jack, why don't you call Maggio. If he's hot to trot, he can arrange state police to monitor Smith and Snow, but I'd advise him to keep his cool and do nothing."

"If Maggio has someone monitor them, it's like alerting them to an imminent arrest."

"Agreed, best to do nothing. That leaves Deb."

"Please, let Leroy take her back to Happy Days now." Jack hung his head. "I can't face much more of her babble. The biggest mystery at Happy Days is why no one has killed her. She's beyond annoying. But our psychologist agreed with Snow. Deb's not crazy, just narcissistic. She plays dumb to get her way."

Sara knew a way to reward Jack, but she thought he'd balk if she told him Rosemary was pretty, smart, and the perfect woman for him. "If you have time, you might talk to Rosemary the analyst for this case."

# CHAPTER 24: Awkward Questions

As Sara drove north with Bug on I-25 after finishing her errands, she thought about Sanders's latest email. It suggested more questions than it answered.

Although he said he planned to fly from Las Vegas to Cancun, he hadn't listed his flight numbers. Usually, he gave her his flight numbers. *Perhaps he was taking a private jet. With whom?*

She was surprised he'd booked their stay at a Marriott Hotel in Mérida not one of the locally owned hotels he preferred. Government agencies insisted those traveling on official business use US owned hotels and airlines when possible. However, Sara thought this trip for the Senate Intelligence Committee was a clandestine venture, and the rule wouldn't apply.

She had also noted he booked the hotel only for Thursday through Saturday nights—while she was there. *Where was he staying the rest of his two-week trip?* Usually, he told her where he was staying in case an emergency arose. Perhaps, he didn't want her to know he had a traveling companion during the rest of the trip. He understood their agreement: their romantic relationship was over if he strayed sexually again.

He had rented a car to be picked up in Cancun on this coming Monday and returned at the Belize City Airport in twelve days. He'd listed her and no one else as an alternate driver. Maybe, he was doing the trip alone. She hoped not. Forget the unrest in the Yucatan and Central America, crime and accidents could happen.

For some reason, Sanders had chosen not to confide in her as he usually did. All she could was to make tonight pleasant and not be late.

***

She found a note on counter when she arrived at home:

> *I'll be back by five-thirty. Salad is in the refrigerator.*
> *Potatoes in oven should be done by six.*
> *Love,*
> *Sanders*

She didn't waste time wondering what errand had distracted him. She noted Sanders hadn't set out any wine for dinner. She hoped he be pleased with the California pinot noir, the clerk at the wine store recommended. She slid the bottle into the refrigerator. Sara was no wine connoisseur and generally let Sanders buy the wines he liked.

She brought out an ironed tablecloth—not placemats—and her good china. She placed sprigs of Rose of Sharon—the only plant still blooming in her garden during this heat wave—on the table.

Finally, she took a quick shower and changed into something comfortable and colorful. *The best I can do when it's over hundred.*

At five-thirty, Bug began to pace at the front door. Less than two minutes later she heard a key turning in the lock and pulled the wine from the refrigerator.

Sanders smiled when he saw the table set with flowers. He laughed when he saw the wine bottle. He pulled a similar bottle from the bag in his hand. "You know me too well"

They kissed slowly.

"We make a good tag team in the kitchen and elsewhere. Let's enjoy some wine and not rush to eat." He opened the chilled wine and poured himself a glass. "Do you want a glass of this? Or would you prefer the cheap rosé which you keep in the refrigerator?"

She smiled as she placed two napkins on the kitchen island and slid onto a stool.

He poured the rosé for her. "I've got something for you in the bedroom." When he returned, he said, "We need to talk."

She opened a file and looked at his plane reservations. He was flying on a chartered flight leaving Las Vegas at eight p.m. Sunday with Victor Ortez.

"Victor is an officer in several banks in the Yucatan. His brother is a member of Chamber of Deputies in Mexico."

Sara frowned.

"It's like our House of Representative in Congress." Sanders sipped his wine.

"What's your cover?"

"You've hit my core problem. If I traveled as a representative of the Senate Intelligence Committee, no one would talk to me. I'm officially representing the Senate Committee on Foreign Relations—particularly the subcommittee controlling USAID and the State Department—on this trip."

Sara sighed. "Well, you were the chief USAID officer in Bolivia when I met you." She stroked his arm.

He leaned over and nuzzled her neck. "I knew almost as soon as I met you that you had a knack for gathering information."

Sara suppressed a smile. Even in private, Sanders never used the word spying.

Sanders must have noted a change in Sara's expression. "You were so cool under pressure." He paused. "So… alluring and …"

Sara pushed his away. *He's trying to be charming but having trouble.* "Anyone with a brain would know you're an intelligence officer to your core."

"You know me too well. Everyone else will accept my cover. I'm on a fact-finding mission for USAID leadership in Washington. Victor will introduce me to businesspeople who want to build industries with good-paying jobs."

"Fine in theory, but is it realistic? USAID is focused on agriculture and public health. Their involvement in drug control made sense when farmers in South America were looking for alternate crops besides coca, but now fentanyl is manufactured from raw materials from China. What are you suggesting the locals manufacture instead?"

He put an arm around her shoulder. "You're outdated. Big industries in the Yucatan are making turbojets and manufacturing clothes. USAID has moved into brokering industrial development of all types."

"Okay." *Time to change the topic slightly.* "When do you leave Mexico and go into Guatemala?"

"I'll travel with Victor around the Yucatan on Monday through Wednesday and pick you up on Thursday. You'll meet him and few of the industry leaders on Friday after we tour the markets of Mérida. On Saturday, we'll go to Chichén Itzá. You leave on Sunday, and so do I." He pointed to his typed agenda.

Sara thumbed through several pages. He'd listed his hotel and business contacts—with phone numbers—for each day as he toured through southern Mexico, Guatemala, Honduras, and Belize. He'd marked his proposed route on a map.

"I feel uncomfortable about you traveling alone."

"I won't be. Victor will drive with me around the Yucatan. He'll leave me at Ciudad Cuauhtémoc, the southern terminus of the Pan American Highway in Mexico. I'll only have to drive alone for a few miles to La Mesilla in Guatemala where the USAID officer for Guatemala will be waiting for me. He wants…"

Sara could tell by the tone of Sanders's voice he was ready to go on for hours. She hated to interrupt him but the aroma from the oven indicated the potatoes were cooked. She looked at the clock. It was six. "While I sauté the lamb chops, why don't you tell me about your plans in Guatemala. What does the USAID rep want to show you?"

"Avocado orchards."

Sara knew she would enjoy such a tour. She doubted Sanders would. "What's their problem?"

"They can't compete with Mexico in the US market and must export their avocados mainly to Europe and the rest of Central America. The locals claim they'd be more competitive if irrigation and road systems were improved."

"Definitely sounds like standard USAID projects." The chops were glistening brown on both sides. "Anything else of interest in Guatemala?"

"I want to meet with businesswomen who are interested in increasing Guatemala's export of locally designed fabrics and clothes to the US. With climate change, they think their brightly colored blouses and skirts could become staples in the summer wardrobes of women in the US."

"Smart. I can't be the only one who would welcome those loose, comfortable styles." She placed the platter with the lamb chops on the table. "Dinner is ready."

***

Sara had only eaten her salad and given Bug two small pieces of her lamb, when Sanders started to expound on his trip. He planned to spend three days in Guatemala before he met the USAID representative and two security officers from the US Embassy at the El Florido border crossing between Guatemala and Honduras.

*Did I hear correctly?* Sara swallowed her mouthful of potato with a gulp. "US-Honduras relations must be rocky if they're sending two security officers."

Sanders chewed his mouthful slowly and sighed "This afternoon the US Embassy in Honduras advised me to cancel my visit. They feel my presence would endanger them."

He got up from the table and began to pace. "I put so much effort in planning this trip. Originally, the committee wanted me to visit not only the Yucatan in Mexico and Guatemala but also Honduras, Nicaragua, and Belize. I decided a couple of days ago my visit in Nicaragua would be inflammatory. Now I can't visit Honduras either."

Sara stood and enclosed him in her arms. "The senators have set you up to fail."

His shoulders heaved up and down as he appeared to be on the verge of crying. "I wanted to see problems at the ground level."

She tightened her hug. *I'm relieved but can't say that.* "So, in your revised schedule, do you go to Belize?"

"Yes."

"I'll be relieved when you reach Belize."

He pushed her away. "I know. You've told me a dozen times you have a bad feeling about this project."

She didn't want to stoke his anger. So, she changed the topic slightly. "I'm surprised there are USAID projects in Belize. It's relatively well-off, isn't it?"

"You're doing it again."

"What?"

"Trying to distract me."

Sara had lost her appetite. She dropped more pieces of lamb into Bug's bowl. "Bug never likes lamb in his dried dog food, but he sure seems to be enjoying the meat tonight."

Sanders ate several mouthfuls before he answered. "Bug should like it. This was good spring lamb not the mutton they use in dog food."

Sara wished she knew what to say to make him feel better. She dreaded thinking about his mood if he didn't get the position he wanted in the State Department. *Nothing to do about that now.* "It cools off after eight, especially in the bosque. Why don't we take a walk?"

# CHAPTER 25: Reaching for the Sky



Being in a bad mood didn't seem to decrease Sanders's sexual appetite on Friday night. The urgency of his desire was fun but made Sara nervous. He'd made love as if there was no tomorrow. *He was afraid.*

They had a slow start on Saturday morning. While he sorted and resorted his documents in a leather briefcase, Sara had wrapped the presents for the christening—the engraved silver teething ring and a big box of practical baby clothes. She had also packed a tote for herself and assembled all of Bug's paraphernalia.

They drove separately to the airport because Sanders wanted to return his rental car and then drive on to Acoma in Sara's car. As they left the airport together, Sanders said, "Carbonne called and apologized, but he and Barbara can't entertain us tonight. What do you want to do this afternoon?"

"The christening will be in the historic church on the Acoma mesa tomorrow. I haven't visited the cultural center at the Sky City Casino in years."

"Agreed. It's too hot to be on the mesa in the blazing sun. We can also take in an early show tonight at the casino."

Sara glanced at Sanders. He seemed to be calm. *Now was the time to ask key questions.* "We haven't talked yet about what I should do in an emergency."

Sanders frowned. "What kind of emergency?"

"Like if I haven't heard from you in over 24-hours."

"I'll have a satellite phone along. As usual, I'll call you each morning around six."

"But satellite phones don't always work in jungle areas. When should I panic if you don't call around six?" Sara looked away from her driving for a few seconds. Sanders didn't look annoyed.

"Remember the file I showed you last night. You brought it along today, right? On the last page I listed emergency numbers and email addresses."

"I remember." He had listed names and numbers of senators on the intelligence and the foreign relations committees and officers in USAID and FBI in Washington and the embassies in Belize and Guatemala and the consulate in Mérida. *None would respond quickly to a problem.* "Who do I call in an emergency?"

"Call the starred number—the number for my FBI contact in Washington. Your code phrase to that contact is *I'm sick.*" Sanders leaned over and kissed her lightly. "Thanks for being my backup."

She knew she shouldn't nag but couldn't resist. "You know it's not too late to call this excursion off. Everyone knows you're qualified for the job in the State Department. This so-called fact-finding trip won't change anyone's opinion of you. They either like your style, or they don't."

***

*Sunday*

Sara, Sanders, and Bug stopped several times as they walked to the San Estévan de Rey Mission Church. Sara thought the adobe church with its twin bell towers looked more like a fortress than a church. Maybe, because of the violence in its history. Priests in the 1600s had enslaved the Native Americans to build it on top of the mesa at Acoma, and the natives had thrown an especially corrupt priest off the cliff near the church.

They entered the church a half-hour before the service because they knew the church was no longer used for weekly services—only for special events. Besides it was too hot to stand in the sun. As they entered, Sanders pointed to the thick adobe wall around the doorway. "It must be almost seven feet thick."

They walked around examining the limited paintings on the interior walls. In general, the inside was more muted than most Spanish colonial churches in the Southwest. There were no pews. Only about twenty chairs were placed a respectful distance from the altar, which had been adorned with a few sprigs of Texas sage. The lavender color brightened the dim church.

Suddenly voices filled the church as Barbara and Carbonne carrying Willow entered the church. In the group following them, Sara recognized Barbara's parents, Barbara's older brother and his wife, and Barbara's aunt and uncle. Sara thought it sad that none of Carbonne's family were present. She knew he had not invited his parents to his wedding to Barbara, but he'd informed them that they were grandparents when Willow was born.

Carbonne announced, "Father Felipe will be here momentarily. He was delayed by a problem at Santa Maria de Acoma."

Sara assumed the priest would not arrive for another fifteen minutes. The other church was in the nearby village of McCartys below the mesa.

No one seemed to miss the priest as they cooed over Willow and admired her white eyelet christening dress, which Barbara had worn when she was christened twenty-six years before. Father Felipe had to clap his hands twice to gain the attention of the group when he arrived.

Father Felipe baptized Willow. Then Barbara's parents led the part of the ceremony—where the godparents pledged their support of the child—because Sara wasn't Catholic and couldn't be a godparent under church rules.

Afterward, the group went to the ancient house on the mesa maintained by Barbara's family. The spread was less grand than for the fiesta in honor of Carbonne's and Barbara's marriage. Sara, Sanders, and Bug slipped away around one to drive to the Albuquerque airport.

***

Sanders insisted Sara drop him off at the door to the terminal. She didn't cry as he gave her a long kiss and pushed her back into the car. As she watched him disappear into the terminal, she wondered what he hadn't told her about the trip and if she'd ever see him again.

Sara then reverted to her stand-by behavior in all crises—get so busy, you don't have time to worry.

***

The halls of the FBI building were dim on this Sunday afternoon. Her footsteps echoed on the floor as Bug led her to her office. She turned on her computer and realized a lot had happened since Friday at four.

*First things first.* She determined all the suspects in the case were alive and well. The agents in the safe house reported Evie was a model resident. She slept in late, read novels during the day, and played poker with them in the evening. She had requested a meeting with Maggio in the attorney general's office on Monday morning. Maggio wanted Sara to be present.

Gus and John had both sent short emails apologizing for their bad behavior during the last week. Sara decided to let them stew and didn't reply.

Sara read the emails from Rosemary and Jack. Neither mentioned anything personal, but Sara thought they must have enjoyed each other's company, or they wouldn't have worked so long on Saturday mining Gus's and John's files.

They had provided enough evidence for her to request warrants for access to the medical records of patients in the memory unit of Happy Days during the last five years and to the computers, phones, and paper files of Evie, Rosa, and Snow. She hoped a judge would grant the warrants quickly. She wanted Maggio to have all the evidence he needed before he decided tomorrow whether to cut a deal with Evie Schoener or Herb Snow.

She saw an official at FDA had sent her a complicated email with several attachments. To answer the email, she'd have to organize all Gus's hunches on the continued use of contaminated food products by Happy Days. She didn't have the energy.

She and Bug needed a break. They went to a favorite grassy spot by the building but didn't dally. It was too hot. Instead, they ran races in the basement. *Hard to believe Bug with his short legs can outrun me in a short stretch.*

As they wandered to the vending machines, Sara phone pinged. There was a message from Sanders:

> *Will leave Las Vegas for Cancun in thirty minutes. Victor*
> *is very slowly saying goodbye to his family now.*
> *Love always,*
> *S*

*Why did Sanders say Victor was very slowly saying goodbye to his family?* She knew Sanders wouldn't include that extraneous detail if it wasn't important. *He wants me—or agents in Washington   to check on Victor's family.* She texted:

> *Don't go. I'm sick.*
> *Sara*

*Why hadn't Sanders texted his FBI contact in Washington directly?* He must have felt he was being monitored. There was no time to think to think about unimportant details now. She texted Sanders's FBI contact in Washington:

> *I'm sick.*
> *Need to know location of all members of Victor Ortez's family*
> *during the last 24 hours.*
> *Stop takeoff of Ortez jet from Las Vegas.*

Sara was surprised when Ray Curtis—a young agent who had worked with Sanders in Brazil—called two minutes later. He was not the agent listed.

"Hi, Sara. Surprised to get me?" Ray didn't pause. "We know Victor's wife and parents are safe at his home in Mérida. His daughter—Carina—is a student at University of Nevada-Las Vegas." There was a long pause. "Her roommate thought Carina had spent last night with a *new friend*. Victor's wife wouldn't answer questions on the location of the son—Roberto. Text Sanders to get off the plane. The code is: *I need you now*."

Sara texted:

> *I need you now.*
> *Love,*
> *Sara*

"Done." Sara was terrified but didn't want to waste Ray's time by asking why he hadn't directly texted Sanders. "Now what?"

"You're still a cool cucumber. Listen as I talk to others."

Sara heard several clicks. "Tower, don't allow Gulfstream G200 jet number MEX566 to leave the gate." The voice was lower than Ray's voice. She thought she heard Ray in the background in another conversation. The low voice again. "I don't care if the main door is closed. This jet can't leave." A third voice with a Spanish accent entered the argument. Sara wondered if the third voice was the pilot's. Finally, the official with the low voice said, "Ground observed a flat tire. I'm shutting you down."

Then Ray's voice again. "Sara, you don't need to hear the details, but the jet won't roll onto the tarmac. One of our agents was tired of the argument and punctured the tire. Don't ask how."

Sara was even more scared now. *Had Ray closed her out of the loop because he knew hostage negotiations were about to begin?* She doubted Victor would release Sanders if his own son or daughter was being held hostage.

The minutes seemed long. She picked Bug up and cuddled him. She didn't even try to work on the local case, but she kept checking her emails just in case a relevant message appeared. She chuckled to herself. *What was a relevant message?*

# CHAPTER 26: Failed Hostage Negotiations

Her phone pinged. The text from Ray was short.

*Watch this feed on your computer.*

Sara pushed the highlighted area and saw the closed door of a plane on her screen. The lighting was dim. She thought the camera must be attached to the wall of the jetway. A man, evidently farther down the jetway, was trying to yell above the background noise of the airport runways. Sara had to concentrate to understand what he was saying. Only sporadic words were clear. "Not until you open…" "Have daughter." "Not until open…" "No." Mainly, Sara heard grinding mechanical sounds from several directions and the roars of jets taking off.

Suddenly, Sara saw a helmeted women with a Kevlar vest race down the jetway toward the door. The woman opened the side door of the jetway adjacent to the plane and an individual also in protective gear leaned forward, pounded on the door to the plane, and then retreated. The woman ran back up the jetway past the camera.

The grinding sounds continued as did the fractured calls from the man on the jetway—but out of the camera's range—for several minutes. The man stopped yelling. When he resumed, his voice seemed to be coming from the doorway by the jet., but Sara couldn't see him. His voice was still hard to hear above all the mechanical sounds. His "Let us help…" sounded as if negotiations were not progressing well.

Bug was tired of being petted and jumped off her lap. *Can't blame him.*

Sara looked at her watch. She'd been staring at the screen for thirty minutes. She forced herself to sort papers on her table and generally neaten her office.

After thirty more minutes, the door to the main cabin opened. Sara thought she heard a shot. *Hope not.* Then another shot. Four men in SWAT gear charged up the stairs and into the plane.

The scene on her screen was stagnant. Almost no noises came from the plane. Two women with *Las Vegas Fire EMT* embroidered on their shirts brought a stretcher up the steps and onto the plane. Five minutes later, they carried the stretcher out. A white sheet was draped over a body on the stretcher.

Sara gulped and prayed.

The EMTs returned to the plane. After five minutes, a man in a torn blue shirt emerged from the main entrance to the plane. It was Sanders. His left arm was in a sling and blood stained his shirt. The EMTs helped him down the stairs.

*Interesting they avoided the ramp and hence the public area of the terminal.* Sara texted the number where she'd reached Ray Curtis before:

*How serious is Sanders's injury?*

On screen, three more men in SWAT gear surged into the cabin. The background noise continued, and Sara couldn't hear anything distinct from the cabin. A man in protective gear stepped out of the plane. He backed up and focused a gun on two crew members—at least both wore white short-sleeve shirts and black slacks, but one was a woman and wore heels—as they exited with their hands raised above their heads. Two men in protective gear emerged behind the crew and pushed the crew down the stairs.

Watching the feed was excruciating. Everything was happening at a slow pace. Sara still had not received a response on Sanders's condition. By her calculations, one passenger and four SWAT team members were still on the plane.

After several minutes, a rather rotund, bald man with his hands handcuffed behind him emerged from the plane. He was pushed down the stairs of the jetway by a man in protective gear. Sara assumed the man was Victor Ortez and the dead man must have been either the pilot or the co-pilot.

Sara was surprised the camera kept transmitting until she saw two SWAT members carry briefcases and boxes from the plane. She thought one of the briefcases—a brown leather one—was Sanders's case. A third man followed with a small box. He called, "All clear," as he exited onto the stairs.

The screen went blank. Sara's phone pinged. The text was short:

*Clean wound to upper arm. Under medical care now. He'll
call you tonight.*

Sara wished everyone didn't expect her to be so logical and cool, but she knew no one wanted to waste time updating her when she couldn't do anything useful. She also knew her nerves were shot. She couldn't concentrate on Gus's files. She picked up Bug.

Bug licked her hands. His black eyes seemed to beg her. There was only one thing to do. Get a cheeseburger and fries at McDonalds. Bug liked it best when they ate together in the car. Then they'd go home and watch *PBS Masterpiece Theater* at eight and wait for Sanders's call.

***

Sara's home phone rang at nine-thirty. Usually, she didn't answer the phone when it rang in the middle of her favorite show, *Masterpiece Theater*. Tonight, she ran to the phone and yelled, "Sanders."

"Sara, I'm fine."

He didn't give her time to show her concern. *Means he's feeling guilty for misleading me.*

"We thought Victor Ortez had acted strangely during the last twenty-four hours." Sanders sighed. "But then I approached him to be my guide in the Yucatan because the FBI and Policia Federal Ministerial—the Mexican equivalent of the FBI, better known as PFM—thought he might have contacts in the drug cabals."

Sara interrupted, "So, you never thought we'd be going on an excursion to the Yucatan?" She tried to control her voice, so it didn't sound as annoyed as she felt.

"Not exactly. I—really my whole team—thought Victor wouldn't show his hand—allow gang members to capture me and to make demands for my return—until we were in the Yucatan."

*Odd explanation.* She wanted to ask whether she also would also have been bait when she arrived in Mérida next Thursday. Reason over emotions prevailed. "What was Victor demanding on the plane?" She gulped. "Let me rephrase. Tell me what happened once you arrived in Las Vegas. I want to understand this mess."

"Ray Curtis was waiting for me when I departed my flight from Albuquerque."

"I should have known Ray wasn't in Washington when he patched me to the feed from the camera at the jetway."

Sanders sighed. "I suppose I should have told you more, but..."

"Continue with your story. Why risk meeting Ray at the airport? You two could have been seen together."

"We had been monitoring the Ortez family for weeks. We—particularly the PFM—believed the drug cabal might take one of his family members as a hostage to ensure Victor's cooperation. We thought it would be his son or daughter because Victor and his wife aren't close. Two days ago, the PFM realized that Victor's son Roberto—a student at the Autonomous University of the Yucatan—hadn't show up at his usual haunts in Mérida in the last week. His mother made excuses when a friend—who was an undercover agent—called."

Sara had to give Sanders credit. His scheme was thorough. That only annoyed her more. "Did they find the son dead or alive in Las Vegas?"

Sanders sniffed loudly. "How did you guess Roberto had fled to the US?"

"Remember, I worked with Ray, too, in Brazil. He lowers his voice when he's lying. The way he suggested the daughter was with a *new friend* made me suspicious." She paused. "I'm asking questions now, not you. What was so urgent that Ray had to meet you at the airport before you went to the terminal for private jets?"

"A photo of Roberto in drag. Ray thought I'd not recognize Roberto and felt I shouldn't have the picture on my phone."

"Okay. Then why did you text me not Ray shortly after you boarded the Ortez jet?"

"I recognized the cabin steward as Roberto in heels when I boarded the plane. I had to assume my phone messages were being monitored. It was more logical to send a quick message to you than to a work associate at that point. I also thought you'd figure out my coded message faster than anyone else."

*Risky decision. I almost didn't.* "Okay, how did it turn nasty on the plane?"

"Victor insulted his son and called him a 'gutless wonder' and other names. Roberto became hysterical and screamed in Spanish. The essence of what I understood was: The pilot and co-pilot were working for a drug gang based in the Yucatan. Local gang members had his sister—Carina—and would leave her body at the airport if Victor didn't cooperate."

"Doesn't make sense. Why make a scene in Las Vegas? It would be easier to dispose of you in Mérida."

"You're thinking like the gang members. Victor isn't a gang member. He told us afterward he'd decided the only chance of his, mine, and his daughter's survival was if the plane never left Las Vegas. He knew how to provoke his son into spilling what he knew. He also felt he had to make crew believe he was cooperating."

"Okay." After a long pause, "How?"

Sanders must have recognized her silence indicated her disbelief and added, "Victor knows I speak Spanish, but he switched to Spanish and said, 'If I shoot Sanders now, you and your friends will know they can trust me because then I'll be a felon in the US. Is that enough to get my daughter released?'"

"What did the son and crew do?"

"The co-pilot pushed Victor toward the cockpit. I couldn't hear the conversation. I just saw Roberto grinning like an idiot as he stared at me with dilated pupils. Occasionally, he would coil a curl in his wig around his fingers and say, 'Don't you worry. They will not kill you yet. Frederico in Mérida must talk to you first.' I figured he was high on cocaine and disguised himself as a woman frequently."

Sara snorted. "Your profiler missed that Roberto was transgender or a drag queen?" Sara wished Sanders would speed the story but guessed telling his story was cathartic. "Ray let me watch the feed of the camera focused on the main door to the cabin. When did the pilot finally release the door so it could be opened?"

"Don't rush the story. I knew the crew didn't want to kill me yet. It was also apparent the co-pilot—not Roberto or the pilot—was the real boss. I also knew the clock was ticking. I could hear thumps on the rear and front of the plane. I figured the FBI and airport personnel were emptying the cargo compartments and moving stairs toward the cockpit. If the microphones I had planted in several sports when I boarded the plane were working, they knew my situation was bad."

*About time he admits he was afraid.* "Weren't you scared?"

He ignored her comment. "When Victor returned, he pushed his son toward the cockpit. 'Roberto, beg them to release your sister. They wouldn't listen to me.' He slid a gun into my hand."

"Was it loaded?"

"Yes, Victor was supposed to use it on me. Less than a minute later, the lights went off in the cabin. I figured the ground crew was through negotiating and had turned the power off to the plane. I knew a SWAT team would arrive soon."

Sara thought a second. "Didn't it quickly get hot on the plane? It was a hundred here today. It must have been a hundred and twenty in Las Vegas."

"Very hot. That's why the pilot opened the door to the plane. The co-pilot stomped into the cabin waving a gun. I took aim and shot him but I'm not as fast as I used to be. He got off a shot before I did, but I knew enough to roll. Then the SWAT team raced in."

# CHAPTER 27: Sanders Remembers

Sanders spent Sunday night in Las Vegas for three reasons. One, it was logical. He and Ray needed time to debrief the characters involved in the attempted kidnapping.

Two, he couldn't face Sara. Her voice had become shriller as they talked on the phone. She was angry because he'd been less than honest about his plans in the Yucatan. She'd get over it. She knew the importance of secrecy in his work. However, he was worried. Since their experiences in Brazil, Sara had become less game to participate in his intelligence gathering. He feared she was close to issuing an ultimatum.

Third, he was weary and tired of talking. He lay in a hospital bed and reviewed the last six hours.

***

After he'd shot the co-pilot, four SWAT team members had rushed on board the plane. They had isolated Roberto and the pilot and summoned EMTs as he questioned Victor.

Victor had quickly admitted he'd brought his son to Las Vegas the previous week and enrolled him in a drug rehab clinic. However, Roberto had bolted from the clinic after two days and gone to stay with his sister—a student at the university of Nevada-Las Vegas.

Victor had rambled a bit as he told the rest of the story. On Sunday morning, he had gone to his daughter's apartment prepared to take his children to brunch. Two men met him at the door and flashed pictures of his children tied up and gagged. The older man had said, "All you had to do is get Sanders on the private jet this evening. My associates will release your children after the jet lands in Mérida."

The EMTs had interrupted Victor's story as they examined Sanders's arm and pronounced the co-pilot dead. Sanders had refused the EMTs' requests to leave the plane and had resumed questioning Victor.

Victor had closed his eyes when Sanders had asked, "When did you decide the men had lied?"

"As soon as I saw the crew. The pilot, who had flown me and my son to Las Vegas from Mérida, looked nervous. The younger man whom

I had met at my daughter's apartment had replaced the regular co-pilot. The steward was…" Victor swallowed hard. "…Roberto dressed in drag."

Sanders had been incredulous. "Why didn't you warn me?"

Victor had looked surprised. "I did. I sent the picture of my son in drag to the number you gave me Didn't you get it?"

***

As the EMTs carried the body of the co-pilot from the plane, the SWAT leader had pointed at Sanders. "You leave next. No excuses."

Sanders had stumbled down the steep stairs by the side of the plane and had been led to a room where Ray was waiting. He and Ray had laid out their game plan. Ray and two FBI agents would question Roberto and the pilot. Local police and airport security would check closets and unused rooms in the airport because the co-pilot had said Carina would be found in the airport. Sanders would go to the hospital for treatment.

***

Ray had worn a body cam as he interviewed Roberto and the pilot. Of course, the EMTs in the ambulance and the nurses in the surgical prep area had objected as Sanders listened to the feed from Ray's body cam, but he had ignored them.

Ray's main problems had been the pilot wouldn't talk, and Roberto wouldn't stop jabbering. He claimed he and his sister had been tied up and gagged on Saturday evening by an older man and the man who became the co-pilot on the flight. All Roberto knew about the place where they'd been held was it had at least two rooms. He and his sister— both with their hands tied—were kept in a small bathroom with a tile floor, a toilet, and a sink. He could hear his captors in the next room. The men had offered him and his sister food only once after they took photos of them.

Roberto had guessed it was around two on Sunday afternoon when the men had given him his makeup bag and a uniform and ordered him to dress as a female flight steward. Then the older man had driven Roberto, his sister, and the co-pilot to the airport in a gray SUV. When he dropped off the co-pilot and Roberto at the private terminal, the older man had said, "I'll leave your sister tied up in the van. If your father cooperates, the police might find her before she dies of heat."

Ray had ordered the local police and airport security to immediately switch from searching the airport to checking all vehicles parked in the airport, with an emphasis on gray SUVs.

The anesthesiologist hadn't argued with Sanders, she just jabbed him with a needle.

***



J. L. Greger

Sanders had awakened around six in the evening.

The co-pilot had been identified. He did not have a police record, but he was suspected of being a hit man for gangs in the US. The pilot still had not spoken, except to request food.

Ray had decided Roberto was only an errand boy for the Mérida drug gangs and knew little. Thus, he'd had acceded to Victor' request and had Roberto admitted to a locked drug rehab unit.

Victor's daughter had been found in a gray van in a distant parking lot at the airport. Before she had passed out, she had managed to kick out both rear side windows. However, her prognosis was doubtful. No one could survive long—at least without brain damage—in a locked vehicle when the heat was over a hundred degrees.

Sanders had decided it was time to call Sara.

***

After his conversation with Sara, Sanders decided he would delay his return to Albuquerque until Tuesday because Sara needed time to cool off. He ordered a dozen pink roses and a box of dental bones be delivered to her office. Sara liked pink better than red roses. Dental bones were Bug's favorite treat.

Sanders also decided Victor could be turned into a reliable source of information for the US because Victor wanted a future for his surviving child.

# CHAPTER 28: Jack Catches Up

*Monday*

Sara didn't look away from her computer screen when Jack entered her office on Monday morning. He decided to be cautious. "How was your weekend?"

"The christening was nice." She kept staring at the screen.

He decided to goad her a bit. "Did you and Sanders have another big send-off at airport?" Although Sara and Sanders generally didn't act affectionately toward each other, he'd noticed they were not reserved when saying goodbye at the airport.

"I don't want to talk about my weekend."

He suspected a lot had happened. Sara wasn't terse without a reason.

She finally looked at him. She looked tired with bags under her eyes. "I can't give details, but I won't be flying to Mérida on Thursday."

He remembered the last time Sara looked as bad as today. It had been when Sanders had visited two weeks ago. Considering his dating record, he knew he had no right to criticize, but Sanders didn't seem to bring much happiness into Sara's life. Carbonne had said then. *What was it?* "You want Sanders to lead national information gathering activities, but he's a hard man to live with."

Sara looked back at her computer screen. "I'm having trouble pulling info out of Gus's files for FDA."

"You didn't seem to have any trouble getting info from his files yesterday to build a case for warrants for the records of everyone connected to the memory unit at Happy Days."

"Rosemary did all that sorting. I just worked with Maggio and wrote the warrant requests."

"This morning, Winslow and I delivered those warrants, picked up all the files covered by them, and delivered copies of documents to Maggio."

"Thanks. Did they all cooperate?" Sara was still scanning documents on her screen

"Evie Schoener was delighted. Rosa Gonzalez didn't seem surprised and was quieter than usual. Snow and his lawyer were reluctant but cooperative. Alejandro Smith was another story. He blustered and made threats until his lawyer advised him to shut up."

"What about Maggio?"

"He was disappointed you didn't prepare a summary for him."

Sara groaned. "I told him I had to get info for the FDA and didn't have time to digest the info we got from the new warrants before our meeting at one." She shook her head. "Twirp. No one else would have even gotten the files for him before the meeting."

Jack chuckled. He'd not heard Sara criticize anyone in the New Mexico Attorney General's Office before. *She really was in a foul mood.* "We both know Maggio is as green as I am. But he's dumb, and I'm not."

Sara smiled at Jack. "You're not green anymore. I bet several of the senior agents will request you as a partner any day now. I know the leader of the FBI SWAT team here has asked Carbonne if you'd be interested."

Jack tried to hide his annoyance. *Why had Carbonne told Sara and not him?* He knew the reason. Carbonne regarded Sara as a big sister and often tested ideas with her.

Sara finally relaxed. "Have a seat. You're talking to Gus this afternoon and he's not what he appears to be."

"What do you mean?" Jack didn't want to mention Rosemary's name for fear that Sara would give him another lecture on how *nice and smart* Rosemary was. That might be true, but Sara didn't realize how hard it was to get Rosemary to talk about anything not in computer files.

He lucked out. Sara kept to the subject and didn't mention Rosemary. "Gus is not a prankster or dirty old man when he uses the internet. He sends emails as if he was using a university account. His emails are businesslike with no curse words or attachments of cartoons. However, the emails *to* Gus were interesting—especially those from women. Several bordered on pornographic or were threats."

"How did Gus respond?"

"He didn't. He deleted without answering most of his emails. However, he kept many of the emails from Cookie, Evie, and Ruth in a file he called *IPO*. Unfortunately, they were mainly copies of the documents Ruth and Cookie already gave us."

Jack nodded as he took notes on his phone. "Who did the threats come from?"

"Five from Rosa Gonzalez. Not threats per se. More like lectures on the privacy of medical records. One from Evie echoed those sentiments. Then there were two complaints from Deb Kline and one from Karen Wright. Deb believed he was 'ruining the social life of others with his pranks.' Karen Wright sent a similar—but less whiney—complaint to him after last year's Christmas party."

"Not surprising."

"Yes, but John's friends—Sandi and Bob Jones—sent two emails complaining about Gus's 'disruptive behavior' at parties and another noting 'husbands didn't like how he flirted with their wives.'" Sara shook her head. "I couldn't tell whether Bob or Sandi sent the emails because they appear to share an email account, which both use."

Jack had the awful feeling Sara wanted him to interview Deb Kline and Karen Wright as well as Gus this afternoon. He picked up Bug and rubbed his ears. *No need for everyone in the room to be unhappy.* "What do you want me to do?"

"Listen to my problem. As I look at what Rosemary pulled out of Gus's computer and paper files, I realized I didn't have the data the FDA needs to prosecute staff at Happy Days—particularly Rosa Gonzalez and the chef, whom Cookie replaced,—of knowingly buying and serving contaminated food repeatedly."

"I don't get it. You seemed sure."

Sara shifted in her chair. "We have evidence Happy Days purchased an inordinate amount of cheap peanuts. We also can show an unusually large percentage of past residents of Happy Days died of liver cancer and/or cirrhosis—according to their death certificates. That's probably enough for FDA to prosecute American Peanut Supply and Peanuts Wholesale, Inc. because they knew their warehouses had mold problems. But I can't find any proof that Rosa Gonzalez and the previous chef knew the peanuts were contaminated—except that they were priced ridiculously low. The aflatoxin analyses Gus obtained are helpful but probably are not enough."

"Didn't Gus show the aflatoxin analyses he got to Rosa? Didn't she order more nuts after he notified her?"

Sara smiled. "You understand what you need to locate—dated evidence that someone notified Rosa of the problem before she ordered more nuts. Course, it would help if we found a document from Rosa or the last chef indicating they'd received the notice." Sara shrugged. "But the latter is wishing for the moon."

***

Jack expected to find Isaac's house had been turned into a frat house with John and Gus staying there. He was shocked.

As Jack approached the front door of Isaac's house, he saw multiple new cameras and an elaborate shiny-new lock with an elaborate intercom system. He walked to the side and saw two more cameras and a new tall wire fence surrounding the back yard. A handprinted sign on the fence said: ELECTRIFIED—*DO NOT TOUCH*. The security system rivaled those on houses with expensive collections.

When Jack returned to the front yard, John was waiting at the door.

"Who did you get to install this elaborate security system? They must have charged you and arm and a leg."

John smiled. "You forget I'm an engineer by training. After Sara left Tuesday night, I began working on improving the security. I didn't want Isaac's house damaged by intruders looking for me…and then Gus." He pointed to the control panel by the door. "Amazing what's available online."

Jack heard a snapping noise to his left. The sofa was gone, and the living room had been turned into an office with two folding tables. A laptop, a printer, and a few pages lay on one table. Gus sat at the other table with a three-ring notebook and another laptop.

Gus inserted a page and snapped the notebook shut. "Isaac picked up my and John's computers from the FBI Building on Saturday after the nice technician—Rosemary—had copied everything."

*Why does everyone preface their comments on Rosemary with nice?* "Does Sara know you have your computers?"

"Oh yes. I've been sorting my files trying to find answers to Sara's questions since Saturday." Gus shook his head. "Kinda discouraging to realize AI did almost as good a job as I did but in less time." He smiled. "But I've found at least two items AI missed." He motioned to Jack to be seated.

John nudged Jack's shoulder. "Would you like something to drink? We have a lot to show you."

Jack turned to see John offering a bottle of water or a bottle of seltzer. "I thought you guys would be bored, watching TV, and drinking booze."

John handed him the water. "We're not fools. I removed all booze from the house on Friday. We all need to think clearly."

Gus laughed. "D*** teetotaler. Good thing he's cheap. Instead of pouring all our booze down the drain, he locked it in a closet in the garage and won't tell us where he put the key. It's harder on Isaac than me."

Jack sat. "What do you have to show me?"

Gus opened his notebook. "If you check Ruth's bra, you'll see I inserted slips of paper in the padding."

*This is weird.* "Why?"

"I knew someone searching for evidence on the case would never look in my trophy collection. On the other hand, they wouldn't throw my collection away because they'd use it to prove I was senile. It was the perfect safe place to store important information. And Ruth's bra has bigger cups than Evie's."

*Weirder than I thought.* "Do you have copies of those messages?"

"Yes. They were in my shoe."

*This is seriously weird.* "Weren't you worried the messages in your shoe could get wet and be ruined?"

"It seldom rains here. I only kept notes in my shoe when I was transporting them." He leaned down and picked up pair or trainers stashed under the table. "These were designed to make a man look taller." He pulled out the insole and pointed to a hollowed-out area. "I had copies of two messages in my shoe when the three us went to the bosque because I wanted to talk about them. Until I got here, I didn't have a chance to pull them out."

*A psychiatrist should examine this guy.*

Gus handed Jack a wrinkled, xeroxed page. It was handwritten and dated from two years earlier. "This note is to Rosa Gonzalez from the last head cook two days before she quit."

> *Don't order more cheap peanuts. They smell funny like the*
> *ones before. I told Mr. Smith because you don't listen to my*
> *complaints.*
> *Betty*

Gus handed Jack a second wrinkled, xeroxed half-page. The handwriting looked rough and uneven like that of the previous note. "I can't date this one."

> *Those peanuts stink. The have a white powder all over them.*
> *Can I pitch them?*
> *Betty*

“How did you get these?”

“Evie regularly searched Rosa’s desk and wastebasket.”

“What?”

“She took real risks for me.”

“Where are the originals?”

“I told you—in the lining of Ruth’s bra.”

Jack shook his head. “Old man, were any of your trophies real? Or are they all ways to hide messages.”

Gus grinned. “Wipe that smile off your face. You won’t do as well at my age. I think I have a couple more messages like these, but I can’t find them.”

John nudged Jack’s shoulder. “I told you Gus was more interesting when he talked business than when he talked about the ladies.”

“I heard you.” Gus straightened in his chair. “I wouldn’t have bothered if Olivia hadn’t died. She was the best.” He looked like he’d cry. “I promised her I’d get everyone responsible for her death.”

John cleared his throat in an obvious attempt to get Jack’s attention. “Guess it’s time for my report. After I watched Rosa Gonzalez for a couple of months, I decided she was a frightened woman who was taking orders. Then I got Ruth to help me assess the corporate structure of GYM. The person making serious money off the business was Alejandro Smith.”

Jack nodded. “I saw the documents indicating Snow and Evie got kickbacks from him when patients went to the memory unit. What can you tell me about Smith?”

“Has a temper. I heard him yell at Rosa on several occasions.”

Gus interrupted. “Dresses well. John wouldn’t notice, but I can tell a designer suit when I see it.”

John shrugged. “Expensive house and habits. He has a Cessna plane and likes to gamble in Las Vegas.”

Jack gasped

John smiled. “You at the FBI aren’t the only who can search federal data bases. I followed him several times when he left Happy Days and went to the airport. I checked the FAA database.”

“You guys must have been bored at Happy Days.”

John shrugged. “You should check Alejandro’s financial records. I suspect he’s a big gambler, but I couldn’t get to those records.”

Jack nodded and checked his notes. “Gus, Rosemary noted you had received several unpleasant emails from Deb Kline, Karen Wright, and the Jones.”

Gus snorted, "All emails from Deb are unpleasant. Can you be more specific?"

"They all claimed you were ruining the social life at Happy Days with your antics. Karen admitted to Sara she had been close to Ab once, but your antics made it impossible to rekindle her relationship with him."

Gus bit his lip. "Not true. Ab didn't want to be close to any woman and didn't want to raise Karen's hopes. He knew she'd be better off with… someone else."

Jack noticed the pause but decided he didn't want to learn unnecessary details about the love life of seniors at Happy Days. "How about Deb?"

John cleared his throat. "Gus was protecting me. After a drink or two, Deb is…"

Gus winked. "Demanding. Scares the hell out of John. Look how she stalked him to this house. But she's too dumb to know about methanol. I figured the Joneses emailed me because they were tired of hearing Deb's complaints."

John cleared his throat. "Maybe we should tell Jack about our big secret."

Jack tensed. "What?"

Gus laughed. "You don't need to be scared. It's a storage unit we rented."

## CHAPTER 29: Prosecution Is a Team Sport

Sara arrived at the attorney general's office complex an-hour before Maggio's conference with Herb Snow. The receptionist whispered, "Good luck," when she directed Sara to Maggio's small office.

When he spied Sara, Maggio pulled a file and slammed a drawer shut in his metal file cabinet. "I expected better cooperation from you."

"What do you mean?" Sara tried to keep her voice level. She figured this young lawyer could barely handle this case. He would blow it if he got emotional.

Maggio's face got redder. "You didn't give me a complete report." His hands shook as he glanced at the file. "Data are missing."

Sara kept her voice low and steady as if she was talking to a remedial student. "That's why you're meeting with Evie Schoener and Herb Snow. We suspect they have the info we need to make the case against Happy Days, its parent company GYM, and its chief officers. You must decide who has the most info to offer—and hopefully is the most innocent—and offer them a deal for their info."

"Don't lecture me. My boss already did." He threw the file on his desk.

*Control your temper little boy.* "You're lucky. AI…" She thought he might not know what AI was in his agitated state. "AI—artificial intelligence—is faster than any analyst in locating data in files, but we're still experimenting with AI at the FBI office in Albuquerque. I thought it was amazing what it pulled out of Gus Rinaldi's voluminous computer files. Surely you found enough info to create a plan."

"My boss nixed my plan this morning. She wants me to cooperate with the federal DA and cut a deal with Evie Schoener." He pounded his fists on the table. "Everyone knows my case will be stronger if I have a doctor—granted only a clinical psychologist—as my chief witness, not a social worker. No one in this state trusts social workers. I'm being set up to fail."

"I think Evie Schoener has more key evidence to share for our cases. My partner is talking to Ab Hess's friends."

"Who's Ab Hess?"

Sara swallowed hard. "The man murdered with methanol. The incident which really made your case viable." She decided not to lecture him further. "Anyway, my partner is talking to Ab's friends—Gus Rinaldi and John Lindberg—now. They claim Evie Schoener got many key pieces of info for them."

Maggio's phone rang. "Yeah." Maggio listened. "So, what?" He put his hand over the mouthpiece and turned to Sara. "Why should I let another lawyer—a Ted Cottingham—attend my conferences with Herb Snow and Evie Schoener?"

Sara held up her hand to keep Maggio from saying more. "Ted Cottingham is a federal assistant DA for New Mexico. Don't you remember? He participated in the video conference last Friday. He may prosecute the murder case and is involved in the potential FDA case against Happy Days." She decided to do Maggio a favor. "Don't cross him."

Maggio grimaced as he removed his hand from over the phone mouthpiece. "Mr. Cottingham, I'd be delighted if you joined us. I agree with you. I just pointed out to Sara Almquist that we should make a deal with Evie Schoener, but I want to see if we can get any information from Dr. Snow first."

***

Sara didn't join Maggio, Snow, and his lawyer at the teak conference table. She chose a seat along the wall opposite Snow and his lawyer. She was there to listen and lip read, if possible. She also wanted to continue a search she'd begun in the thirty minutes after her unpleasant discussion with Maggio. She had consulted with Maggio's boss for ten minutes about old cases involving CYFD—the state agency responsible for protecting children, youth, and families.

She was surprised when Maggio didn't start the meeting on time but nervously sorted through his files until Ted Cottingham appeared. However, Maggio didn't introduce either Sara or Cottingham to Snow and his lawyer before he initiated an obviously rehearsed statement. It sounded more like an opening statement in court than the onset of a negotiation.

She noticed that Maggio was almost obsequious to "Dr." Snow and figured Maggio must have wanted to be a doctor not a lawyer. Then she wondered if Maggio was setting a trap for Snow and his lawyer, but she doubted Maggio was that clever.

She glanced at Cottingham, who had sat next to her. He seemed more intent on reading the message on her laptop screen than listening to Maggio. He handed her a note:

*Don't let Little Jerry go on too long before you drop the CYFD bomb. Snow is more apt to talk then.*

After ten minutes, Sara decided that Maggio had pulled nothing new from Snow. She cleared her throat loudly. "I need clarification on a point."

Maggio reddened. Snow's lawyer looked annoyed.

"Dr. Snow, I remember a case against CYFD from a few years ago. A social worker…" Sara decided not to name Evie. "…released two children to their family after a psychologist determined the parents were mentally sound." Sara shrugged. "Two days later, one child was killed and the other maimed by the father."

Snow turned white. Snow's lawyer looked annoyed. "That is not relevant."

Sara forced a smile. "Let me continue. I believe Dr. Snow you were the psychologist, but your name never appeared in any news stories. The social worker's name was spread across the headlines. You both left CYFD shortly afterward."

Snow conferred with his lawyer. The lawyer must have noticed Sara's and probably Cottingham's stares and raised his hand to hide his mouth when he spoke.

Snow's voice was shaky. "I'm not sure of the case you're referring to. I consulted on many cases at CYFD. I didn't leave because of any one case. I was tired of their mismanagement."

"I doubt your answer. Alejandro Smith hired you as consultant for GYM after you had left CYFD and had been hired and fired by a clinic in Santa Fe."

Snow's lawyer stood. "I repeat this information is not relevant to the current discussion."

"I think it is. The person who recommended Dr. Snow to Happy Days was Evie Schoener—the social worker who protected him during the CYFD investigation."

Cottingham tapped her elbow.

"Maybe, I should add that you and Evie played a game the last time. Neither of you talked. So, the State of New Mexico couldn't make its case against either of you in the death of the child. We don't want a repeat of that situation."

Snow's lawyer whispered to his client and then turned to Maggio. "We'd like to continue the discussion with you tomorrow."

Maggio's lips quivered. Sara knew she was overstepping her authority. She was an investigator with no authority to make deals, but she was afraid what Maggio might say. "Good. We plan to talk to another witness who is willing to provide the state with evidence. Tomorrow we can decide if you have anything *useful* to offer."

Cottingham leaned over and whispered in her ear. "That was a nice gift for Little Jerry. Let's see if he has the sense to accept the gift."

Maggio stood. "I…I don't know."

Cottingham under his breath said, "D*** fool." He stood. "Gentlemen, we'll meet tomorrow at one." He walked over and grasped Maggio's upper arm and led him out.

Sara thought it best to avoid further conversation and followed.

***

Cottingham, Maggio, and his boss met behind closed doors for ten minutes before Sara was admitted. As soon as Sara entered, Maggio snapped at her. "You had no right."

Sara held up her right hand. "I apologize but I didn't want you to promise Snow anything. The FBI agents watching Evie believe she's ready to talk because she fears Alejandro Smith."

Maggio shook as he yelled, "I'll put you on report."

His boss leaned toward Maggio. "Did you hear anything I said in the last few minutes? When Sara stopped by my office and started asking about the CYFD case, she jogged my memory. D*** mess. I didn't have time to talk to you."

Maggio shook as he stared at her. "You had time to text Cottingham."

"True. I didn't have to remind him of the headlines that went on for months. It was before you came to this office. It would have taken too long to get you up to speed. I'm sorry."

"I'm sorry, too, if I embarrassed you." Sara looked at the floor.

"I'm not sorry." Cottingham laughed. "If Sara hadn't spoken, I would have had to say more. Her offer was nonbinding." He pointed at Maggio. "Now you're up to speed. Let's see what you can wring out of Evie Schoener."

***

Sara was impressed by Maggio's next performance. Evie Schoener strutted into the conference room confident she had a deal. After five minutes, she was shaking and blurting out all sorts of info about Happy Days. However, she was reticent to say anything about Alejandro Smith.

Maggio leaned toward Evie. "I'm tired of being jerked around. Here's what you're going to do. You're going to answer questions from the FBI for the next eighteen hours. If they tell me, you gave them enough to convict Alejandro Smith, I'll make a deal with you. No jail time but you give up your license as a social worker and will be put on probation. If the FBI is not satisfied, I'll make a deal with Herb Snow."

Cottingham leaned over and whispered in Sara's ear. "Maggio has developed teeth. Can you deliver?"

"Don't know." Sara thought a second and turned to Evie. "Any evidence you give us on Snow's behavior in CYFD or how he was hired at GYM might reduce your sentence."

***

Sara didn't feel like talking to Sanders. He knew she could have been the target of a kidnapping attempt in Mérida. *Not fair for him to assume I was willing to take the risk.* Then she doubted her own motives. *Was she willing to take Maggio's order to work tonight because she wanted to avoid Sanders? That was childish.* She emailed Sanders:

> *Finally making progress on the case. At least the prosecuting attorneys are no longer at war. I will work late tonight unless you plan to arrive. Then, I'll gladly change my schedule.*
>
> *Being shot is traumatic. Pamper yourself.*
> *Love*
> *Sara*

## CHAPTER 30: Jack Is Tired Already

Jack tossed the key Gus had pulled from the heel of his shoe in the air. "Is there anything else in your shoes?"

"No."

"Which one of you wants to come with me when I go to your secret storage unit?"

John spoke first. "Both of us." He nodded to Gus. "If Deb could follow you here, so could Rosa Gonzalez or Alejandro Smith. We feel safer together and think you should have all our data."

"Can't be that much. The FBI collected your computers and all the files in your apartments at Happy Days."

Gus waved his right hand. "You forgot John removed a box of stuff from his apartment before he left last Monday. I kept lots of stuff in the storage unit for the last two years."

Jack suspected he was walking into a trap but asked anyway. "Why did you rent a storage unit?"

Gus looked at him with disgust. "To keep our data safe. We've been convinced for the last two years that it was only a matter of time before someone broke into our apartments." Gus smiled. "And to keep my T-Bird safe."

John interrupted, "While you drive, I'll call Isaac and tell him to go the FBI building after his shift."

Jack saw both men were breathing heavily through their open mouths. They weren't acting; they were afraid. "Let's go."

John picked up a few folders and a gym bag. Gus handed Jack his three-ring notebook and picked up another box and a garbage bag which seemed to be stretched by two or three pillows and blankets. The two men looked like they were ready to camp out in the FBI building. Jack didn't feel like arguing and hurried them to the FBI van.

Before Jack pulled the van away from the curb, Gus checked the back and side doors and John "electrified" the system. Again, Jack didn't ask questions.

***

Jack assumed Gus had rented a small unit. He snorted when Gus unlocked the padlock, and John raised the garage door to the unit. Gus's 1962 Thunderbird Sports Roadster and John's Lexus SUV were parked inside.

John shrugged. "Isaac's garage has room for only two cars. We kept Gus's compact car at Isaac's house because it gets the better gas mileage than my Lexus. Friday night, I loaded all Gus's and my boxes into the Lexus. In case, we had to make a fast get away."

Jack's phone vibrated. He had arranged for ABQ Police Real Time Crime Center's cameras to follow his trip from Isaac's house. An analyst watching the camera shots along his route had spotted a car—a 2022 red Camaro—following the FBI van along its route.

Jack didn't want to scare the elderly men. *God knows what they might do.* "We might have been followed by a red Camaro. Let's pack the boxes in the FBI van and get going."

John pulled out keys and jumped into his Lexus SUV. Gus rushed to the FBI van and pulled out a box. "Better if we leave here in a different vehicle."

Jack agreed and helped Gus unload the contents of the FBI van into the Lexus SUV. Then he drove the FBI van into the space left when the John backed the Lexus into the lot. Gus locked the space and handed the key to Jack.

John drove his Lexus out of the parking lot. Almost instantly, Jack spied a red Camaro parked about a block from the storage lot's exit. "John, drive past it at a little under the speed limit so we can get the license plate number."

Gus wrote down the license as Jack snapped a photo and transmitted it to the Real Time Crime Center. The center quickly confirmed it was the car that had followed the FBI van earlier. The center also directed a way back to the FBI building that would maximize the Lexus passing cameras in the system.

As they pulled through the gate into the back parking lot at the FBI building. Gus whistled. "We made it. Is the Camaro still parked where we last saw it?"

"No about a minute ago it rushed off, but it hasn't gone by any of the cameras in the Real Time Crime Center system yet."

John sighed. "So, he got away."

"I didn't say that. The car is registered to Alejandro Smith's wife. The analyst thought the driver was a man or a woman with short hair."

"Will APD arrest the driver?"

"For what? The Real Time Crime Center will watch for the car's reappearance and will alert the owner of the storage units to be on the alert for suspicious behavior." Jack directed John to park his Lexus at the loading dock. He'd already asked Rosemary to join the two old men in a small conference room near Sara's office.

***

Thirty minutes later, Jack found John and Gus scanning new files into Rosemary's computer. Rosemary smiled when Jack entered. "The same AI program that analyzed Gus's other files will scan these new files. Sara left me clear notes on what questions the FDA wants answered. Gus is sure that info is in his paper files—somewhere."

"How long will it take?"

"By tomorrow morning, we'll have answers for the FDA." She pulled Jack from the room. "I've never seen such an eager crew. These two came prepared to spend the night loading the data. The only problem is I must yell, or they pretend not to hear me."

Jack shrugged. "They're not pretending. Their hearing is poor. But don't leave them alone. They can be sneaky."

"Sara told me about their past pranks. I understand Isaac Newson will be joining them soon." She stepped back into the conference room. "Take your time guys. It wastes a lot of time when documents aren't scanned properly, and we must repeat analyses." She stepped back out into the hallway. "I'm eager to meet Isaac Newson. He's a legend around here. You should see the reprimands he sends agents."

"I'll pass." Jack changed the subject. "Did Sara say when she expected to get back to her office?"

Rosemary tittered. "I heard you passed out during one of Isaac's worst autopsies. Several of the old agents laughed when they heard of your first encounter with Isaac, but they weren't really laughing at you. They were feeling relieved that they hadn't been assigned to watch that autopsy."

Jack didn't want to continue this conversation. "When did Sara say she'd be back?"

"She didn't but said Cottingham would be stopping by because he wanted to watch Gus and John in action. He's another legend among analysts. Bet, he'll be assessing what types of witnesses they'll make. Everyone says he's a bad ass."

Jack phone vibrated. Sara emailed:

*Bringing Evie Schoener with me. Maggio wants to know if she's worth a deal. Here's what we must do:*

*1. Talk to the agents from the house. They may have new info on Evie.*

*2. Get details on Herb's and Evie's actions during a botched CYFD case a few years ago. The NM Attorney General's Office has shared their files on the case. (attached)*

*3. Define the roles of Alejandro Smith and Rosa Gonzalez in hiring Evie and Herb. Confirm the deals they made. Notes in my files.*

*4. Find the head cook who preceded Cookie.*

*5. Order pizza and lots of soda. Gus and John like regular cola—not diet. It's going to be a long night.*

Jack perused the attachments. The info looked new to him. This case—really three cases— was getting more complicated every day. He also realized that all the effort today might not help in identifying who had murdered Ab Hess. Just thinking about the cases made him tired.

Rosemary opened the door when she thought she heard Gus and John arguing. Just the thought of supervising them increased his weariness.

## CHAPTER 31: Sanders Learns What is Important

Ray looked around Sanders's hospital room and pointed at Sanders's arm. "Hurt much?"

Sanders leaned forward in his wheelchair. "Yes, but I declined pain killers this morning because I wanted to be sharp for this interview." He motioned Ray closer. "I'll promise Victor almost anything to turn him into a trusted informant. How's the daughter?"

Ray whispered into Sanders's ear. "She almost died but was moved from the ICU—under an alias—to a nearby room two hours ago. Victor knows nothing." He stepped back and motioned Victor in.

As Sanders thanked Victor for his help the previous day, Ray made a call. Five minutes later, another agent escorted in a hand-cuffed Roberto.

Roberto averted his eyes as soon as he saw his father. Victor didn't seem to notice. He stepped forward and hugged his son. "Son, I forgive you, but you must take charge of your life. No more excuses." Victor glanced at Sanders. "He's agreed to have you committed to a locked drug rehab unit. You won't be released until you're drug-free and a psychiatrist has diagnosed you as capable of facing charges."

Roberto raised his eyebrows. "F*** for what?"

Sanders was ready. "We know you served various small functions for a drug gang in Mexico in return for drugs. The Mexican police think you set up your father's friends for robberies."

"No f***."

Victor grabbed his son's arm. "Don't lie. My friends' homes were robbed when they were guests in my home or at an event with me or your mother." He shook his head. "I suspected you, too. That's why I arranged for you to come with me to Las Vegas last week."

"You lied." Roberto's face was red. "I thought you were taking me on vacation, but you checked me into a f****** drug rehab unit. Then Carina wouldn't help me either. She was trying to force me to return to it. I showed both of you."

Victor grabbed his son's other arm, so the young man had to look at him. "Agent Ray Curtis convinced me you were compliant with your sister's kidnapping and the attempted kidnapping of Mr. Sanders."

"So what? He's a f****** cop. She's a *La Malinche*."

Victor winced. "Ray warned me you were defiant. I know they…" He waved a hand at Ray and then Sanders. "…are right. I can't make any more excuses for you. Treatment and prison time here will be less severe than in Mexico."

Roberto spit at his father. "You always pampered Carina."

Sanders rolled his wheelchair toward the door. "Victor, you, and I need to go down the hall." He pointed to the agents. "Can you take care of our bad boy for a while in this room?"

***

Ray pushed Sanders's chair down the hall and stopped in front of a room with a sign: *DO NOT DISTURB*. Sanders touched Victor's arm. "This will be a shock for you. Ray only told me a couple of minutes ago."

Ray opened the door. A woman lay on the bed with an IV line attached to her arm. Her urine was dripping from a catheter into a bag. Her body was covered by a sheet and her eyes were half-closed.

"Carina," whispered Victor as he ran toward her bed.

She moaned, "*Papá.*"

Ray informed Sanders that Roberto's version of their kidnapping differed from Carina's story. She'd been held alone in the bathroom. The first she saw Roberto after the kidnapping was during the drive to the airport. "However, she claimed he'd saved her life. He'd left a bottle of water in a well of the back seat."

Sanders frowned. "I thought she was tied up—both hands and feet."

"She was, but she was smart and agile enough to kick out the back side windows and scream for help." Ray walked nearer the bed and put his hand on Victor's shoulder. "We almost didn't find in her time. The doctors say she should take it easy for a couple of weeks but shouldn't have any permanent damage."

Victor knit his brows. "Why didn't you tell me sooner?"

"We had to get her statement and see how Roberto reacted to you."

Sanders thought the answer was incomplete, but Victor seemed to accept it. "She says Roberto saved her life by leaving a bottle of water for her."

Ray backed away and whispered into Sanders' ear, "Doubt that."

"She and Victor are happier thinking he did."

Ray shook his head. "Calling your sister *La Malinche* after Cortez's Aztec mistress is strong stuff."

***

Sanders sat in a conference room at the FBI's Las Vegas field office. As Sanders's expected, Ray had led the investigation in Las Vegas skillfully. In fact, Sanders felt slightly insecure as he reviewed Ray's accomplishments.

The driver of the gray van had cleaned the steering wheel, the door handles, and all the controls on the dashboard of the gray van. Similarly, the kidnappers had cleaned all surfaces in Carina's apartment. However, Ray had ordered FBI technicians to search the garbage from Carina's apartment complex. They found several clear fingerprints—besides hers, Roberto's, and the co-pilot's—on soda bottles in a trash bag, which they identified as coming from her apartment.

Agents had used the fingerprints to identify the older man and then determined he'd left Las Vegas on a flight to Cancun before the charter flight with Victor and Roberto would have taken take off. They had contacted the Mexican police to arrest him. Like the pilot, he refused to talk. Unlike the pilot, he had a long police record and was currently suspected in several cases in Mexico. The Mexican police didn't need to release him quickly.

Ray had also arranged for Roberto to be flown to a federally-funded rehab facility for prisoners in Colorado within an hour of leaving the meeting with his father. Sanders knew Ray had acted quickly to prove to Victor that the FBI would keep their promises to him.

Ray entered the room. "You must be eager to get back to Sara. She kept her cool and transmitted your message to me without making any demands."

Sanders nodded. "That's the problem. She never complains or yells at me. She just gives me silent stares when I return from what she calls *foolish trips*. I don't want to return to Albuquerque tonight and face her stony reception."

Ray stuttered, "I...I had...I had no idea that you two had problems. She never let on."

"Not problems per se. I just know enough to stay away for an extra day. Besides, she's busy with a convoluted case involving the elderly. I don't want to hear about it."

"Why? You told me about several of her cases when we were stationed in Brazil. They sounded interesting and often bizarre."

                                                        

"This case involves retired faculty who didn't mind their own business."

Ray laughed. "Do they remind you of yourself and Sara?" He handed Sanders several pages. "Here's what still needs to be done here." He pointed to the first page. "Victor doesn't think Carina should return to UNLV but should enroll in another university under a false name. She says she doesn't want to run. What do you think?"

Sanders shook his head. "Sounds like an argument I would have with my daughter." He shook his head. "We'd ask Sara for advice. My daughter trusts Sara's judgment more than mine."

Ray pointed to a second page. "We shouldn't keep Victor here any longer than necessary or the gangs will suspect he's now our informant."

Sanders picked up a newspaper from the table. "I read the report you planted in the *Las Vegas Record Journal*. The FBI looked like it successfully foiled a kidnapping attempt with one killed and one arrested. I noticed you listed me as a State Department official."

"Congressional leaders didn't want to be mentioned."

Sanders nodded. "You identified the co-pilot who was killed and Roberto but didn't mention the pilot or Carina."

"Point one. You missed the article on Carina." Ray opened the newspaper to a back section. "We reported Carina Ortez was found in a locked car, but didn't mention she was tied up. Most readers will assume she was drunk or high on drugs. You'll note we only said she was in critical condition at the hospital."

"You left it open for several outcomes."

Ray held up two fingers. "Point two. We think the gangs will think the pilot talked and has been put in protective custody because he wasn't mentioned." Ray shrugged. "Might loosen his lips."

"That gets us back to the problems of what to do with Carina and Victor."

***

"Victor, what did you decide?"

"It's up to Carina."

Sanders turned to Carina. "What do you want?"

Carina grabbed her father's hand as tears ran down here cheeks. "My brother hates me. Mother and I aren't close. *Papá*, you will be safer if I can't be used to blackmail you. I want to complete a degree in the US and live here." She kissed her father. "When you get unsigned postcards, you'll know they're from me."

Sanders interrupted. "You can never send them from your home state."

The young woman nodded.

Victor wiped his eyes. "You'll be safe. And if God is willing your brother will be clean in a couple of years."

"And you *Papá*?"

"I'll continue my business as usual, but I'll see Sanders and his friends occasionally."

Sanders spoke slowly. "Carina, the hospital will announce you died of heat stroke. We will inform your mother that you were cremated. Agents have collected the items you wanted from your apartment." He looked at Victor. "Your father has arranged for you to have a large bank account."

"How?"

"He conveniently lost a lot of money at a casino last night. Two US Marshals are waiting for you in the next room. Ray and I will step out so you can say your goodbyes."

***

Sanders felt hot and lightheaded as he left the room. He started to fall and grabbed Ray's arm. "I think my wound is infected. Get me a doctor fast, but without any fuss."

# CHAPTER 32: A Long Night

Cottingham pulled Sara aside before she and Jack entered the conference room where Evie and her lawyer was waiting. "Open the door. I want her to hear me say I'm talking to other witnesses. That should prime her to talk."

"How long do I have with Evie?"

"As long as you need. I want to watch Gus Rinaldi and John Lindberg without them realizing I'm from the US attorney's office. See how they think."

Sara suppressed a giggle. "Then I won't have long to pump Evie."

Jack coughed. "I think their frenetic activity will wear you out in ten minutes."

Cottingham played with his earplugs. "We'll see. Besides I will also be listening to your interview with Evie."

Sara opened the door. "Evie, I'll be with you in a moment."

Cottingham said loudly. "Take your time I'll be talking to the other potential witness."

***

"Evie, state officials know you and Snow lied to protect each other in the CYFD case. We aren't going to discuss the current case until I get the truth from you about the CYFD case."

Her lawyer licked his lips. "It's not relevant."

"It is to the prosecutors. They want to prevent Evie and Herb from tricking them again." She kicked Jack under the table.

Jack struggled with his words. "Yes, hmm. It surprised me, but you wounded the pride of lawyers in the attorney general's office."

Evie swallowed hard. "It's all in the records at CYFD."

"I'd like to hear it in your own words."

Evie pulled out a cigarette.

Sara wanted to make Evie feel comfortable, but knew she'd go into coughing fits if this small room was filled with smoke. "Please don't smoke."

Evie closed her eyes and spoke as if in a trance. "A teacher from the kids' school called CYFD twice before they called APD. The police came immediately, saw the sores—probably rope burns—around the kids' wrists and ankles, and arrested the father. Even though I had a large case load, I got the assignment. I asked Herb to interview the kids while I interviewed the mother and teachers and arranged for the kids to be sent to a foster home. But the father was released a week later because both Snow and I missed the father's arraignment."

Sara looked at notes in the CYFD file. "But you both showed up at a later hearing. You reported the children should stay in the foster home."

"Didn't matter. Snow reported the kids needed counseling on appropriate play behaviors and missed their parents. He was a clinical psychologist with a Ph.D., and I was an overworked social worker The kids were sent back to their parents. Two days later the father strangled the six-year-old girl and beat the eight-year-old boy." Evie stared straight ahead.

Sara noted that Evie spoke in a monotone, unlike her usual speech pattern. "Why didn't you turn in Snow for malpractice?"

"He pointed out to me that I had missed a court date and had talked to the mother and teacher but not the kids. He suggested if we both kept our mouth shut and resigned, the case would be forgotten quickly."

"Why didn't you speak up when the press started publicizing the case?"

"I was guilty of not doing my job. I was depressed. Then Alejandro Smith called and made me an offer."

Sara thought about Evie's gauntness and compulsive smoking. *This woman is self-destructive.* "Before or after the press stories?"

"After the press had killed my self-confidence. I took the job at Happy Days immediately even though the pay rate was low for my level of experience."

"Okay." *It was time to get her to talk about Smith.* "You got a bonus every time a resident who was under the guardianship of GYM went into the memory unit. Did Alejandro Smith mention this deal when you first met him?"

"Not exactly. During my interview, Alejandro stated the prime function of a social worker was to identify residents who needed special care. A social worker who succeeded at this task would get bonuses; one who failed would be fired." He then pointed out he had fired the current social worker, clinical psychologist, and medical director because they relied on families to transfer their relatives to the memory unit instead of being 'proactive.'"

"Did his statements bother you?"

"Not until he *clarified* several points. Like he thought it was easier to meet 'patients' needs' when GYM—not relatives—was the legal guardian of the patients. He also claimed clinical psychologists were more 'flexible' than physicians or nurse practitioners and should decide admissions into the memory unit. Finally, he asked me to suggest a clinical psychologist who understood 'the economic importance' of memory units to businesses like GYM."

Evie whispered in her lawyer's ear. He nodded. "Ms. Schoener feels she's demonstrated she is cooperative and has the info you need. She wants assurances that she will face no charges stemming from any of her CYFD cases. She signed a rather detailed non-disclosure statement as demanded by Mr. Smith." He pushed the document toward Sara. "She wants assurances that she will not be charged with stealing from her employer or any other crime because of info she gave Gus Rinaldi or gives to you. She also wants assurances that she can't be charged in any way for damages to patients who entered the memory unit at Happy Days while she was employed there." He flashed a big smile. "I don't believe you can make those assurances."

Sara heard her phone ping. Cottingham's text message was short.

*Meet me in observation room at once. Maggio or his boss are on their way.*

*Gus & John are smart and will make good witnesses once they understand I'm the boss.*

***

Maggio looked a mess as he rushed toward Sara. "You interrupted my one fun activity every week—a pickleball game with the crew at work."

Sara thought this explained his wet hair, slightly stained shirt, and wrinkled pants. He hadn't had time to go home to change and had showered at the gym. "Well, you were the one who wanted to make a deal with Herb Snow tomorrow. That forced Jack and me to interview Evie tonight. She explained her part in the CYFD mess and has started to explain her arrangement with Alejandro Smith."

"Why bother me?"

"Her lawyer knows my assurances didn't mean anything. He wants to talk to the prosecuting lawyer before she says more." Sara thought how to word the next statement. "It looks to me like consulting psychologists, not overworked social workers, will be the chief villains in the flawed state system. Snow is in the first group."

Maggio's lip quivered. "Cottingham lectured me already on the phone while I was driving here. He said I was too inexperienced to smell a winning hand and should take your advice." He craned his neck. "Where is he?"

He's in the observation room with Jack. "He wants them to make a deal with you and forget the potential federal side of the cases."

"Yeah, he said then he could correct for my mistakes."

Sara doubted Maggio understood all the possibilities. "You know Evie could have been the one who put methanol in Gus's bourbon and the murder case may be tried in federal court. Cottingham doesn't want to jeopardize it."

Maggio reddened. "So, he's covering for your ineptness."

Sara silently counted to ten. "I think you'll find Jack and I have amassed an impressive array of data that can support the attorney general's case on elder abuse and the federal case on intentional food contamination. But there are limits on what we can do in a week."

She led Maggio into the observation room and was relieved when Cottingham suggested she and Jack take a break while he got Maggio "up to speed."

***

Cottingham nodded to the window in the observation room. "Our witness and her lawyer have become more nervous in the last fifteen minutes." He cleared his throat and pointed to Maggio who was typing rapidly on his laptop. "He found a standard agreement used by the New Mexico Attorney General to grant immunity to key witnesses. He's modifying it to fit Evie's needs."

Maggio didn't look up but growled. "He's convinced me to let you run this session." He stood up and walked to a printer, which was spitting out a five-page document. He picked it up. "I'm ready."

***

Evie's lawyer quickly agreed to Maggio's offer. Sara suspected Evie either was sure she wasn't a serious suspect for Ab's murder, or her lawyer had forgotten that the state could transfer this murder case to a federal court because it was related to other federal charges. That wasn't Sara's concern.

The first document Evie handed Sara was the diary she kept during her years as a social worker at CYFD. It was filled with interesting notes on psych consultants who billed for work they didn't do and administrators who assigned unreasonable caseloads to social workers. Sara thought the diary and the accompanying emails were a gold mine for the attorney general's office, but of little value to the FBI. "Why didn't you take this info to the attorney general?"

Evie sat without even moving an eyelash for several seconds. "No one would listen to me. They'd just claim I was another unhappy state employee."

"I assume you kept a similar diary while you worked at Happy Days. When did you become suspicious of that operation?"

Evie pulled out another notebook from a tote. "I knew I'd stepped into a hornet's nest during my first interview with Alejandro Smith." She opened the notebook. "You can see my notes start with my interview. But Alejandro is a smart man. He made statements and offers but put nothing in writing. All written documents came from Rosa Gonzalez." She turned to a page with a tab. "After about a month I asked Rosa why she blindly did as Alejandro ordered."

"Surely, she didn't answer you."

"You're wrong. Rosa sighed. 'I defied him once. He told me—I was replaceable.'" Evie gave a pathetic smile. "That's when I checked her background. Like me, she knew only GYM would hire her with her previous work history."

Sara and Jack thumbed through Evie's notebook as Evie explained that she recommended Herb Snow to Alejandro because Snow was what Alejandro wanted. She also knew Snow was lazy and would keep no records. "He could never threaten me." She claimed she had little contact with the any of the nurse practitioners who served as medical directors in the memory unit over the last six years. "They all seemed interested only in the physical condition of patients and deferred many decisions to Herb."

"Didn't you think that strange?"

"Very. I didn't even want to think how Alejandro had threatened them."

"Okay, you've reviewed the characters at Happy Days. Now explain how the scheme worked."

"I did honest assessments of residents and suggested those who needed to move to assisted living—usually because of complicated medical regimes, the inability to walk, and/or poor memories." She swallowed hard. "Of course, I knew Snow would move those who had no close relatives and apparently adequate financial resources to the memory unit."

*Basically, consistent with the written statement we already have.* "So, you facilitated Alejandro's plan to fill the memory unit?"

"I guess, but I only regret one case—Olivia Bend. She was so unhappy in the memory unit that she stopped eating. And she could have lasted a year longer because Gus Rinaldi was willing to care for her." She wiped a tear from her face. "That's why I supplied all sorts of info to Gus. I admired him because he refused to be intimidated."

Sara reached across the table and patted Evie's hand. "But you were and still are intimidated by Alejandro Smith. Why?"

"He's the CEO of GYM—one of the largest chains of senior living centers in the US. If he blackballs me, I'm through professionally."

"Yes, but you'll probably lose your license as a social worker anyway. What do you really fear?"

"He told both Rosa and me that directors of his centers often died of heart attacks."

Sara turned to Jack. "Better check his employees nationwide. I only had checks run on his operations in New Mexico and Arizona." She turned back to Evie. "CHD is common among middle-aged individuals in high stress jobs. Sounds like working for Alejandro is high stress."

Evie bit her lip. "It's the way he said it. He smiled as he spoke."

*We're getting close to pay dirt.* "You've got to do better than that if we're going to keep you under wraps after tonight."

Evie whispered in her lawyer's ear. He nodded twice. She pulled out a page of blue stationery from her notebook and handed it to Sara. The note was handwritten:

> *Evie,*
> *It's been a long time since we studied social work at Texas Tech. I've found being a social worker isn't like what I thought it would be.*
>
> *I learned through the grapevine that you accepted a job from Alejandro Smith. Be careful. Remember Barbara Ann Howe—the giggling blonde in our class. She died of a drug overdose while working for Smith in a facility in Abilene. None of us believed she ever used drugs. Her husband found a note on her computer after she died and sent copies to a*

"Here's a printed version of the email from Alejandro Smith."

*You are foolish to complain about sexual harassment. I can
fire you for substandard work or find other solutions. I suggest
you resign quietly.*

Sara handed the pages to Maggio. "This note suggests Smith has a temper but…"
Maggio groaned. "Got anything else?"
Evie shook her head.

# CHAPTER 33: Jack Is Warned

*Tuesday*

"Thanks for staying with the guys last night. I couldn't concentrate after interviewing Evie."

Sara looked better than when she and Bug had staggered out last night at nine. The bags under her eyes were gone, and she'd walked into the room briskly.

He understood why these cases were tiring for Sara. He didn't have her unique knowledge of public health and science. Thus, he wasn't as effective a partner as he would like to be on the elder abuse case being pursued by the New Mexico Attorney General or the food contamination case being investigated by FDA.

However, he thought Sara's real stressor was Sanders. She had said almost nothing about the attempted kidnapping in Las Vegas. News coverage had been minimal. CNN had run a banner—*FBI stops kidnapping attempt by two deranged men in Las Vegas*—with pictures of a private jet and unidentifiable man being led away by FBI agents. They hadn't named Sanders and referred to him as a State Department official. After a short, closed-door session with Sara, Carbonne had muttered under his breath, "One of these times, Sanders won't survive his calculated risks. And Sara knows it."

Sara was also overly nervous about Cottingham. He didn't think she needed to be. After Sara left, Cottingham told Jack and Maggio, "We need more like Sara in law enforcement—thinkers not gun-toters." Jack had also noticed how Cottingham smiled when Sara talked. Maybe he liked her personally. Or maybe he was just relieved when he didn't have to listen to Maggio.

Jack decided Sara was ready to engage in a real discussion after she settled Bug in his bed with a bone. "I've been checking on Smith. His business record—at least on the surface—is impressive. He's a self-made man who built GYM from a small nursing home in New Mexico fifteen years ago into a chain of thirty senior living centers in ten states."

She flicked on her computer. "Tell me about his bad side."

                                    

"Smith has been sued for about every unfair business practice known, but all the suits have been settled out of court. All his past employees are reluctant to talk. Most said he had 'a bad temper.' A couple added he was 'vindictive' but would not explain." Jack looked at his notes. "He also is considered a 'high roller' in Las Vegas. That suggests he might have overextended his credit at times."

Sara looked away from her computer screen. "Rosemary found nothing unusual in the financial records for Happy Days or GYM in New Mexico."

"I'd like to get a warrant for the financial records of his facilities in west Texas. They've been the source of the most lawsuits." He leaned closer to Sara. "I'd also like to work with IRS and examine Alejandro's tax records."

Sara's jaw dropped and she stared at Jack for at least ten seconds. "Why?"

"Last night Cottingham mentioned he liked this case because he'd never worked with FDA attorneys and investigators before. He said he was 'intrigued by the possibilities.' Maybe he'd like to work with the IRS, too."

Sara closed her mouth. "That's a good idea. Unfortunately, neither of us have the accounting skills to be useful participants in a search with the IRS." She paused. "It may be a niche you want to grow into. Why don't you lay out your ideas for Cottingham?" She returned to scanning her computer screen.

Jack nodded. "Nobody here does. And I don't want to stuck working with Maggio on the elderly abuse part of the case. I'll learn nothing, except how not to behave."

Sara turned her chair to focus on Jack. "I understand, but you've got to accept some cases aren't really solved. Only a bandage is put on an obvious surface problem." She shrugged. "I think the elder abuse case is a winner. I suspect Happy Days is just the tip of the iceberg. But if the New Mexico Attorney General was serious about the case, he wouldn't have assigned Maggio to it."

"What does that mean for us?"

"We keep careful records, tell Carbonne everything, focus on helping the FDA nail Happy Days for purchasing food they knew was substandard, *and* solve who killed Ab."

"How do we handle Maggio?"

"We give him what we've got. We've almost forced him to cut the deal with Evie not Snow. Now it's up to him. I doubt he'll be willing to tangle with Smith. His lawyers in expensive suits will impress Maggio too much."

"That's not enough."

She patted Jack's hand. "I don't have the energy to go over Maggio's head and build the case with AG." She tapped her index finger on Jack's hand. "It's too big a risk for you. Maggio must have connections—with his personality—or he would have been fired by now. Talk to Carbonne if you doubt me. Now let's figure out what type of data we need to identify who poisoned Ab."

"I think our best evidence is the DNA on the bottle of bourbon." Jack scanned his phone. "That means Gus, John, Karen Wright, Ruth Lopez or one unknown individual is the poisoner." He frowned. "If we assume Gus's memory of who entered his apartment during the last week is correct, Bob or Sandi Jones is the most likely source of the unknown DNA. They complained about Gus, and both refused to give DNA or be fingerprinted."

Sara nodded. "But the poisoner could have worn gloves. For example, Rosa Gonzalez was surprisingly cooperative when she ordered her staff to all be fingerprinted. She and her staff are smart enough to wear gloves. We know they all had access to methanol from various sources."

He watched Sara as she sorted pages and rearranged piles on her desk. "What are you trying to achieve with all that sorting? My grandmother would say you're acting like a sow building a nest for her piglets."

Sara stopped. "You're right. My father would have said that, too. I'm guess I'm nervous, I'm picking up Sanders at the airport at eleven. Normally I let him rent a car and join me here, but…"

"He was shot and almost kidnapped. You're feeling sorry for him. I understand." Jack realized he didn't understand but it seemed like the right thing to say.

Sara picked up a note on a scrap of paper. "I think I ordered DNA analyses of the panties in Gus's collection but don't remember getting the results from Winslow." She shook her head. "Why don't you check?"

"What will we gain?"

"I'd be annoyed—like pissed—if a man kept my underwear in a trophy collection. Maybe not enough to poison him but…"

"We don't have better ideas."

***

Gus was more of a gentleman that Jack expected. He claimed he couldn't remember the names of the women who had owned three of his trophies. He freely admitted again the other sets were those of Olivia Bend, Ruth Lopez and Evie Schoener.

In desperation Jack yelled loud enough for John to overhear. "Gus, stop being gallant. You're risking not only your life, but John's and Isaac's lives as well."

John leaned across the divider between his and Gus's desks in the once living room of Isaac's house. "I think one was from the scrawny kitchen worker at Happy Days."

Jack sighed. The woman he talked to on the loading dock fit the bill. *What was her name?* "Gus, what attracted you to Lola Lopez?"

Gus's lower jaw dropped. "She was desperate. She needed money to buy basic supplies." Gus hung his head. "She also caught me studying the packing slips." He looked around as if he remembered when he was caught. "Cookie hangs a file in the kitchen at the entrance to the loading dock. Everyone deposits packing slips in it and..."

John interrupted. "What's he's trying to say is he and Cookie had a deal. He could look at the packing slips after she'd notified him when questionable ones were there."

This story coincided with what Cookie had said. "How did Cookie notify you?"

Gus sighed. "She gave Lola a note to deliver me at a meal. It didn't take long for Lola to realize I always appeared on the loading dock after she delivered those notes. She watched me enough to know I wasn't stealing. She offered to take photos of all the packing slips and forward them to me. She could do it without being noticed."

"The deal?"

"I buy her a new phone and pay for its use."

"Is that all?"

"I felt sorry for her. I took her shopping."

John interrupted, "When?"

"When you and Ab were busy." Gus smiled. "I wanted to treat her and took her to Dillard's—my ex-wives' favorite store—and bought her a red bra and pantie set and a tiger print set. A week later, I found a bag hanging on my door. She returned tiger print set after she wore it. I guess she'd heard about my trophy collection." He looked defiantly at Jack "That's it. You've gained nothing."

"You now have only two—not three—women to identify."

"Hmmf." He bit his lip. "Can we discuss the other two privately?"

*That's strange. Why doesn't he want John to hear his confession?*

John must have thought the same. He stood. "I can take a hint. I'll be in the kitchen making lunch."

Gus waited until John left. "I never slept with Lola, but I slept with the other two women. You could ruin their lives."

"How?"

"You'll figure it out. One was Linda Wright. She was so dejected when Ab kept avoiding her. It was only a couple of times. Then I learned Ab thought John was the right man for her."

"I take it John doesn't know."

"He must never know. John and Linda would make a good pair."

"And?"

"The other was Sandi Jones. She was unhappy because her husband was often violent with her. She quit our affair because she thought her husband would kill both of us if he learned the truth."

"Again, I assume John doesn't know."

Gus nodded. "John is so naïve. He thinks they're the perfect couple."

Jack stared at Gus. *Wonder what other surprises this old coot will deliver?*

## CHAPTER 34: A Series of Half-Truths

Sara was aghast. Sanders was too weak to effectively turn the rotating door that separated the hallway from the flight gates to the reception area at the Albuquerque airport. *His wound must be worse than I was told.* She rushed forward and grabbed his arm. "Do you need a wheelchair?"

He whispered in her ear. "Don't fuss. The severity of my injury was never reported. I can't act injured. The young blond man behind me is an agent and a nurse practitioner. Don't lose him." He pulled away and announced. "I don't have any bags."

*Strange.* Sanders had left Albuquerque with a rolling carry-on bag and a heavy briefcase. *Better carry on this act.* "It's so hot. I think we should pick up cold beverages before we leave the airport."

Sanders sat on a bench as she purchased two bottles of water. The blond man continued to the baggage claim area and was pulling a rolling bag which looked like Sanders's bag from the carousel when they walked past on their way to the parking garage.

*Better stall a bit.* "Gee, I was thirsty. I've drunk all my water. Do you want me to get rid of your bottle, too?"

"Yes." He sank onto the nearest bench.

Sara noticed his bottle was half-full. She took her time strolling to the garbage bin and wandering back to Sanders. "I always enjoy watching people at the luggage carousel. I try to guess which are coming home, which are starting a vacation, and which are going to work. Today most have on long pants. I think this group has lots of businesspeople."

"Hmmf."

*I'm trying to stall gracefully. Give me a break.* She smiled. "After a couple of days in Vegas, you must be eager to…" *The guy finally has his bags.*

"See Bug. Let's go." Sanders stood.

*Sanders must be tired. He's not faking well.* "It was hard to find a parking place this morning in the garage. My car is in aisle B." Sanders sighed when the young blond jumped into a black car near the building's exit. *This could be a long, slow walk.* She didn't try to fake conversation.

***

As soon as she closed the car door, Sanders said, "I hurt. We were in such a rush to get me out of the Las Vegas airport unseen on Sunday, the EMTs didn't look at my arm carefully. And the surgeon Sunday missed something. Yesterday I spiked a fever. A physician had to clean my wound and fix the damage."

"Do you need to go to the hospital?"

"No. Take me to the FBI building. The blond agent will meet us there."

Sara voiced the obvious question. "Should you have stayed in a hospital in Las Vegas?"

"No. I can rest better at your house, and we wanted to avoid questions."

"Does *we* include Ray Curtis, FBI agents, or senators from the Intelligence Committee?"

"All of the above. All are grateful. I did what had to be done."

"Good." *If I say more, I'll annoy him.*

***

Carbonne closed the door to Sara's office and tousled Bug's ears. "I understand you installed Sanders and his entourage in the small conference room."

She felt like crying. "I didn't know what else to do until I understood the situation."

He sank into a chair at her small table and gave a tired smile. "No problem. Upper echelon of the FBI—an agent named Ray Curtis—informed me an hour ago that I should cooperate with Mr. Sanders when he arrived."

*Gee, Ray has risen in the ranks since Brazil if he's in the upper echelon now.* "Sanders shouldn't have flown today but my nagging is useless. And the blond is a nurse practitioner At least, he's pleased with himself. He delivered what he promised."

"He always was a risk taker but…"

"He's not logical anymore. He wants to direct information gathering for all of the State Department so bad." She paused. "He doesn't care if he dies trying." She paused again. "I should be crying my eyes out, but I can't cry anymore."

"What will you do?"

"Accept the situation. He thinks my acting unconcerned is his best cover. So, I've got to concentrate enough to work on the case." She frowned. "Besides, I'm so annoyed with him, I don't want stay home with him and be his nurse."



J. L. Greger

"He's a fool."

"No. He's right. I'll be happier if I'm busy. Jack and I have come up with a plan to get DNA samples and fingerprints from two unwilling suspects."

"Will that be enough to finish the Ab Hess murder case?"

"Not quite." She felt like smiling and did. "We are ninety percent sure the intended victim was Gus Rinaldi. Ab Hess was just unlucky. That's progress."

Carbonne stood and patted her shoulder. "Cottingham called. He said Jack was 'developing well.'" He walked to the door. "Funny thing. He also asked whether 'you were serious about anyone.' I think you have an admirer—another obsessed workaholic."

***

"I thought it was time for us to gossip about the men of Happy Days." Sara raised her pink plastic glass of iced tea and saluted the three women she'd invited to John Lindberg's apartment.

Ruth giggled and raised a blue plastic glass in response. Karen and Sandi stared at their yellow and lavender plastic glasses, respectively.

Sara had worked too hard planning this event to give up. "You all know John, Gus, and the late Ab Hess. Linda, do you think one of them got so enthralled with playing pranks that…" She frowned. "…he went too far?"

Linda blinked. "How would I know?"

"Psychologists say your initial gut reactions are apt to be right. You three knew the men well and I'm confused by them. So, what was your first thought?"

Linda gulped.

*This woman has never been spontaneous in her life* "Come on." Sara raised her glass again.

Linda grabbed her yellow glass. "He finally got a taste of his own medicine."

"It's your turn now, Sandi."

Sandi lifted her lavender glass. "I agree with Linda." She took a big swallow of tea.

*Finally, got Sandi's prints.* "Ruth, didn't you think that, too?'

Ruth looked like she would cry. "No, I'll always have a soft spot for Gus. He knows how to show a woman a good time." She shook her head. "But he'll never get over Olivia."

*That's a downer. Got to keep them talking.* "Okay. We now know Ruth's a romantic. I bet you other two have been less fortunate in love.

My boyfriend is a daredevil. He came back injured from his vacation this morning. I was so angry at him for lying to me… I decided to have this little party with women who would understand." *That lie—well half-truth—sounds logical.* She pushed a plate of chocolate chip cookies toward Ruth. "Here. Have another cookie. Calories don't count when you're complaining about a man."

Ruth cleared her throat. "You're wrong. I had one boyfriend who hit me when he drank too much." She swallowed a cookie in two bites.

*God bless Ruth. Exactly where I wanted this conversation to go. Got to egg them on.* "My mother always said there were only two acceptable reasons for divorce—the man drank too much or hit you. What are your thoughts, Sandi?"

Sandi looked at her lap. "My mother thought a man who paid the bills was the perfect man." She looked up. "I didn't have a career like you three. Divorce wasn't an option."

*How do I foster more honest comments? Maybe the obvious.* "Who do you think poisoned the bourbon—the stuff Linda and Ruth gave Gus?"

Ruth giggled. "Not me. I'm not dumb enough to think I can do the impossible and teach a man anything."

Linda gasped. "I think this tea party was an excuse to get us to talk." She frowned. "I should be annoyed, but I'm not. I'm glad you're trying so hard to find Ab's killer. He was a good man."

Sandi stood. "I won't tell Bob about this fake party. It would make him angry."

***

Jack emerged from the bedroom after the three women left. He clicked his tongue. "We didn't get much for all our effort."

Sara carefully dropped the lavender plastic tumbler into an evidence bag. "I disagree. We finally got Sandi's prints and DNA. She also basically confirmed Gus's comments on her husband. You'll notice she didn't return to her apartment."

"True."

"Now for the next skit. Are you ready?"

"No." He picked up two jugs of windshield wiper fluid. "This is dumb."

"It's only humiliating if you fail. Besides, John couldn't suggest anything else that Bob would accept."

***

Sara watched through the peep hole as Jack rang the bell of the Jones's apartment. Bob answered.

"Hey man, I was thinking."

Sara thought Jack's attempt to sound natural was contrived. Bob must have, too. He began to close the door.

Jack put his foot in the doorway. "I found this new product for cleaning car windshields. It's safer than the old stuff." He shoved an almost empty bottle into Bob's hands. "Look at the label. It works well on my car's windows. I figured you might want to use this in the future."

Bob turned the bottle over to read the label. "No methanol."

"Why don't you take the new bottle?" Jack pulled a full bottle from under his left arm with his right hand. "I'll take the one I partially used." He pulled the almost empty bottle by its lid with his left hand from Bob's hands. "Like I said, I appreciate your help." Jack took a step backward.

Bob smiled and closed the door.

# CHAPTER 35: Follow the Money

Jack whistled as he drove out of the parking lot at Happy Days. "What took you so long in getting back to the car?"

"I didn't leave John's apartment until you left the floor." She paused. "Cottingham has come up with an interesting suggestion. A DA in west Texas was building a case against Alejandro Smith for fraud. He gave up after a suspect died of a drug overdose—probably suicide."

"Bet Evie and Herb Snow already know about that case. Any chance we can tie the two cases together?"

"That's what Cottingham was thinking. The basic scenario is similar. The parent company for the senior center in Amarillo was GYM. It was packing its memory unit with wealthy individuals with no close relatives." She frowned. "The local state DA set up a sting. He recorded the psychologist for the facility requesting info on two prospective patients' accounts from a local bank. The next day, the wealthy—but seemingly normal—patient was admitted to the memory unit and the patient with no funds—but with Alzheimer's Disease—wasn't."

"What ruined it?"

"The psychologist died a couple of days later. Suddenly, the cooperating business officer couldn't recall anything."

Jack pulled into the order lane at a McDonalds. "If Cottingham takes our case out of the hands of the New Mexico Attorney General, we won't have to deal with Maggio anymore."

"Just order diet coke for me." Sara sighed. "But we don't want to do Cottingham's dirty work. Worker ants—like us—get smashed when two elephants—like an US attorney and a state attorney general—fight."

Jack placed the order. "It might be fun. What would Sanders say?" He handed the cups of beverages to Sara and dropped the bag of food onto Sara's lap before he drove to a parking space.

Sara ate several fries before she replied. "He'd agree, *but* I think we should focus on assuring Evie's continued cooperation and not worry about politics." She sipped her soda. "There's something she's hiding. A key…"

Jack ate a fry. "They're greasy and disgusting, but I love them." He ate several more fries. "We never explored how Evie knew about the financial situations of residents of Happy Days."

"Not completely true. I learned Happy Days requires monthly bills be paid through direct access to residents' accounts. They claim checks are cumbersome and often late. I even have a list of the direct accounts used to pay bills at Happy Days."

"When did you get that?"

"When we got the financial records for Happy Days." Sara rapidly scrolled through records on her laptop. "Aha. Here it is." She scrolled some more. "Rosemary pulled this info, but I didn't know what to do with it." She studied her screen. "Of the twenty residents in the memory unit now, twelve have accounts in the same bank—Second National Bank of New Mexico." She pounded a few keys. "GYM is the guardian for eight of those twelve. We also have the names of forty deceased patients from the memory unit who had accounts with this bank."

"Do we confront Evie or the bank first?"

"Good question." She typed on her laptop. "This is Cottingham's show now. I'll get his advice."

Jack finished the fries and wiped his hands before he fiddled with his phone. "The main office of the Second National Bank of New Mexico is only a few blocks away."

Sara didn't look up from her laptop. "Cottingham says to give him thirty minutes. In the meantime, I'm reminding the agents monitoring Evie to not allow her access to phones or the internet."

"Why the delay?"

"Cottingham is getting warrants for the fifty-two present and past accounts in the bank."

"Is he that fast?"

"I suspect he has more than one judge on speed dial. He's also expecting me to kill time in the bank until he gives me the go ahead."

Jack laughed. "It should be easy. I always wait more than ten minutes before I see anyone with more authority than a teller in banks."

***

Sara was amazed how quickly she and Jack were ushered into the bank manager's office after Jack flashed his FBI badge at the receptionist. In less than five minutes, the trust officer—Audra Brown—appeared, too.

Sara explained the FBI was investigating elder abuse and was interested in the accounts of fifty-two individuals. She showed them the warrant a judge had already issued for the financial records of Happy Days and explained that was how the FBI knew fifty-two people had or once had accounts in the bank.

The trust officer—an attractive woman of about forty with brown hair and eyes—snorted. "That doesn't mean you can see the financial records of those individuals."

Sara punted and tried to bluff until the new warrant arrived. "True, but we want to be sure these account numbers are accurate."

The manager—a large man with a full head of gray hair—leaned back in his chair. "I agree with my trust officer, but I suspect you're already in the process of getting the needed warrants. While we're waiting, I can check your list of account numbers to see if they are accurate." He motioned to Jack. "You can watch."

***

Audra stood as soon as the manger agreed to check the account numbers. She nervously stepped from one foot to the other as if she needed to go to the bathroom. "I must make an urgent call."

*We've found Evie's collaborator.* "Ms. Brown, I'm afraid you can't make a phone call until we get the new warrant. If you need to go to the restroom, I can accompany you. But leave your phone on the desk."

"Really." Audra sat down.

Sara babbled about the process it took to get a warrant while watching Audra study her boss and Jack.

After several minutes, the manager turned to Jack. "The numbers look correct."

Audra tensed. "I think I'm going to vomit." She stood and raced out of the office toward the front door.

"Audra, don't be foolish."

Jack ran after Audra and tripped her. He leaned down and helped her up. Sara couldn't hear what he whispered, but Audra suddenly became calmer.

Sara's phone pinged. "I've received the warrants."

***

Audra was leaning over her boss's desk crying. The bank manager was leaning back in his chair—as if he was trying to distance himself from her.

Sara spoke slowly hoping they would focus on her. "Pretend you agreed to provide info on the amount of funds in accounts of residents at Happy Days to an employee of Happy Days or GYM. That would be illegal without the proper documents. But the punishment might be negotiable if you admitted everything."

                                                    

Audra's lips quivered. "I would never…"

"Perhaps you felt you had no choice. It would be in your and the bank's best interest if you were honest now with us…" Sara decided to bluff. "…and the US attorney."

Audra continued to fidget.

The bank manager's face became redder, and his eyes bulged more as Sara spoke. He leaned toward Audra. "These agents are serious. So am I. Tell them what you know. The bank will support you if you are innocent."

Audra shook her head. "I can't."

"We know about the case in Amarillo where Alejandro Smith escaped exposure because a psychologist died, and a bank officer had a memory lapse. If you are honest with us, we will get you and your family protection."

Audra moaned.

Jack turned to the bank manager. "Tell me about her family."

"She's divorced with a teen-age daughter." He waved his hands. "I need to talk to a lawyer. I think he'll advise me to put Audra on leave until this is resolved."

"Let's give her a chance to respond before you act."

Jack turned to Audra. "You're making things much more difficult for yourself."

Sara noticed the manager was becoming agitated. He was pacing now. *Better get him to find those records before he figures out, he could be charged, too. And Audra might be more talkative if her boss isn't around.* Sara stood and pointed to the bank manager. "Please help me get the info covered in the warrant." She pushed him out the door of his office and then turned to look at Audra. She lowered her voice so the manager couldn't hear. "Here's what we need to know: Did Alejandro Smith force you to provide info? Were either Evie Schoener or Rosa Gonzalez involved?" She glanced at the bank manager and then glared at Audra. "And how were you threatened?"

Audra stared defiantly back at Sara.

"Don't think my partner will be easier on you. He's got a hot date tonight and will be glad to deliver you to a holding cell rather than waiting for your attorney to make a plea for you."

Jack added, "Spending the night in the ABQ jail isn't fun for a middle-class, non-Hispanic woman."

Sara laughed. "I'll make arrangements for you to be held in jail if you haven't started answering questions before I return." She turned to the bank manager. "I'm so sorry to inconvenience you but you may be saving the life of an elderly individual."

***

As the bank manager obtained the records she'd requested, Sara read an email from the nurse practitioner caring for Sanders.

*Patient is no longer fevered. He is resting comfortably with your small dog lying by his side. I will stay with him tonight.*

*He doesn't want you to rush home. I've ordered carry-out food to arrive at six-thirty.*

Sara perused the computer printouts on the twelve patients currently in the memory unit. Nine had at least a hundred thousand dollars in their accounts, but three had less than twenty thousand.

The bank manager explained the closed accounts of the forty who had died were harder to access. Sara waited. When he handed their computer printouts to her, she choked. Eighteen—with GYM as their guardian—had about twenty thousand dollars in their accounts when they died. Nine with close relatives in the state and Olivia Bend had died with more than fifty thousand dollars in their account. The rest had died with their accounts almost totally depleted. *Looks like Jack will get his chance to work with accountants.*



J. L. Greger

# CHAPTER 36: Recovery

The nurse practitioner waved for Sara to stop as she turned the corner onto her street. "I need to talk to you in private." He glanced over his shoulder at Sara's house. "Sanders should have stayed in the hospital in Las Vegas, but he was insistent on managing every detail."

"Tell me something new." Sara knew she sounded uncaring, but she didn't want the man's respect just his medical advice. "Do you think he'll be all right at home, or should I insist he go to the hospital?"

"That's what he's afraid you'll do. Besides, he's stabilized now." The nurse practitioner shook his head. "Do you know why he's so anxious, but won't take antianxiety drugs?"

"Hop in. He could look out a window and see us. I'll drive to the end of the cul-de-sac." Sara looked at the nurse practitioner. He was young and energetic. "Being almost kidnapped and shot would make anyone nervous. Is he more nervous than most of your patients?"

"Yes, but in an odd way. He's concerned his bosses will think he's too old for field work."

Sara parked the car. *Sanders is too old for field work.* She decided it would be disloyal to state her opinion. "Before this incident, he helped prevent an armed coup in the Brazilian state of Amazonas. I was there for part of it. That situation would make anyone anxious."

"I was briefed on his impressive record. Unlike most older patients he doesn't want to talk about the past, only the future."

"How old are you?"

"Twenty-nine."

"You don't understand the concerns of a man in his mid-fifties. They—especially if they've been successful—aren't old enough to have lost dreams for the future, but they know they don't have the physical strength of their thirties. I suspect his wounds hurt more than in the past."

"He can become a noted teacher at Quantico. I understand he'll be doing more than just occasional lectures starting this fall."

*Those who can't, teach. How many times had Sara heard Sanders use that expression?* "Teaching isn't his dream job. And he's not a patient man."

*Now all he can do is wait for others to decide his fate.* "I suspect he doesn't want the use of antianxiety drugs on his medical record."

"There's nothing to be ashamed about the use of them."

"What are symptoms that indicate he must use them?"

"Talking about suicide. Men often act quickly after they think about suicide, especially men used to violence."

Sara started the car. "I get the message. I know the cure, but I can't deliver what he needs. I doubt antianxiety drugs will help."

***

Sanders was sitting in her recliner with Bug settled on the nearby sofa when Sara entered her house. She leaned down and kissed him. *Truth is overrated sometimes.* "Did you drive your caregiver crazy today? I don't see him."

"He went for a walk. Unfortunately, he's staying tonight because he's got me on an IV line."

"What for?"

"He's vague—antibiotics, pain killers, and I don't know what else." Sanders rubbed his arm. "I'd like to get off the line. I can't do much with Bug when I'm attached."

"Okay. I'll talk to him. If he can treat your infections with oral antibiotics, I'll suggest he let you gut the pain out." She kissed him again. "But you may regret getting what you asked for. That upper arm has been wounded twice since I met you. You may have built up a lot of scar tissue."

He waved his right arm. "Anything to get loose."

"And for entertainment tonight. I want to hear all the *juicy* details about the trip to Mexico you didn't take. You know the details you hid from me." *Those details will probably upset me, but it may be his only chance to show off all his plans.* She looked at her watch. It was almost six. "What type of food did you order?"

"The nurse practitioner wanted Southwest food. I think he ordered brisket burritos, chicken quesadillas, and ribeye steak enchiladas from Cocina Azul."

"I'll make a big bowl of salad." *Let's see if Sanders can do simple task without wincing.* "Please set the table."

***

The nurse practitioner removed Sanders's IV line after supper and went to bed. He planned to leave early in the morning if Sanders didn't spike a fever.

Sanders grabbed his laptop and sat on the sofa as soon as the paramedic closed the door to his bedroom. He began to hum as he scanned messages and typed.

Sara snuggled up to Sanders. "What's the problem between you and your nurse practitioner?"

"No problem." Sanders didn't bother to look up. "He's just of the mind set that drugs can fix all problems, and I don't believe it."

"Okay, that makes sense." She didn't pause. "Now tell me the important details about Vegas."

He kissed her cheek. "Victor will report regularly on his observations in the Yucatan."

"What was the price?"

He kissed her cheek again. "You're a good guesser. Roberto won't be charged until he completes rehab in Colorado."

Sara waited for more explanation. None came. "What will be the charges?"

"Depends on Roberto's attitude. If he remains defiant, which I think is likely kidnapping of me."

"Why not kidnapping of his sister?"

"We want to avoid mentioning her name since she died before we could rescue her. It makes it easier for the family." Sanders started to peck at his laptop.

"I don't buy it. The case is stronger for kidnapping her. Smells like the witness protection program. I bet that's why Victor is cooperating."

Sanders turned Sara's head and kissed her deeply. "You're not involved in this case. Just listen to the official line. The pilot was sent back to Mexico because he's wanted on multiple charges there."

"And then you can keep a low profile because you won't have to testify against him."

"Correct."

Sara sighed. "At least you didn't say *perfect*. Have you noticed everyone under thirty now says *perfect* not *correct* or *right* when they agree with you? It grates on my ears."

Sanders snickered. "Maybe I should remember to say *perfect* when I answer questions during interviews. It will make me seem younger."

Sara shook her head. "Sounds like your action in Vegas was a success. I'm glad I didn't have to pretend to be enjoying the ruins and markets in the Yucatan while I was nervously waiting to be kidnapped."

"Perfect," He choked. "I didn't think my plans were that obvious."

"Just to me. Now here's the important question. How do you plan to keep busy without driving me crazy during the next month?"

"Remember the camera I bought the last time I visited you. I've signed up for classes. Bug will become the most photographed dog around."

"I don't see you as a master of cute photos."

"I thought the nurse practitioner advised you to focus my interests on pleasant topics."

Sara looked askance. "When?"

"When you talked to him in your car before you came into the house." He laughed. "I know you can read my mind, but you forget I can read yours, too."

She kissed him.

# CHAPTER 37: New Partnerships?

*Wednesday*

Jack whistled as he knocked on Sara's office door. "No Bug?"

"Sanders thinks Bug is a better subject for his photography than I am." She studied him for a second. "You look like the cat who swallowed the canary. What's up?"

"Didn't you get a message from Cottingham?"

"Yes. Several last night. *The man's a worse overachiever than Sanders.* This morning's message was simple. We are to show up at his office at eight-fifteen. Other agents will bring Audra to one of his conference rooms at nine and Evie to another at nine-thirty."

"That's all?"

"He did some wheeling and dealing with the attorney for northern Texas—that…"

"I know that covers Amarillo. C'mon what else?"

Sara wanted to laugh because Jack was almost whining. "The US attorneys of these two districts will be investigating the management of five facilities owned by GYM. They suspect they will find evidence of elder abuse, fraud, and perhaps murder in several memory units as they examine those facilities."

Jack bounced with excitement. "And?"

"Cottingham will have you temporarily assigned to work on this multi-state project, if Carbonne agrees."

Jack stopped bouncing when she said *if Carbonne agrees.* "Oh."

"I already talked to Carbonne. He will release you—provided you continue to support efforts to identify the murderer of Ab Hess."

Jack shook his head and looked at the floor.

Sara again wanted to laugh at Jack but didn't want to hurt his ego. "Cottingham agreed to the stipulation because he thought murder charges here against Smith would strengthen the case against him in Texas." She laughed. "I bet him a lunch that he wouldn't get what he wanted because I don't think Alejandro Smith murdered Ab Hess."

Jack finally sat down. "Working on a big interstate investigation with lots of accountants will…"

"Provide you with more exposure and experience. Just remember—be careful what you wish for, or you may end up like Sanders and Cottingham."

Jack looked down. "You mean…"

Sara touched his arm. "This isn't the time for a philosophical discussion about life goals. At least, you won't have to work with Maggio. I don't know much about the deal Cottingham struck with the New Mexico Attorney General, but Maggio won't be working on this case."

***

*When the stars are aligned right, things magically fall into place.* Jack and Cottingham spent the morning shuttling between rooms—one with Audra Brown and her lawyer and one with Evie Schoener and her lawyer. Sara sat in another room and listened to the interviews through her earplugs. Mainly she worked on her laptop to provide Jack and Cottingham with the info they needed to manipulate the two women.

Both women seemed eager to answer questions. *Forget magic.* Cottingham was convincing when he said, "Your only chance of a reduced sentence or no sentence is to talk before employees at other GYM facilities do."

Sara enjoyed listening to the interviews. It was nice not to be the person responsible for dragging details out of witnesses. She found Alejandro Smith's understanding—as described by the two women—of the relatives of patients in memory units to be impressive and alarming. Smith believed "twenty-thousand dollars was the minimum estate distant heirs would accept without complaints." Thus, he had instructed Evie to notify Snow when the accounts of residents in the memory unit were depleted to thirty thousand. Sara could find no indication any distant relatives had complained or even asked for details on their relative's death *after* they received notice of their inheritance, even though several of the deceased had been worth almost five hundred thousand dollars when they originally entered the memory unit.

Evie claimed she didn't know what Snow did with the information she gave him. Sara checked the records of patients who had died in the memory unit of Happy Days. Pneumonia, coronary heart disease, sepsis, extreme weight loss, and dehydration were listed as causes of death on the death certificates. All common causes of death among aging patients. Only two, besides Olivia Bend, had been autopsied. Sara could see no differences in the types of deaths among patients with relatives who visited frequently and those who had only distant relatives and were under

GYM's guardianship. *Perhaps AI can tease out a relationship.* She emailed Rosemary.

Audra admitted Alejandro had invited her to a working lunch shortly after her daughter had been featured in a news story about the challenges of disabled students. "He seemed to know I was strapped for funds. He offered to pay me a thousand dollars whenever I 'streamlined' the process for Evie, who was drowning in paperwork at Happy Days." She was silent for fifteen seconds before she added, "I knew he was asking me to act illegally unless Evie had the proper power of attorney documents, but it was easy." Audra claimed she never met with him again.

In general, the women's comments were consistent. They were paid in cash and were instructed to communicate in person, not by emails or phone. To facilitate communications, Evie established a checking account in the bank. Audra was told she should not communicate with anyone, except Evie, at Happy Days. Alejandro instructed Evie to file standardized forms with Rosa Gonzalez and Dr. Snow. Rosa never asked for more details on patients, except those who disrupted meals or social events. In contrast, Dr. Snow who disliked spending time at Happy Days, requested weekly updates on patients from Evie.

Evie hadn't mentioned how Alejandro knew when to pay her and Audra. Sara emailed Jack to determine that point.

Evie voice deepened as she replied. "He gave me cash when I had lunch with him about twice a month. You can identify the dates. I marked AS on my calendar."

It took Sara a while to locate Evie's calendar in the pile of files Evie had delivered. When she did, she laughed. The lunches generally lasted three hours and were usually followed by an hour visit with "GR." Sara assumed Gus Rinaldi.

Sara was pleased when Cottingham finally asked a key question to Audra. "Why did you wait so long to admit the truth?"

Audra blinked back tears. "When the press in New Mexico made a big deal about elder abuse in memory units about six months ago, I told Evie I wanted to quit. A few days later, my daughter came home with an envelope. It contained a clipping about the suicide of a doctor at an Amarillo senior center and a clipping about suicides among handicapped teens."

The same question evoked a less emotional response from Evie. "I asked him a few questions during our second lunch encounter. He put his hands around my neck and murmured, 'Aging isn't pretty, but you don't want the alternative.' After that, Gus and I became friends."

"I'd hoped to interview Sandi and Bob Jones this afternoon, but I'll have to spend the afternoon writing warrants instead."

Jack flopped in a chair next to Sara. "Good. I don't think I'm up to any more interviews."

Sara smirked. "I think you'll have something worse to do. I'm preparing a request for an arrest warrant for Alejandro Smith for secondary felony charges—for his threats to Evie and Audra. You will serve the warrant and unprofessionally mention you're in a hurry because you're also serving a warrant to Dr. Snow. Cottingham will coach you on how you should goad Smith."

"What will that achieve?"

"Cottingham will arrange for Smith's arraignment to occur tomorrow morning. He and his lawyer won't have much time to prepare. We think Smith will do something foolish beforehand and attack Snow."

"Who is we?"

"Cottingham and me. So, you and Leroy Elroy will have to watch Snow constantly for the next twenty-four hours but leave him in his house."

"After we arrest Snow for murder, won't he be held in jail?"

Sara winked. "You aren't going to serve Snow with any warrants today. It's part of our trap to get Smith to act."

Jack winced. "Smith will know the charges for threatening Audra and Evie aren't enough to hold him in jail until a trial. He'll keep his cool."

"Not *if* you get him riled. And if Smith acts against Snow, the judge will order Smith to await trial in jail or at least to wear an ankle bracelet. That should make Snow nervous enough to strike a deal with Cottingham when he's charged with murder of residents in the memory unit."

"Awful lot of *ifs*." Jack shook his head. "Cottingham expects a lot. I'm not that good an actor."

"You're creative. You'll find a way to rile Smith."

***

Cottingham leaned into the small room where Sara was working. "Jack's on his way to Alejandro Smith's office with agent Leroy Elroy. Do you think he can pull off the bluff?"

Sara looked away from her screen. "I'm sure he'll try. The judge is balking about the warrant for Snow. It's not easy to prove a medical professional speeded the death of patients with Alzheimer's or Parkinson's disease."

"D*** judge."

"Don't blame him. Although I think Snow hastened the death of several of his patients when their accounts neared the twenty-thousand-dollar limit set by Smith, I doubt you can convict him without the testimony of a nurse in the unit." She suddenly typed rapidly on her computer. "I included the pharmacy records in our last search warrant. An analyst might be able to calculate all recorded drug usage in the memory unit and find a discrepancy in the drugs on hand in a month when a patient in the memory unit died." Sara bit her lip. "But the difference between a therapeutic dose of morphine or similar compounds and an overdose that kills is small."

"Try."

***

An hour later, Cottingham returned. "I talked to Carbonne." He closed the door but remained standing. "I guess I should admit to you I wanted you—not Jack—assigned to me for this project. Carbonne explained you have some *unique professional* responsibilities with the FBI because of your personal relationship with Eric Sanders." He looked at the floor. "If those change, I'd like to increase our interactions."

*It's not often a single man of an appropriate age flirts with me.* "I enjoy your company, too."

He gave a boyish smile. He really did remind her of the guy she had a crush on in high school. *I'm more nervous than flattered.* She guessed Cottingham was as manipulative and controlling in his personal relationships as in his professional life.

She tried to flash a warm smile. "I did my best on the warrant request for Snow. It's iffy. I'm going back to the FBI Building to work on the Ab Hess murder case. Clearing that may be the best way I can help the bigger case."

***

When Sara was depressed, she took Bug for a walk. Today Bug was with Sanders. She decided the next best pick-me-up was Winslow.

He started to smile as soon as Sara entered the lab. "I hoped you'd stop by. I can now account for all the fingerprints and DNA on the bottle of Wild Turkey. We knew Gus, Ab, Ruth, and Linda touched the bottle. So did Bob Jones."

"Good. It fits. Bob was in Gus's apartment. Bob had access to methanol in windshield wiper solutions. Is there evidence of someone wearing gloves handled the bottle?"

Winslow squinted. "You know that's impossible to tell."

"Yes, but sometimes you can see prints have been partially obliterated by a smooth surface."

"Oh, I see what you mean. Not really, and I couldn't testify on that."

"Although Bob is probably the murderer, I think Sandi would do whatever he ordered. That means I must break one of them. It's always hard."

Winslow's eyes widened. "I'd think it would be exciting as you waited to shout *gotcha.*"

*He's young.* "Not usually." She thought a second. "What about the DNA on the panties?"

"Unidentified DNA—not Gus's—besides Evie's was on her panties."

Sara texted Jack:

> *Get a DNA sample from Smith. We may have his DNA*
> *on Evie's panties. Should clinch her claims.*

"Winslow, you're a wonder."

## CHAPTER 38: Jack's Worse Fears

Alejandro Smith was not in his office. His secretary refused to indicate his location until Jack showed her his FBI badge. Then she admitted he'd gone home fifteen minutes earlier and was leaving on a private jet in two hours. "He didn't state his destination. Usually when he's in a bad mood, it's Las Vegas."

Jack found riding shotgun with Leroy alarming. Leroy bolted from every stop sign to fifty miles per hour in a less than a minute even in residential areas. He swerved around other cars as if he was playing a computer game. Jack was relieved when he saw Smith's red Jaguar parked in front of a two-story house with a four-car garage for two reasons. He'd survived the ride, and Alejandro probably hadn't left for the airport yet.

The maid denied Smith was home, but a man yelled from the second floor. Leroy barged past her and ran up the stairs to the balcony which ringed the open atrium.

Jack recognized the potential for Smith's escape was great, but he was used to Sara's more measured response to a crisis. He showed his badge, ascertained no one else was in the house, and advised the maid to wait outside. She pointed to a door at the far end of the balcony and scurried out the front door. By that time, Leroy had opened three of the five closed doors along the balcony.

Jack waved to Leroy to not open the last door. When Jack reached it, Leroy stood with a shot gun in one hand and a key ring in the other. Jack could hear a man talking inside the room. Jack knocked on the door.

"I told you not to bother me."

Leroy handed a bump key to Jack and nodded.

Jack announced, "FBI. Mr. Smith, we have a warrant for your arrest."

Silence.

Jack played with the key for only a couple of seconds before the door swung open. Smith was reaching into a briefcase. Jack yelled, "FBI. Don't do anything foolish. We're..."

"Armed and aimed at you." Leroy smirked as he pointed the shotgun at Smith. "Just raise your hands nice and gentle. My partner here is used to white-collar crime. Me—I'm used to the gangs."

Smith raised his hands. Jack frisked him and found one gun in an ankle holster and one in the briefcase. "Mr. Smith, we know you have at least five registered guns and are authorized to carry concealed weapons. Thus, I will hand cuff you before I read your rights. Then you may call your lawyer and arrange for him to meet you at the FBI Building."

Smith's voice was loud and clear. "You're in big trouble, Boy."

"Afraid you're wrong, sir. We have a warrant for your arrest. Unfortunately, you won't be arraigned until tomorrow morning."

After Smith listened to the charges against him, he laughed. "I don't want to wait around for an arraignment for minor charges by two money-grubbing s****."

***

Jack looked nervously at the mirror. Cottingham was behind it and judging his actions. Jack wished Cottingham wasn't in such a hurry. He'd insisted Sara interrogate Sandi and Bob Jones while he and Leroy handled Smith. Cottingham had made it clear he wanted Smith and his lawyer to be so distracted by the agents' actions that they didn't have time to think.

Leroy had already started the plan. He was snickering as Winslow slowly laid out the minor tools needed for collecting DNA and fingerprints on the table. Jack knew the main routine was up to him. As expected, Smith and his lawyer wore expensive linen suits. "How about a cup of coffee while we wait for the assistant DA? He should be here momentarily."

Smith ignored him. Jack stood, poured the coffee anyway, and knocked the full cup onto Smith's lap. Smith jumped from his chair cursing.

Jack had made sure of two things before the skit. The coffee was lukewarm and wouldn't scald Smith. There was an inadequate number of paper towels in the room. Thus, the coffee soaked into Smith's suit while he waited for Leroy to bring more towels into the room.

Winslow—as directed—was slow in swabbing Smith's cheek and fingerprinted his right fingers twice because he claimed the first prints were unclear.

Finally, Jack said, "I don't know where the assistant DA is. I notified him you wanted the arraignment moved to today because you planned to attend a meeting in Las Vegas tonight. Can you tell me about the meeting?"

Smith whispered into the lawyer's ear before he said, "That's unnecessary."

"Mr. Smith, may I see your passport."

"No."

"I must insist. The judge will have to decide if you are a flight risk."

"My lawyer can arrange any bail *you* demand."

"Mr. Smith, the judge—not me—must make that decision."

The door swung open. Cottingham entered. "I have good news. The judge rearranged his schedule for you. If we miss this new time slot, you can't be arraigned until eight tomorrow."

Smith jumped to his feet. The lawyer hesitated.

"A car is waiting."

***

The arraignment was pure theater.

An array of cameras and reporters caught Alejandro Smith's entry into the federal courthouse in a stained and wrinkled suit. Jack noted that Cottingham had on a better suit than usual. *Little doubt who tipped off the news stations.*

Smith and his lawyer had little time to peruse the warrant before entering the courtroom. It featured charges based on sworn statements from Audra Brown and Evie Schoener, stating Smith had paid them to do illegal actions and had threatened them. However, it also stated Smith had paid Snow to act illegally—to kill individuals in the memory unit of Happy Days.

Smith choked in surprise when the judge read the last part of the warrant to him in court. His lawyer challenged it and requested Smith be released on his own recognizance.

Cottingham delivered his final surprise. *Sara and Rosemary had come through, as usual.* Smith and his secretary had lied. His flight was headed for Tijuana, Mexico—not Las Vegas. Cottingham declared Smith was a flight risk. The judge agreed.

Cottingham magnanimously agreed Smith could be released if he wore an ankle monitor, gave up his passport, and turned over all his guns to the FBI. However, if Smith committed other crimes, he would be forced to await trial in jail.

The judge agreed to the stipulations.

*Cottingham has set the trap with Snow as the bait.* Jack hoped Snow would realize the danger and quickly admit what he'd done to gain protective custody in another state. *It seemed unlikely.*

# CHAPTER 39: Sara Fries a Small Fish

Sara decided Sandi and Bob Jones were more apt to tell the truth if they were brought by agents to the FBI Building and placed in separate rooms than if she went to their apartment. Sandi's earlier comments suggested her husband was easily annoyed. Accordingly, Sara decided to make Bob wait in the smallest room available while she interviewed Sandi.

Sara asked one of the agents bringing the Joneses to the building to sit in on the interviews because Cottingham had insisted Jack be present at Alejandro Smith's arraignment. *The rush isn't necessary. You'd think this was two weeks before an election and he was running for office.*

***

Sara wished herself good luck and started to interview Sandi by saying, "You know men get grouchy with age. Have you noticed it's hard to please Bob sometimes?" She pushed a plate of cookies closer to Sandi after she took one.

Sandi grabbed a cookie. "Bob has been a good provider and father, but he's always thought I was too friendly with others."

"Mmm. You mean with men?"

Sandi nodded. "He doesn't like anyone who makes a scene."

"What constitutes a scene?" Sara waited fifteen seconds. "Do you mean someone like Gus who acts up at parties and uses a squirt gun?"

Sandi nodded. "He was so annoyed with Gus after one party, he made me write an email to Mrs. Gonzalez complaining about Gus."

"Were you offended by Gus's behavior?"

Sandi didn't look up from the table. "No, I thought Gus was funny as he impersonated Groucho Marx and wore big fake eyebrows and used a squirt gun like Groucho's cigar."

Sara put her left hand on Sandi's shoulder. "Then why send the email?"

"I had to…or Bob would guess."

Sara waited for Sandi to take a gulp of water. "Guess what?"

"Guess I'd been foolish?"

"How foolish? Did you sleep with Gus?"

Sandi was silent.



J. L. Greger

"We found a pair of panties and a bra in Gus's apartment with your DNA."

Sandi leaned over the table holding her head in her hands. "Gus saw me crying one day after Bob had yelled at me for being stupid. He waited until Bob and John went off on an errand and invited me to his apartment. We cuddled mainly."

Sara knew it was an unnecessary question, but she wanted to understand Sandi's motivation. "Then why did you leave your panties and bra with him?"

"He said he wanted to remember 'our sweet moments together.' I couldn't say no." She sniffled. "Bob never says nice things to me. Gus was so sweet."

*This woman is really starved for affection.* "Did Bob know?"

Sandi straightened in her chair. "No, but he suspected something." She bit into another cookie. "He kept complaining I was making a fool of myself laughing at Gus's pranks. A couple of weeks ago, he said I had to prove myself."

"What did he mean?"

"Well, maybe I should go back a bit. John and Bob were ready to service two women's cars, but they needed rags to clean up any spills. I didn't have any old towels. Neither did John, but he thought Gus would have an old towel. When I went to get the towel. Bob insisted on going with me. Just before we reached Gus's apartment, Bob said I should distract Gus because he wanted to look for something. It didn't make sense."

"What happened?"

Gus invited us in and led me to his bathroom to decide which towels were the most decrepit." She chewed a bit of cookie. "I took my time—as Bob requested—in choosing two ugly, salmon-colored hand towels. When we got back to the living room. Bob was pacing around the room and in a hurry to leave."

"Did he explain?"

"No."

"Why do you think this errand to get a towel was important?"

Sandi's occasional sniffle now became loud sobs. "Bob started drinking more after we learned Ab had died." Sandi hiccupped. "And he keeps repeating, 'D*** Gus is a fake. He even faked his drinking.'"

*That may not be enough to convince a jury.* "Did Bob say anything else?"

Sandi gulped. "The scary part. 'Gus didn't drink enough of the d*** Wild Turkey."

Sara quickly got Sandi to sign a typed transcript of the interview. Sara presented it to Bob.

He read the transcript slowly. "Knew the b**** couldn't be trusted. I want a lawyer."

She called Cottingham. Bob Jones was his problem now. She doubted Cottingham would waste much time in closing the Hess murder case because he had a bigger fish to fry. At least, now Sandi would have a chance to build a better life.

***

She called Jack and asked. "Do you need help?"

There was silence for a moment. "Yeah, from God. Snow is still refusing to admit anything. He and his lawyer don't seem to realize Smith will act tonight or at the latest tomorrow. I begged Cottingham to let us provide Snow with protective custody, but he said, 'Unless Snow talks, he doesn't qualify as a key witness.' Technically he's right."

"Do you want me to talk to Snow?"

"What can you say that I can't?"

"I can be blunter because I don't care that much if Cottingham blackballs me."

"But Sanders does. He needs you to have a clean image if he's to get the position he wants."

# CHAPTER 40: Artificial Intelligence versus Humans

Sara felt guilty as she walked to Rosemary's cubicle. She had assigned the analyst many tasks but given her little guidance and insufficient praise for her accomplishments. *I've been so swamped trying to follow leads in this three-ring circus of a case. Cottingham has been in such a hurry.* Her excuses didn't justify her inattention to Rosemary who had been on the job less than a month.

She looked over the gray fabric divider around Rosemary's cubicle. Rosemary was hunched over a computer. Her long brown hair was pulled back severely from her pale face. Her right foot tapped the floor—a nervous tic maybe—as her index finger moved along a long column of figures. She looked like a teenager studying for exams in high school—not an FBI analyst with a master's degree in computer science.

"Rosemary, I thought you'd be interested to know we've solved the Ab Hess murder case. So, I have time to help you answer FDA's questions."

Rosemary looked up and blinked. "I don't need help. After Gus and John got all their paper files loaded onto the computer system, it's just been a matter of giving the AI system the right key words. Besides, you put me in contact with FDA officials who helped me refine my searches." She again focused on her computer screen.

*Strange. She didn't ask who the murderer was. She didn't offer to share the data.* Sara cleared her throat. "I find its helpful when FBI agents and staff discuss their findings."

Rosemary ignored her and continued to scan her screen.

Sara cleared her throat again. "Please show me anything you found which indicates that Rosa Gonzalez or the previous cook at Happy Days knew the peanuts were contaminated or knew that American Peanut Supply was being investigated."

Rosemary sighed. "I can do better than that, I can show you a timeline."

"I'd like to see both the timeline and actual evidence."

"FDA officials didn't seem to want to see more than the timeline. Why do you?" Rosemary flipped her hair back over her shoulder.

Sara bit her tongue. "Print out the timeline and let's examine all the data together."

Rosemary winced.

"I know it seems silly, but it's necessary. The lawyers from American Peanut Supply and GYM will look at all the data carefully. If they find mistakes, they'll try to get all your work thrown out in court."

"I hadn't thought of it that way before." Rosemary placed a printed copy of the two-page timeline on her desk and moved her chair so Sara could scoot a chair next to her.

Each page had a vertical line down the middle of the sheet. Entries were printed in red on the left side labeled *FDA*. The right side was labeled *FBI*. Entries were in blue or black.

Rosemary pointed to the first entries on the left side of the page. "These are the initial reports to FDA that American Peanut Supply was selling aflatoxin-contaminated peanuts." She pointed to the fourth entry. "This is when the FDA's laboratory confirmed the complaints. The next entry is FDA's recall notice."

Sara looked at the right column. "I see Happy Days purchased peanuts twice from American Peanut Supply during the period after FDA received the first complaint. Why are some entries in blue ink and other black?"

Rosemary tapped keys on her computer. "I have good evidence—invoices and packing slips—of the purchases printed in black." Copies of the invoices appeared on the screen. "I got these from the financial records of Happy Days." She highlighted the prices. "You'll note the second batch of peanuts was cheaper than the first."

"Odd. Prices seldom go down. Did you happen to compare these prices to the going rate at the time?"

"FDA officials did." She tapped a few keys. "A graph of average wholesale peanut prices over a ten-year period appeared on the screen. "The initial price Happy Days paid was a little below average. The second batch was ordered only a couple of days before the recall. The price had been reduced by sixty percent."

"I thought FDA required companies to notify customers when food was recalled—at least of major recalls. Did Happy Days receive such a notice?"

"AI couldn't find any recall notice in all our records, but American Peanut Supply listed Happy Days as one of the vendors contacted on this date. I marked it in blue because the company couldn't supply anything but a form letter and a list that only recognized the first purchase of peanuts by Happy Days."

"Odd. What did FDA officials say?"

Rosemary smiled. "They thought it was interesting."

"You've really done a beautiful job of laying out this case. No wonder my friend in FDA is pleased."

Rosemary seemed to ignore Sara's comment and pointed to a series of entries in black in the right column. "These indicate when patients in Happy Days were first diagnosed with liver cancer and when they died."

Sara recognized several names in the list. "Were these patients all in the memory unit when they died?"

"No. FDA made it possible for me to examine all the deaths in Happy Days since it opened ten years ago." She again tapped several keys. A graph appeared. "Usually, one resident per year died with liver cancer—at least according to their death certificates—in the years before the purchase of the bad batches of peanuts starting about six years ago."

"Are the diagnoses supported by biopsies or autopsies?"

"Sometimes. If yes, they're marked in black. If not, in blue." Her knee bounced as her right foot tapped the floor rapidly. "Anyway, in the last five years the death rate from liver cancer increased to about four deaths per year." He finger moved across the timeline.

Sara squinted at the page. "What about these purchases from Peanuts Wholesale five and four years ago?"

"Your friend at FDA was excited when I found receipts from Peanuts Wholesale in the records of Happy Days. I also determined one of the batches of peanuts that Gus had analyzed came from Peanuts Wholesale. FDA officials determined Peanut Wholesale was created by a VP of the American Peanut Supply a couple of months before the FDA recall was issued. Peanuts Wholesale continued to do business after American Peanut Supply closed." Rosemary's knee was bouncing rapidly.

Sara continued to quiz Rosemary. Her answers were logical and thorough "Looks like you nailed FDA's case against American Peanut Supply, Peanuts Wholesale, and Happy Days. Now we've just got to show who at Happy Days is responsible."

Rosemary looked puzzled. "It's obvious. All the invoices were signed by Rosa Gonzalez. All the packing slips by last head cook—Betty Wagoner. None by the current head cook—I think she's called Cookie."

Sara stood. "Gus thought he had a note from the last head cook to Rosa."

"Yes, AI found it." Rosemary pointed to a blue entry. "It's not dated. I'll pull it up." She tapped a few keys.

> *Don't order more cheap peanuts. They smell funny like the ones before. I told Mr. Smith because you don't listen to my complaints.*
> *Betty*

"I think I'd better talk to Betty Wagoner."

"I hoped you'd say that. I looked at the Happy Days payroll for three years ago and got Betty's address. I contacted the owner of the house where Betty rented an apartment. The owner said Betty walked out sometime in the week after she quit her job at Happy Days over two years ago. Her stuff was claimed by a sister named Patricia O'Hara."

Sara choked. *Cookie said her name was Pat O'Hara.* "I think I should update Cottingham and see if I can learn more about Betty Wagoner." *Time to reward Rosemary. She's earned it.* "Would you like to go along as I talk to a few people?"

"No, AI systems are often accused of fabricating data, but they don't lie as much as most people. Talking to people makes me nervous because I can't figure out when they're sincere. I'll keep tweaking my AI system. It seems to think Gus imagined he had more data than he did."

*Rosemary is smart and nice, but she isn't right for Jack. Jack is more outgoing.* She wouldn't try to do any more matchmaking between them.

***

Sara checked her emails. *Cottingham again.* She opened his message.

> *Bob Jones agreed to plead guilty to manslaughter in the death of Ab Hess. Be at the arraignment tomorrow at nine.*
>
> *Bob Jones is seventy now. I'll save the prison system money and suggest he be sentenced for only ten years. Then he should be released before he needs nursing home care.*

Rosemary was right on one point. Humans often were less than honest. Sara figured Cottingham was more interested in his conviction rate than Bob Jones or the prison system.

She read an email from Sanders. He'd updated her several times today about his photography. An AI program would assess his enthusiasm for photography was less than genuine.

# CHAPTER 41: Jack Feels Dirty

Jack was tired of watching the Snow house, eating cold pizza, and only sipping water because bathroom breaks were unpleasant. His hadn't gotten out of the car in hours. *It was so unnecessary. If Snow admitted what he'd done, he and I would be in a safe house now.*

Snow had laughed when Jack had warned him Smith would try to kill him in the next twenty-four hours. Snow had said, "You can't get me to admit to anything that easily. If you had a case, you would have arraigned me."

Jack had gulped. Snow was partially right.

∗∗∗

The highlight of the wait had been listening to Leroy's dirty jokes and the calls from Sara. She had called at two in the afternoon to tell him Bob Jones had admitted to poisoning the Wild Turkey Bourbon. *At least, one part of this case was over.*

She had called at five to tell him about her work with Rosemary. He was surprised by only one thing—Sara didn't mention how nice or smart Rosemary was.

Rosemary had been unable to find any evidence that Rosa gave any orders to Snow or received reports from Snow. Rosa's only documented contact with Snow was the annual renewal of his contract with a one-page assessment of his work. Sara moaned, "The evaluation was the same every year—Rosa checked average in five assessment boxes—and signed it."

Sara complained, "Evie's written and computer correspondence with Rosa doesn't seem consistent with all the comments about Evie being a stool pigeon for Rosa." Rosemary hadn't found any written or computer correspondence from Rosa to Evie, except for questions about "disruptive residents," like Gus and Deb. Evie's weekly computer reports to Rosa always were lists of data: the census in the units, deaths—with no mention of cause—in each unit, and movement of residents into the assisted living and memory units—usually without explanation. Rosa's evaluation of Evie's work was like Snow's evaluation—average boxes checked for five questions. Nothing else.

Jack had laughed when Sara said, "I think Rosa believes in the phrase—*Ignorance is bliss.* But I don't think it will work for her because she was the boss for all of Happy Days, including the memory unit."

Jack was surprised Sara didn't give one of her usual lengthy explanations. *She must be tired or worried about Sanders.* "Shouldn't you get home to Sanders?"

"He sent me several pictures of Bug." She hesitated. "I don't think photography is going to be a long-term hobby for him." She paused. "Oh, I almost forgot. A former nurse from the memory unit called a few minutes ago. I don't know if I believe her, but she claimed she argued with Snow once about the dose of a pain killer he was giving a patient. But Rosa fired her for being drunk on the job shortly after the incident. She sounded drunk on the phone a few minutes ago."

***

*Thursday*

Around four in the morning, Snow emerged from his house with his white standard poodle. As the dog pranced by the car where Jack and Leroy were pretending to sleep, a black car swung around the corner and came hurtling toward Snow.

Jack aimed a spotlight at the windshield of the speeding car and turned on a siren. Leroy yelled at Snow to run for cover.

The driver of the black car must have been blinded for a few seconds and didn't notice the prongs that projected from the two stop strips, which Jack and Leroy had placed across the street. The vehicle hit the prongs on a strip at full speed, skidded, and jumped the curb onto the sidewalk.

The heroine of the morning was the poodle. She bolted and pulled Snow behind a tree in a neighbor's yard.

Leroy ran to the black car and flung open the driver's door. While Jack frisked the driver and recovered a handgun from his leg holster and a shotgun from the seat of the car, Leroy saw Snow running away from behind the tree. "Snow, you b******, stop running or I'll shoot."

As Leroy ran after Snow, Jack handcuffed the driver and locked him in the back seat of the unmarked FBI car he and Leroy had sat in for hours. Jack almost felt sorry for the driver. The car reeked. Jack retrieved the spiked strips from the street when he heard sirens approaching.

The APD car sped by Jack and joined Leroy in pursuit of Snow. Jack didn't see the arrest, but he heard Leroy's curses as he and one officer led a handcuffed Snow and the poodle back to Jack.

                                                        J. L. Greger

The other APD officer parked his car by the FBI car. "You were lucky to have Mad Dog Leroy as your partner tonight." He looked the back seat of the FBI car. "You want us to handle the driver."

Before Jack could answer, a tall, gaunt woman slammed the door of the Snows' house and strode toward him. The woman almost spit at Jack as she said, "I'm Herb's wife. This is the third time this week Smith's friends stopped by. How are you going to protect us?" She grabbed the leash for the poodle. "I'll tell you what I know if you come inside."

Jack followed her.

Snow's wife claimed her husband never spoke of his work but had seemed "nervous" during the last week. When their high-school age daughter had found a threatening note in her locker on Monday, Snow had suggested one of her friends was playing a prank.

The wife handed the note to Jack. It had been made by pasting cut-our letters to a sheet of paper.

*IF YOU TALK, YOUR DAUGHTER DIES. TEENS DIE OF DRUG OVERDOSES EVERY DAY. THE POLICE WON'T INVESTIGATE.*

Snow's wife considered the second threat to be that someone had stolen the poodle. The daughters had found the poodle without its collar four blocks away when they searched for it after school.

Jack gave the note to the FBI lab team who had just arrived and asked them to look for fingerprints on the gate to the Snow's back yard. It was unlikely the perpetrators had worn gloves yesterday in ninety-five-degree heat.

After Jack had talked to the family, Jack and Leroy focused on Snow. He said only four words: "I want my lawyer."

Leroy smiled. "Good. I don't like standing next to you in the open waiting for another of Smith's hit men." He pushed Snow into the back seat of another FBI car which rushed off to the FBI building.

Jack talked to Cottingham on the phone as Leroy and an APD officer thoroughly searched the driver and his car. The driver had a thousand dollars in his pocket, didn't have licenses for his guns, and had a long arrest record. Cottingham decided to relegate his case to local authorities, even though the case against the driver would be stronger if attached to the other federal cases.

Cottingham also instructed Jack and Leroy to inform Snow's wife that she and the children should not leave town until after her husband's arraignment. When they did, she snorted. "Too bad." She looked at her watch. "My daughters' flight has already left. They will be with my family by noon today."

Leroy had grinned. "You're my kinda woman."

***

Jack felt grimy—physically and emotionally—as he stationed Snow and his lawyer in a conference room in the FBI building to wait for Cottingham's arrival. As Jack sat in the observation room for the conference room, he read his emails.

Cottingham had gotten a warrant for Snow's arrest for one charge of second-degree murder. Its validity was tenuous because it was based on the allegations of a nurse—the drunken one Sara had mentioned—about a death three years ago in the memory unit. In another email, Cottingham had assigned Sara and him an impossible task. They were to identify which of the deaths at Happy Days were due to intentional overdoses of drugs and which were of natural causes. Jack figured his role would be to interview everyone who had ever worked in the memory unit during the last six years.

At eight, the door to the conference room swung open. Cottingham stepped inside and motioned for Leroy to parade Alejandro Smith past. Cottingham focused on Snow. "I could release Smith with an ankle bracelet to monitor his activities *or* I could send him to Colorado to be held in a federal prison. It all depends on you. What do you think your wife and daughters will say when I tell them, I was forced to allow Smith to be released with only an ankle monitor because you wouldn't talk."

Jack gagged. He knew the judge had already decided Smith should be sent to medium security correctional facility in Colorado to await trial because there were no such facilities in New Mexico. Cottingham suggestion that Smith's imprisonment in Colorado was up to Snow was dishonest. Pitting his family against Snow seemed unnecessary. *Then again, Cottingham was reducing Jack's work.* That only made Jack feel dirtier.

## CHAPTER 42: What about Rosa?

*Thursday*

Sara felt happy as she pulled her car into the back parking lot at Happy Days at six in the morning. It was only seventy degrees—the coolest it would be all day. She was avoiding Cottingham's whirlwind of activities at the FBI building. *He was more driven than Sanders. Poor man.*

Rosa would not be at Happy Days yet, but Cookie would be. Sara wanted to confront Cookie without an audience.

***

"Who is Betty Wagoner, the previous head cook here?"

Cookie guided Sara from the dining room where Lola was setting the tables and past the line cooks who were frying eggs and flipping pancakes to her small office. She waved to a metal folding chair and plunked in her desk chair. "My older sister."

"Where is she?"

"With God."

Sara was unsure how to pull out the whole story. "Why didn't you mention her earlier?"

"I didn't have all the details the police would need."

"Okay. Tell me why you came to Albuquerque."

"My sister called me the day she quit working at Happy Days. I was still in the Marines. She was upset. She had just learned the peanuts she had served the residents for years were what she called *dirty*." Cookie closed her eyes and leaned back. "Betty was not well educated—just a good cook. She didn't know about aflatoxin, but she knew peanuts shouldn't leave a powdery coating on her hands. She thought if she rinsed them, they'd be okay."

"Why did she suddenly become alarmed after years of serving bad peanuts?"

"She had gotten another large batch of peanuts, evidently more than two-hundred pounds. They smelled worse than the last batch, which she hadn't used up yet. Rosa Gonzalez had ignored her previous complaints about the peanuts." Cookie straightened in her chair. "She called Rosa's boss—Alejandro Smith. A big mistake."

"What happened?"

"Smith told my sister to forget the peanuts. An hour later, Rosa stormed into Betty's office and said, 'If you're smart, you'll quit today and leave town immediately.'"

"And?"

"I couldn't calm her. Two weeks later, I got a call from her landlady. Evidently Betty had left her apartment shortly after she called me. No one had seen her since."

Sara leaned forward and checked her recorder. "What did you do?"

"Requested a week's leave for a family emergency. I searched all over Albuquerque and in our hometown in Kansas. I filed multiple missing persons reports. Before my leave ended, I put everything in her apartment in storage and paid all her bills."

"Did you ever find her?"

"About a week after I returned to duty, I got a call from the APD." Cookie wiped her eyes. "They had found the body of an obese woman at a homeless campsite. She'd died of a drug overdose. No one knew her last name, but other residents at the camp said she called herself Betty."

"Why did they call you?" When Cookie didn't respond, Sara added, "Surely they found a clue."

Cookie stared straight ahead and spoke slowly. "The autopsy report said she didn't look like the typical homeless person. Pale—not tanned from living outside. No indication of drug use—no needle marks. Obese—most homeless are thin. APD found a cookbook in her stuff." Cookie reached into the bottom drawer of her file cabinet and handed a bag to Sara. An old Betty Crocker cookbook with a torn red and white cover was inside the bag. The inscription on the first page said:

> *Betty,*
> *Merry Christmas.*
> *Love,*
> *Pat*

Sara noted the stains on the book. It had been well-loved and used. "So, APD functioned well?"

Tears trickled down Cookie's face. "Not really. Betty had been dead for over two weeks. It took the police that long to connect my missing person's reports with the body in the morgue."

                                    J. L. Greger

Sara stood and wrapped her arms around Cookie's shoulders. "I understand why you had little confidence in Jack and me when we questioned you last week." Cookie didn't move. Sara remembered Cookie's annoyance when Jack tried to hug her last week, released her grasp, and sat down.

"Things have changed. Alejandro Smith and Herb Snow have been arrested. I need your help to decide what to do about Rosa Gonzalez. Are you up to it?"

Cookie stood and walked around the kitchen and then the loading dock. "Guess no one is listening. Maybe Betty will get justice."

***

Sara felt as if Cookie had been waiting for her. Her well-organized records were kept in a locked file cabinet in a locked closet in her office. She answered Sara's questions almost before she asked them.

Betty—like Cookie—had made copies of the packing slips for all foods that Rosa Gonzalez had ordered. They appeared to reconfirm the records found in Rosa's office. Since Cookie had arrived, Rosa had ordered a large batch of cold cuts, three large batches of avocados, two large batches of coffee beans, and one large batch of pinion nuts.

Cookie shook her head. "I searched FDA recall notices. None were issued for first three products, even though the cold cuts were bad. The avocados and coffee seemed of good quality. So, I studied USDA—particularly the APHIS website of the Animal and Plant Health Inspection Service in USDA. APHIS inspectors in Texas had seized avocados originating in Guatemala that were labeled as coming from Mexico. They also had seized Arabica coffee beans raised in Mexico that were labeled as organic but were not."

"Why didn't you report your suspicions to USDA?"

"The charges were too petty. I figured if I was patient Rosa would make a big mistake."

Sara frowned.

"Don't worry I kept samples from those orders in my home freezer. I also sent small samples to the lab that Gus referred me to. The owner charged me at a reduced rate when I told him I was Gus's friend." She handed a folder to Sara. "Didn't learn much. No mold problem. They found traces of pesticide residues. Means the coffee beans weren't organic. No heavy metal problems but the metal analyses suggested the avocados were more apt to have been grown in Guatemala than Mexico."

Sara had been playing with her laptop as Cookie spoke. "I think the state chemistry lab has tests that may be able to prove your guesses." She looked up. "Now what about the order of pinion nuts this week?"

Cookie smiled. "Rosa made the big mistake I was looking for. I didn't like the look or smell of them. That's why I had Diego store them in a janitor's closet on the second floor, not in the kitchen storage area. I sent a sample to the lab run by Gus's friend, but I've heard nothing yet."

"Did you tell Gus or Diego of your actions?"

"Nope. Both are good guys, but they talk too much. Gus also had this odd habit of..."

Sara choked. "You didn't want to give him your underwear for his collection?"

Cookie nodded. "Not my style."

Sara looked at her watch. It was only seven. "I don't think my favorite lab tech—Winslow—will be in yet. I'll leave a message. And I want another agent with me when I interview Rosa."

***

Carbonne trudged through the back entrance of the kitchen at Happy Days. "This had better be good. Cottingham called me at home. He said you were desperate, and Jack and Leroy were unpresentable. And as a special favor for him, he wanted me to serve as your backup when you talked to Rosa Gonzalez."

"Gee, maybe Cottingham isn't so bad." She giggled. "Are you ready?"

Carbonne glanced at Cookie. "Winslow Red Feather—a trusted FBI staff member—is unloading his gear now. You should stay near him until Sara or I return, no matter who calls you." He turned to Sara. "Let's go."

***

"Rosa Gonzalez, you have a choice. We can interview you here or in the FBI offices. You should know we have already arrested Herb Snow and Alejandro Smith." Rosa retained her proud stance as Sara read her rights.

Before she sat in the chair Sara pushed toward her, Rosa announced, "You are making a mistake. My files—ones you've already seized—prove I had no knowledge of the medical care given patients at Happy Days."

Sara smiled. "Doesn't matter. You are the supervisor at Happy Days. We can charge you with abetting the murder of patients in the memory unit. We might not, if you give us the whole truth. Let's start with your food orders."

     J. L. Greger

"Alejandro gave me a tight budget."

"That doesn't justify ordering aflatoxin-contaminated peanuts from American Peanut Supply and its derivative company, Peanuts Wholesale, after FDA had issued recalls of their peanut products."

Rosa did not bat an eyelash.

"We have purchase orders, lab analyses of the peanuts, and aliquots from each batch. You also purchased intentionally—and fraudulently—mislabeled avocados and coffee beans. The pinion nuts that were delivered last week are being analyzed for mold as we speak." Sara flashed a broad smile. "I think you'd better start talking."

Rosa sniffed. "I obeyed Alejandro's orders."

Sara softened her smile. "I know your job must have been hell. You were paid poorly because of the death in the previous unit you managed."

Rosa looked at her lap. "You know about that?"

"Of course. I assume that's why you took Alejandro's abuse. You were unemployable elsewhere. Why don't you tell me about what happened after Betty sent you the note complaining about the bad peanuts." Sara handed Rosa a copy of the note."

Rosa didn't even glance at the note.

"We know Betty was killed by a drug overdose about a week later."

Rosa stared straight ahead.

"I'm waiting."

"Alejandro visited me a couple of days after Betty resigned. He was angry and burst into my office without calling beforehand. He leaned over my desk and growled, 'I fixed your problem. I've overlooked your side hustle in the past. I won't anymore. We're going to hire a head cook with good credentials—no problems—after a well-advertised search. You aren't going to buy any more questionable food at big discounts.'" She shook violently.

*Let's see if she'll continue to be honest.* "What did he mean when he said, 'I fixed your problem.'"

"I don't know."

Carbonne snorted.

"I'd hired Betty because she wasn't bright. Couldn't use the computer easily. I didn't think she'd realize what I was doing." Rosa bit her lip. "The deals were so good. American Peanut Supply guaranteed their products were good. The problem was silly FDA rules."

*She's still lying.* Maybe I can scare her. "How much kick-back did you get?"

Rosa began to sniffle.

"Stop the act. After Alejandro's threat, why did you order more— I guess I could call them black market items—like avocados, coffee beans, and pinion nuts. Surely, you knew Alejandro would catch you."

"I waited a whole year before I ordered the avocados. I thought he'd forgotten. And I needed the money. Schools for my sons are expensive."

"How much kickback did you receive?"

Rosa whispered. "Fifteen percent of the price Happy Days paid for the nuts and ten percent of the price for the avocados and coffee beans."

*She got peanuts for her effort.* Sara forced herself to not laugh at her own pun. "For a few thousand dollars you endangered the lives of everyone at Happy Days and broke countless laws? I should order your boss to replace you as the director of Happy Days immediately, but your boss is now unavailable. I'm not sure what to do."

Carbonne looked up from his phone. "I've reached the personnel officer at GYM. Rosa, you should be receiving an email in a few minutes and a special delivery letter later today. They will tell you that you are suspended without pay until this investigation in over."

Rosa shook. "They can't."

Carbonne looked at his computer again. "An assistant US attorney says we should bring you to the FBI Building. He and FDA officials will meet you there."

Rosa screamed.

Sara touched her hand. "Half-truths like you gave me won't be good enough. No one is going to buy your claim that you didn't know the batches of peanuts weren't fit for human consumption." She didn't say: *Or that you didn't know Smith had gotten Betty killed.*

Carbonne tapped Sara's arm as they left Rosa's office. "Glad you didn't buy her story either. Cottingham wanted me to remind you that you're due at Bob Jones's arraignment in federal court at nine. It's five to nine now."

# CHAPTER 43: Ambitious Plans

"Rosemary, I hate to jerk you around, but we're going to focus on Rosa Gonzalez—not FDA questions—for the next hour. Rosa's too confident, like she's got something over one of the other suspects—most likely Smith."

Rosemary stood and stretched like a cat arching her spine. "Sounds interesting. Where do we begin?"

"Until I talked to her this morning, I didn't realize two important points. Her sons go to the Albuquerque Academy. Tuition there would equal almost one half of her salary. She claimed her kickback from buying questionable food for Happy Days was only a couple thousand a year. Ergo, she's got another source of money."

"It wasn't part of any records I've seen."

"Think. Are she or her sons listed as beneficiaries to any trust accounts?" Sara frowned. "Did Happy Days purchased products or services from any small, local vendors."

Rosemary turned pale. "Maybe."

"While you do those searches, I'm going to check for details on her husband's death."

***

The police records on the death of Olo Gonzalez—Rosa's husband—were sketchy. Police had hypothesized Olo died defending an Albuquerque businessman called Zito Soto. But there was no follow up. *Typical of investigation into deaths of suspected gang members in New Mexico.*

Sara scanned for information on Zito Soto. Two points looked useful. He had been one of the chief wholesalers of imported produce in the Southwest. His obituary from a year ago listed Rosa Gonzalez as one of his nieces. He appeared to have died of natural causes at the age of eighty.

Sara glanced at Rosemary. "Find anything?"

Rosemary's right knee bounced wildly. "I was swamped with data in the financial records. So, I scanned Rosa's files quickly because her spending didn't seem extravagant. I didn't think it was worth the effort to examine accounts held in trust for her sons."

"And you assumed wrong?" Sara felt hopeful.

"A man named Zito Soto created a revocable trust account for each of her sons with himself as the trustee fourteen years ago." Rosemary traced her finger along a column on the screen. "Twenty-five thousand was taken out of one account each of the last two years. A similar amount was removed from the other account last year."

Sara nodded. "I think annual tuition at the Albuquerque Academy is about twenty-five thousand."

"That high?" Rosemary typed a bit. "Oh, I see the trustee was changed two years ago to someone else with the last name of Soto." Rosemary slid her finger to the bottom of the screen. "As of today, the accounts together are worth almost a million dollars." Rosemary looked at her lap. "I should have found this earlier. There was so much to do."

Sara put a hand on Rosemary's shoulders. "It's okay." She didn't say: *I would have done the same*. It wouldn't be true. "This case is complex. That's why *all* details are important. Why don't you search for more info on the new trustee. I'm guessing Vito transferred the accounts two years ago because he was ill. I'm going to use these new insights to try to scare Rosa Gonzalez."

"Wait. I remember a small local vendor supplied a lot of supplements and herbal medicines to Happy Days. I didn't think it was unusual, but I'll check it now."

***

Sara whispered into Cottingham's ear when she rushed into the conference room. He smiled and leaned back.

Sara didn't bother to sit before she said, "Rosa, I know Vito Soto created accounts in your sons' names after the death of your husband. Those two accounts are now worth almost a million dollars. You were his niece, what did he leave you?"

Rosa gasped. "You got it wrong."

"How am I wrong?"

Rosa looked at her lap.

*Let's see if I can crack her.* "Tell me about your husband Olo. Was he a member of a drug gang?"

Rosa didn't look up. "Yes."

"Was Vito Soto?"

Rosa raised her head. "Uncle Vito was an honorable man. The gangs wanted him to import drugs with his produce. When he didn't cooperate, they ordered Olo to shoot him. Uncle Vito must have sensed the danger when Olo and his friends stopped by one his warehouses. Uncle Vito said, "Think of your sons." Olo then shot one of his fellow gang members. A second one shot Olo, but Olo got off one more shot and killed the other gang member."

*So far, seems consistent with the police reports. Let's see if she continues to be honest.* "What did the police do?"

Rosa cackled. "Called it a gang fight. Said Uncle Vito was dirty. But they couldn't prove anything."

"What did you do?"

"Went to see Uncle Vito. I reminded him of all the years I'd worked in his wholesale warehouse to earn money to pay for nursing school. I pointed out he owed me because Olo died protecting him."

*Sounds like what Rosa would say.* She waited for Rosa to continue.

"He offered me a part-time job to supplement my salary as a nurse at the VA Hospital."

"What did you do for him?"

"My job was to determine the prices other wholesalers were charging for produce in the Southwest. It was slow work before the internet and took lots of anonymous calls to other wholesalers and to retail stores."

"Why?"

Rosa seemed surprised by the question. "Because then Vito knew if he had to lower his prices or could charge more."

Sara's phone pinged. She glanced at the new message and handed her phone to Cottingham. "What did Vito Soto think when you went to work for Alejandro Smith at Happy Days?"

"He thought I'd made a mistake and suggested I find another job." She shook her head. "He offered me a job in one of his warehouses. It paid less than my job at Happy Days, and I told him he was a fool."

Sara thought a few seconds. "I think you found another source of income when you went to Happy Days. A way to use your knowledge of the wholesale food market."

Rosa smiled. "I already admitted I got a percentage on certain purchases for Happy Days."

"Something much more profitable." Sara gave a broad grin. "Have you heard of a company called Herbal Supplements Unlimited?"

Rosa for the first time showed a sign of nervousness. She bit her lip.

"This little company in Los Lunas, New Mexico seems to sell botanicals mainly to GYM facilities. Funny thing—its owners are R.A. Gonzalez and A. Smith. That's you and Alejandro, isn't it?"

Cottingham didn't look up from his laptop. "FDA thinks your company deserves study."

"I want a lawyer."

***

*Friday*

Cottingham didn't seem to be in the mood to do a lengthy interview with Rosa and her lawyer on Friday. "Here's how it stands. We know your company, Herbal Supplements Unlimited, buys up cheap botanical products, repackages them, and sells them at inflated prices." He nodded to Sara.

"Supplements from this company are sold at more than double the prices of similar products. Hence, few consumers buy the supplements, except GYM-owned facilities. FDA records indicate the facility in Los Lunas only repackages already approved supplements. However, my colleagues confiscated powdered biological material— probably dried spinach—at the facility yesterday afternoon. FDA officials plan to open a case against the company after an inspection next week. I suspect your manufacturing process won't meet FDA standards, and your labels will be found to be fraudulent."

Cottingham smiled. "Today, I won't be addressing potential charges that will stem from these inspections. I will be outlining the charges against you because you abetted the murder of patients in the memory unit after the fact."

Rosa straightened. "My records prove I had no knowledge of practices in the memory unit." She smiled and motioned to Sara. "She couldn't find anything in the materials she confiscated."

"We have new evidence from employees in the memory unit."

Rosa whispered to her lawyer. He shook his head.

Cottingham smiled. "He's right. Non-disclosure agreements are moot in a murder case. Two nurses in their resignation letters claimed Dr. Snow administered more pain killers than necessary."

Rosa frowned. "The nurses didn't resign. I fired them for being drunk on the job. Do you have my letters to them? They didn't realize clinical psychologist can legally prescribe and administer medications in this state."

Cottingham glanced at Sara.

"We have the letters." Sara held them up. "The letters are dated for the days after the deaths of two different patients in the memory unit.

The death certificates of these two patients listed the causes of death as CHD and emphysema. An overdose of morphine would lead to respiratory failure and look like the causes of death noted on the certificates." She looked at Cottingham. "Do you want me to continue?"

"Keep it short."

"We talked to three of the past medical directors of the memory unit yesterday. They insisted that they had complained to you about Dr. Snow's incompetence in handling drugs and you ignored them. That's why they quit."

Cottingham sighed. "Let me explain what that means. We can now prove Dr. Snow knowingly induced the deaths of at least eight patients in the memory unit with drugs. This means eight counts of murder. You did nothing to stop him. You reported his work as satisfactory in annual reports after nurses and nurse practitioners had reported his incompetence. Ergo, you will be charged with eight counts of abetting murder."

Rosa shook her head. "You'll never prove it."

"We'll see. You will be arraigned tomorrow in federal court and held by APD in jail until then."

Rosa's lawyer stood. "Are we through? I need to talk to my client before she is incarcerated."

"No, I now will outline the charges the FDA plans to level at your client for procuring and feeding aflatoxin-contaminated food to residents of Happy Days. Currently FDA estimates you caused twenty deaths attributable to the aflatoxin in peanuts served at Happy Days. My associate…" He nodded to Sara. "…thinks technically four of the deaths attributed to liver cancer induced by eating aflatoxin were ultimately caused by a drug overdose administered by Dr. Snow. I don't want to debate the point now, but I will summarize what these charges mean in terms of sentencing."

Sara almost felt sorry for Rosa as Cottingham tallied the potential sentences. She didn't see how Cottingham could negotiate much with Rosa. The difference between sentences that added up to eighty versus one hundred years didn't seem important. Still, he dangled the possibility of a plea bargain in front of her.

***

Sara tried to explain to Sanders the tangled cobweb of charges against Rosa, Herb, and Alejandro. "And once we handle the charges in this state, Smith faces charges in at least two other states."

Sanders smiled indulgently. "You realize Ted Cottingham has landed the type of case that makes a prosecuting lawyer's career. It should get him an appointment at US attorney for another district and eventually put him on the short list for US Attorney General, if his politics is right."

"I figured it would also get the New Mexico Attorney General re-elected."

Sanders laughed. "He'll take it further than just a re-election and probably go for a higher office."

Sara said, "But I don't want to spend the rest of my life working out the details on these cases." She picked up Bug and stoked his silky ears. "Today I realized I didn't like tallying sentences for hundreds of years. What's the point? Rosa, Herb, and Alejandro should go to jail with no probation possible for at least twenty—probably thirty—years. After that, who cares?"

Sanders laughed. "It doesn't work that way. Their lawyers will fight to get them out in ten. What does Jack think?"

"He's excited. He sees it as a way to gain new skills—like in accounting—and build his career. Even our new analyst, Rosemary, is fascinated by 'heaping facts on facts.' She was bored until yesterday and took short cuts in her searches. Now she sees this case—I'll quote her—as an 'infinity puzzle.'"

"Maybe, that's your answer. Let the young ones stay on the case, and you bow out. You solved the murder of Ab Hess and set the stage for the rest. Carbonne will support your decision."

# CHAPTER 44: Happy Couples?

*Three months later*

Sara was beginning to stuff the turkey when Sanders sauntered from the bedroom. He leaned down and petted Bug. "I see Bug is already at work."

Sara smiled. "Bug patiently waited in his bed while I chopped the onions, celery, and carrots, but when I started to fry the sausage and mushrooms, he moved to the kitchen."

Sanders nodded and started to make his coffee. "When do you plan to serve Thanksgiving dinner?"

"Around three, but Carbonne, Barbara, and Willow will get here around one. Jack and his date around two."

"Oh, Jack must be feeling brave if he's bringing a woman to dinner. Didn't he get dumped the last time he allowed one of his lady friends to meet you and Carbonne?"

"No, the young woman just thought the FBI made too many demands on Jack's time."

Sanders chuckled. "Not quite how I remember the story. Do you know anything about this one?"

"I didn't ask. I haven't talked to him about anything besides GYM during the last two months. He's so busy coordinating investigations of the twenty GYM facilities in six states."

Sanders sniffed his coffee. "You talk less about your new partner."

"He only moved to Albuquerque a month ago. Carbonne has been assigning us straight-forward cases on the nearby pueblos."

"Somehow, I suspect Cottingham has influenced Carbonne's assignments to you."

"Well yes, Cottingham likes to have Jack and others run things by me on the GYM cases. It's easier if I'm in Albuquerque." Sara continued to push moist bread stuffing into the turkey. "I know they say you shouldn't stuff a bird, but I think stuffing dries out and has less flavor when it's baked in a casserole dish. Besides, I'll monitor the temperature of the meat and stuffing with a thermometer."

Sanders sipped his coffee. "What's my job today?"

"What do you want to do? The pumpkin pie, vegetable salad, and cranberry relish are already made. The fruit and cheese need to be cut up and arranged on a platter. The table needs to be set. The wine served." She shoved the turkey into the oven, pulled a can of diet cola from the refrigerator, and sat on the stool next to him. "I also want an update on the preparations for your upcoming hearings."

He leaned over and kissed her cheek. "Members of the White House staff and the State Department gave me a long list of possible questions. I submitted written responses."

"You said they really picked at your answers and were drilling you on Monday and Tuesday. How did that go?"

"We'll find out soon. Next week I visit with key senators as the candidate for the assistant secretary position. The vote should occur a week from Friday." He rattled on about advice he'd gotten from senators.

After ten minutes, she said, "I assume I should smile and act confident when I attend your hearing and avoid questions."

"Yes." He stood. "I'll set the table and handle the wine."

***

Barbara carried baby Willow into Sara's house. Carbonne shuffled behind with all the baby's paraphernalia, which he dumped in the hallway for Barbara to sort. "Sara, we've got to talk. Cottingham got what he wanted. Next Monday he'll be appointed the US Attorney for Arizona."

"Will he turn the investigation and prosecution of the GYM cases over to others?"

"Doubt it. Three of the GYM facilities are in Arizona. But it means he won't be strutting through our offices daily."

"Yes, but we'll get more emails and calls. He really is a micro-manager."

Carbonne nodded. "Jack won't have been told. Don't mention it today."

Barbara put her hand on Carbonne's shoulder. "I settled Willow in her car seat and put it on the sofa. I think she'll sleep for an hour, especially if you stay nearby. I'll help Sara in the kitchen."

Carbonne winked at his wife. "You accuse me of too much shop talk, but you want Sara to update you on her new partner."

Barbara flushed. "Of the ten thousand FBI agents, only twenty are Native Americans. I worked hard to recruit this young man from the Zuni pueblo."

"And you pulled strings to get him assigned to the New Mexico office."

Barbara smiled. "I had confidence you would see he got good mentoring from Sara."

"I'm not sure that's true." Sara placed a platter of cheeses, crackers, and fruit on a card table by the sofa. "Excuse, the table, Bug likes cheese. So, I can't put this platter on a low coffee table."

Sanders interrupted. "She's explaining she doesn't have a coffee table because of Bug."

Sara smiled at Sanders and went back to her previous line of thought. "My new partner wants more action than he gets doing straightforward cases on the pueblos. However, I see no reason to immerse him in the GYM cases and expose him to Cottingham." She shook her head. "So, I've encouraged him to work with Leroy Elroy."

Barbara gasped. "The agent called Mad Dog?"

"Don't worry Leroy's okay. He only acts crazy to impress suspects."

***

When Sara answered the door at two, she was speechless. Jack's hand rested on Rosemary's shoulder. He must have noticed Sara's surprise. "Rosemary and I have spent so much time working together, we've gotten used to how each other thinks."

Rosemary didn't look like a high school student anymore. Her long dark hair was in a chic chignon. Her black slacks and sweater were accented with a red scarf. "Dr. Almquist, I was so pleased when Jack invited me today. I never had a chance to tell you how much I learned from you—especially on how to investigate an uncooperative suspect like Rosa Gonzalez."

Jack laughed. "Rosemary, you don't need to gush over Sara." He pushed Rosemary toward Sanders. "This is Sara's partner—the spy. No, I mean intelligence master. He's like Cottingham but talks less."

***

Sanders, Barbara, and Sara guided the conversation toward cooking and travel during dinner. After the meal, Barbara looked at Sara. "I think we might as well allow everyone talk about his or her aspect of the GYM cases for a few minutes."

Jack spoke first. "Sara, I want to know why Snow took a plea deal so fast. When I asked Cottingham, he mumbled, 'Think strategically like Sara.'"

Sara didn't stop clearing the table. "As you know, more than forty people died in the memory unit at Happy Days during the last five years, but the evidence was only clear and sufficient for murder charges in eight cases. Cottingham told me he wanted Snow off the streets fast. But the plea deal he offered Snow was eight intentional manslaughter charges with potentially eighty years in prison and parole possible after twenty years if Snow testified against Alejandro Smith. It didn't please Snow."

"Why did he take it?"

"I talked to Snow's wife. His daughters were being made fun of in school. She told Snow he'd never see the girls again unless he took the plea and hence stopped the publicity on the case. I suggested Snow be held in a low-security federal correctional facility where his family could visit."

Jack leaned forward. "That explains Cottingham's behavior at the other GYM facilities that I've investigated. All the physicians and head nurses have copped pleas like Snow's deal and agreed to testify against Smith. He is now charged with abetting twenty-three murders in memory units in five states. We also have proof he hired someone to overdose Betty Wagoner, but Cottingham has been reluctant to finish the paperwork on that case."

Carbonne winked at Sara when Jack made his last comment. "Oh, I think Cottingham will surprise you and make that decision next week."

Rosemary stopped stroking Jack's arm. "I think eventually we'll find evidence that Smith bribed at least one or two medical staff members in all twenty GYM facilities." She shivered. "Makes me scared to even think about growing old."

"Is it time to adjourn to more comfortable chairs in the living room?" Carbonne walked to the recliner and perched Willow on his knee. "Our state attorney general is a big fan of Cottingham. He thinks these cases will be the impetus for major changes in the management of all senior care facilities in four of the states with GYM facilities."

Sanders encouraged the rest of the guests to follow Carbonne to the living room. "I suspect all of you have made the careers of the attorney generals in those four states. They all will run for governorships or senate seats in the next two years."

Carbonne choked. "Ours won't wait that long."

Jack and Rosemary chose to sit together on the wooden love seat at the far end of the living room. "Did I tell you I ran into Maggio? He's working as a tax consultant in Texas." He shook his head. "What about Rosa—the original crazy like a goat character?"

Sara kept neatening the kitchen. "Rosa thought the FDA and Cottingham couldn't get her and wouldn't cooperate even after the FDA had all the residents and employees of Happy Days tested for liver cancer. There's thirty-three with varying stages of liver cancer, including those who died. FDA put the data from Happy Days into a national database and fined American Peanut Supply and Peanuts Wholesale for millions. The chief executives of these companies are facing prison terms, and the companies are expected to declare bankruptcy. Several accepted pleas, but not Rosa. Her trial begins in January. And she's facing it alone. Her sons asked the courts to make them wards of Vito Soto's son who also controls their trusts. But it turns out, she hidden lots of money from her so-called supplement business. So, she has good lawyers."

Jack put his arm over Rosemary's shoulder and pulled her closer. "Always knew she was the toughest one." Rosemary kissed his cheek.

When Sanders seated himself on the sofa, Bug cuddled up next to him. "Are we through with Happy Days and ready for happier topics?"

Sara pulled a chair up next to Carbonne for Barbara and began to offer guests beverages. "Don't you want to hear the happy conclusions?" She didn't wait for an answer. "Gus and John didn't want to leave Happy Days and knew GYM—which had closed the memory unit—was close to bankruptcy. So, they convinced the residents of Happy Days to create a co-op. Seventy percent of residents bought in. Isaac Newson bought two units and is remodeling them after the medical examiner suggested he retire or face malpractice charges."

Jack started to cough.

Sara guessed his thoughts. "Deb Kline—with encouragement from Gus's water pistol—decided to not join the co-op and moved out."

Jack snorted.

"They hired Evie Schoener—after she stopped smoking—to manage the facility when Gus convinced the other residents she was responsible for saving them from Rosa Gonzalez and Alejandro Smith. Cookie not only heads the dietary department but is making the kitchen at Happy Days a major training spot for veterans. Diego continues to head the janitorial services while he pursues an associate degree in criminal justice."

Jack smiled. "I can see your hand in these happy endings."

Sara laughed. "But it gets better. After Gus discarded his *collection* and responded well to treatment for an early stage of liver cancer, Ruth suggested he move in with her. They are remodeling her apartment along with the two empty adjacent units into a large apartment. Ruth tells me that John and Linda are an item."

Sanders pulled Sara to the sofa. He whispered in her ear. "Do we get a happy ending, too?"

THE END

# THE SCIENCE AND HISTORY BEHIND THE STORY

**Sometimes science and the legal system do not mesh well in murder investigations.** A basic premise in murder mysteries is that an investigator will identify the cause of death and the murderer(s).

However, most people in modern societies die of chronic diseases—coronary heart disease and cancer—which have multiple causes. It is impossible to state whether any one factor alone—such as a poor diet, smoking, alcohol consumption, being overweight, or the lack of exercise—caused a person to die of a heart attack. This is true for several reasons. The effects of these factors are additive. Moreover, lifestyle factors often cluster together. For example, alcoholics smoke more than others. Experts with sophisticated statistical tools can tease apart the *relative* effects of these confounding variables, but generally a scientific expert can't say one variable alone caused the death (1).

In essence that's the dilemma faced by investigators in this novel—***Crazy Like a Goat***. In legal terms, individuals in the novel were murdered by poisons administered intentionally or by criminally negligent behavior. Generally, the last poison administered was cited as the cause of death. The individual administering that substance was the murderer.

However, alcoholism, excess use of certain pain killers and vitamin A supplements, hepatitis B, and metabolic diseases including diabetes could also have damaged the victim's livers. These other factors may have made the murder victims more sensitive to the poisons than others and would probably have killed the victim eventually.

To help readers understand this complicated nexus of science and the law, I've given short summaries of four different poisons that killed characters in this novel.

**Methanol**—sometimes called methyl or wood alcohol—is a clear fluid and tastes and smells like ethanol. It is found in windshield washer fluid (often at concentrations of 30 to 50%), some hand sanitizers and cleaning supplies, canned heating products, and some nail polish removers (4).



J. L. Greger

Ingestion of methanol may induce stomach upset and vomiting. A poisoned individual often is sleepy or appears to be intoxicated. Severe symptoms usually do not appear for hours after ingestion of methanol because methanol toxicity is mainly due to the toxicity of its metabolites—formaldehyde and formic acid. These symptoms include blindness and metabolic acidosis, which can cause death by respiratory failure.

Methanol toxicity is treated by a combination of drugs (usually fomepizole) which slows the metabolism of methanol and dialysis which removes the toxic metabolites from the blood (5).

**Aflatoxins** are poisonous compound produced by molds (certain strains of *Aspergillu*s) that contaminate plant crops and foods, particularly peanuts, other nuts, and dried fruit (6). The toxins per se are colorless and odorless, but the molds producing them are visible.

Chronic long-term ingestion of aflatoxin causes cirrhosis of the liver and hepatocellular carcinoma (7). People with hepatitis B may be sixty times more prone to liver damage when they consume high levels of aflatoxin.

**Alcohol**—ethanol—consumption is directly linked to increased incidence of several types of cancer, including breast, colorectum, esophagus, liver, and mouth (8). There doesn't seem to be a difference in the toxicity of ethanol in beer, wine, and liquor, just a difference in the concentration of ethanol.

**Morphine and other opiate pain killers** are poisons. Opiates including natural (e.g. morphine), semi-synthetic (e.g. oxycodone) and synthetic (e.g. fentanyl) forms are used for pain relief (9). They have a high potential for being addictive and in theory their use is highly regulated.

The margin of safety—the ratio between the amount of a drug that is lethal to 1% of the population but effective for 99% of the population—for many opiate pain killers is small. Age and diseases that reduce kidney and liver function tend to reduce the margin of safety. These factors further confound investigations of medical malpractice as occurred in this novel.

**A complicated set of laws and regulations control the actions of FDA and state health agencies.** The author tried to make the actions of Sara Almquist and her cohorts in this novel consistent with these rules without being tedious. One set of rules is particularly confusing.

Supplements (e.g. vitamins, botanicals with historic uses) are not treated as food or drugs under the Dietary Supplement Health and Education Act of 1994 (10). Accordingly, FDA has the authority to act against any adulterated or misbranded dietary supplements—as mentioned in Chapter 43—only after they reach the market. FDA doesn't evaluate effectiveness of the products generally.

***Loco como una cabra* is a humorous Spanish idiom.** It translates in English to *crazy like a goat.* People using the idiom are saying the individual is acting erratically.

The basis of this idiom is unclear. Goats are curious and seem willing to eat almost anything. Their agility allows to them to climb and balance in precarious places, including trees. Investigators have suggested goats were as intelligent as dogs in some studies (11). They aren't crazy.

The actions of many of the characters in this novel were erratic but often clever. They weren't crazy, except *like a goat.* The word goat in this novel has no hidden meaning in terms of satanism or the popular expression G.O.A.T—greatest of all time.

## References


1. The role of confounding variables in the assessment of neurobehavioral effects of chronic solvent exposure. *Neurotoxicology* [1996] 17(3-4):761-7. PMID: 9086499.

2. Symptoms & causes of cirrhosis. https://www.niddk.nih.gov/health-information/liver-disease/cirrhosis/symptoms-causes

3. Liver cancer causes, risk factors and prevention. https://www.cancer.gov/types/liver/what-is-liver-cancer/causes-risk-factors

4. Windshield washer fluid: A winter hazard. https://www.poison.org/articles/windshield-washer-solution)

5. Methanol toxicity. https://en.wikipedia.org/wiki/Methanol_toxicity

6. Fungal presence in selected tree nuts and dried fruits. *Microbiol Insights* [2015] 8: 1–6. PMID: 26056470


                                   J. L. Greger

7. Aflatoxin toxicity.
https://www.ncbi.nlm.nih.gov/books/NBK557781/

8. US Surgeon General issues new advisory on link between alcohol and cancer risks. https://www.hhs.gov/about/news/2025/01/03/us-surgeon-general-issues-new-advisory-link-alcohol-cancer-risk.html.

9. Opioids. https://nida.nih.gov/research-topics/opioids#opioids

10. Dietary supplements. https://www.fda.gov/food/dietary-supplements.

11. Goat. https://en.wikipedia.org/wiki/Goat

# ACKNOWLEDGMENTS

I appreciate the efforts of Lorna Collins for carefully editing this manuscript and of Barbara Hodges for creatively designing the cover. Thank you.

The cover artist, Barbara Hodges, and I acknowledge the inspiration for the cover was *The Scream* by Edvard Munch and several of the painting of Vincent Van Gogh. We thought those works suggested the frenetic nature—maybe craziness—of several characters in this novel.

None of my books would be possible without the patience and love of my dogs: Bug, Elf, and Star.

# ABOUT THE AUTHOR

J. L. Greger is a biology professor from the University of Wisconsin-Madison turned novelist. The pet therapy dog, Bug, in her mysteries and thrillers is based on her own Japanese Chin. She includes tidbits about science, the American Southwest, and her international travel experiences in her **Science Traveler Series**.

***The Flu Is Coming***. In the first book in the series, a woman scientist traces the spread of a deadly new flu virus among the frantic residents of a quarantined New Mexico community. (New Mexico/ Arizona book award finalist)

***Murder…A Way to Lose Weight***. A dean in a medical school helps police discover whether an ambitious young "diet doctor," disgruntled patients, or old-timers with buried secrets are killers. (Winner of the 2016 Public Safety Writers Association contest and New Mexico/Arizona book award finalist)

***Ignore the Pain***. A woman scientist learns too much about the coca trade and too little about a sexy new colleague while on a public health assignment in Bolivia.

***Malignancy***. A woman tries to escape the clutches of a drug lord and accepts a risky assignment as a science consultant in Cuba. (Winner of the 2015 Public Safety Writers Association contest)

***I Saw You in Beirut***. A woman's past provides clues for the extraction of a nuclear scientist from Iran. The author's experiences as a science and education consultant in the United Arab Emirates and Lebanon are featured.

***Riddled with Clues***. A homeless man and a woman scientist are targeted by drug gangs after she listens to the strange tale of an undercover drug agent about his war experiences. The memories of an actual CIA agent in Laos during the Vietnam War are featured. (New Mexico/Arizona book award finalist)

***A Pound of Flesh, Sorta.*** The police and a woman scientist can't decide whether a package contaminated with the bacteria that causes the bubonic plague is a plea for help by a whistleblower or a threat from gang leaders awaiting trial. (New Mexico/Arizona book award finalist, New Mexico Press Women Communications award)

***Dirty Holy Water.*** A woman who usually serves as a science consultant for the FBI learns there is a thin line between being a victim and being a villain when she becomes the chief suspect in a bizarre murder case. (New Mexico/Arizona book award finalist)

***Games for Couples.*** Did lethal compounds in a cultured meat product—meat made in a test tube—kill a man in a clinical trial? Or did the toxic competition between biotechnology companies and spite of battling couples cause his death? (New Mexico/Arizona book award finalist)

***Fair Compromises.*** Sara Almquist and her FBI colleagues rush to find the culprits who endangered the lives of a hundred attendees at a political rally by poisoning the food with botulism toxin. Their target was a woman candidate for the US Senate. (New Mexico/Arizona book award finalist)

***Bungle in the Jungle.*** The US consular office in Manaus, Brazil, is a "Bungle in the Jungle." Can Sara Almquist and the new Acting Ambassador to Brazil figure out how the staff became enmeshed in the illegal international trade of drugs and cultural artifacts? (New Mexico/Arizona book award finalist)

***Escape from a Dark Cave.*** Sara Almquist, an FBI scientific consultant, investigates the murder of a young man near a historic cave in New Mexico. As she reconstructs the victim's final days, she learns the autistic victim found the cave to be soothing. She finds the cave to be depressing. (Public Safety Writers Association award and New Mexico/Arizona book award finalist)

***The Man Who Looked for Death.*** Who can an FBI agent and a scientist trust as they investigate a murder in the ghost town of Golden Gully? The medical examiner thinks the victim was tortured for several days before he was killed. However, the ten residents in this remote town in the Gila National Forest deny knowing the man. The local sheriff's office is less than cooperative.

***Crazy Like a Goat.*** Scientist Sara Almquist and her FBI colleagues investigate the murder of a retired professor. Why did someone poison his booze? Did he know too much about the dark side of a successful chain of senior living centers? Or had he played too many pranks on his friends and neighbors?

J. L. Greger also wrote ***Come Fly with Elf.*** In this picture book for children, a tiny Papillon dog called Elf dreams of flying in a hot air balloon. She has written two collections of short stories: ***The Good Old Days?*** and **Other People's Mothers.**

See more at: http://www.jlgreger.com

www.ingramcontent.com/pod-product-compliance
Lightning Source LLC
Chambersburg PA
CBHW020110310726
48970CB00002B/561